# Don't Want No *Humans* 'Round Here!

The creature was wearing a glass bowl over its head; otherwise it looked exactly like the other two. It turned slowly, staring at us. We stared back.

Farrunner took three strides toward it, then turned to face us. He was big and powerfully built, and possessed of a sinewy quickness that belied his size. His black and gray striped belt showed the scars of previous deathduels. "I post a challenge!" he growled.

Howls were coming from all around the ring. The mood was definitely for blood, but killing these creatures every time one turned up wouldn't solve any of the riddles.

I stepped forward. "According to Irongut these creatures don't provide much sport. Perhaps I can tempt you with something better."

"I'm listening."

"I challenge *you* to a deathduel."

Farrunner grinned.

# THE WEIGHER

## ERIC VINICOFF

## MARCIA MARTIN

BAEN BOOKS

THE WEIGHER

A shorter and substantially different version of this story appeared in *Analog* magazine in 1984.

A Baen Books Original

Baen Publishing Enterprises
P.O. Box 1403
Riverdale, N.Y. 10471

ISBN: 0-671-72144-5

Cover art by C.W. Kelly

First printing, November 1992

Distributed by
SIMON & SCHUSTER
1230 Avenue of the Americas
New York, N.Y. 10020

Printed in the United States of America

Dedicated to Robert A. Heinlein

# CHAPTER ONE

Groundplant was a springy, rust-colored blur under my driving paws. I was running at my best long-distance pace, not quite as fast as when I was in my prime, but not dallying either. The wind whistled through the pounding drum-rhythm, while it ruffled my fur and cooled my burning muscles. I sucked in quick, deep lungfuls of it, enjoying the rich variety of forest scents.

The commonland trail followed a narrow gap of meadow between two barren brown mounds which were fancifully named God's Fangs. Ahead I could see the trail winding down the wooded slope to the bend in the river and Coalgathering. Leaves were dying as winter approached, adding yellow and brown to the red-shaded foliage, falling from gaunt branches to brighten the ground. A pelt of fog lay over the forest beyond the river, but the morning air on this side was clear and breath-misting cold.

Overslept again, curse it. I had never been much of a morning person, and always staying up late reading didn't help. Even making the best speed my middle-aged bones could manage, I was going to be late opening my stall. At least I wasn't the only one. I could

1

smell that Flatpaws the tanner and a couple of other late risers had passed recently.

I started down the slope. To my left, a claw of the eastern Low Mountains range reached out almost to the Muddy River. At its paw were the mining territories which accounted for Coalgathering's name and existence. The town lay ahead and below, a haphazard clustering of dirt streets and black-shingled roofs.

The open pit mines with their spiralling rim roads looked like some god had tried to drive monstrous screws into the ground. Owners and *tagnami* were already attacking the pit bottoms with picks and loading the black rubble into runleg-pulled wagons. The noise, the choking clouds of dust, and the gaping wounds in the land were an ugliness I had never gotten used to. The mining territories didn't have much vegetation or game, but Blacksnout and the other miners were by far the richest people in town; they could afford the best breeder stock. Beyond the mining territories the ground leveled off, and the trail became a wide dirt road rutted by wheels. I caught up with a coal-laden wagon rattling toward town. A *tagnami* was loping beside the pair of runlegs, herding them with snarls and nips. Runlegs made poor hunting, tasted terrible, and were only slightly smarter than the boulders they resembled.

"Get those abominations out of my way!" I yelled irritably.

The *tagnami* glanced over his shoulder, saw me, and yelped, "Yes, Ma'am!" Snarling at the runlegs, he drove them over to the right side of the trail. I hurried past the wagon.

I slowed down to a trot as I neared the North Gate and inspected the town wall. The glossy, black strongwood logs were ten strides tall and a half stride thick, with sharpened tops. The wall wrapped around three sides of Coalgathering, ending at the riverbank above and below the town. The only gaps in the row of logs were the wide graystone arches of the North and South Gates.

The wall must have been an impressive sight when it was first built. But it had deteriorated over the years, and its poor condition was a growing headache for me. It was still sturdy enough to keep out dangerous beasts, but just barely. In several places the logs were loose in their foundations and many of the crossbeam nails were rusted through.

I dreaded the job of getting the necessary repairs made. The wall was still the biggest common project ever completed in Coalgathering's turbulent history. It had gone up before my time, after six years of squabbling and eleven deathduels, using up no less than four Weighers. Getting unanimous agreement on *anything* from over four hundred adults was a spine-snapping task. My own pet project—paving the streets, so we wouldn't have to mudwade during the wet season—was tied up by the eternal pawful of adults unwilling to pledge their *twilga* even for something so generally useful.

But I would keep on haggling, and if necessary, I too would meet stubborn holdouts on the challenge lawn. Aggravation was a way of life (and death) for a Weigher.

The wrought-iron gate was open. I stood up on my hindlegs and walked under the stone arch. The first thing I noticed upon entering Coalgathering was, as usual, the reek. Even after a night of airing out, the town-smells set my fangs to aching. Trying to ignore them, I headed for the middle of town.

Coalgathering was crowded, noisy and busy. The stalls and pens were all built out of strongwood and stone, but no two of them looked alike. They were as close to each other as their owners could stand to have them, and the spaces in between had become winding streets. Some bushy tangletrees remained to provide shade. Two boats were tied up at the docks, loading coal. Both thunderfish pullers were thrashing in their harnesses, blowing tall plumes of dirty water, anxious to be away from the shore.

Most of the stalls and pens were open for business. Artisans were at work or hawking their wares. Professionals were plying their professions. Taverners were pouring, savants were studying, claw-trimmers were clipping, and so on. Many adults were browsing and/or buying, and *tagnami* were scurrying about on errands. All the activity made me personally edgy and professionally pleased. Activity meant disputes and disputes meant work for the town Weigher.

Like most towns, the middle of Coalgathering was the challenge lawn. It was roughly circular, about twenty-five strides across. The groundplant was lush and almost scarlet—supposedly kept so by the constant infusions of blood. The lawn wasn't currently in use.

The Weigher's stall had a place of honor on the edge of the challenge lawn. It wasn't as large and ostentatious as the miners' stalls, but it came close—and it had a lot more prestige. It sat on a raised foundation, with three smoothstone steps leading up to the doorway. The strongwood lower-walls and pillars were carved with important Weigher proverbs, and weather-finished in lavender (my favorite color). The chimney rose through the peak of the pyramid-shaped roof. Since rain hadn't threatened overnight, I had left the leather upper-wall flaps rolled up to let the river breeze air the stall out.

It looked just like it had when I closed up yesterday. But as the saying goes, never trust your eyes when you have a nose. I dropped to four legs and loped once around the stall, sniffing for any intruders. No fresh scents of people or animals.

I wound the clock and hurried through the rest of the opening-up routine. Then I settled gratefully into the chair behind the big old desk. The chairs around the

hearth were for clients. A pair of tall cabinets brack-
eted my view of the challenge lawn; their shelves
were crammed with leather-bound volumes of past
weighings. The wood was all shine-finished sandwood,
and the chairs were covered with smooth watersnorter
hide. Business had been good lately.

Leaning back, I silently prayed to Kraal for a few
heartbeats to catch my breath and ease my aching leg
muscles.

No such luck. I was idly checking my foreclaws,
wondering if it was time for a trim, when I heard paws
stomping up the steps. A shadow interrupted the crisp
golden sunlight slanting through the open upper-wall.

"Slasher! It's about time you opened! I've been
stalking your stall like a nightflier on the hunt for the
last hundredth-day!"

I recognized my first client of the day by his scent
and hollow-jug voice even before I looked up. "Good
morning to you, too, Treesap," I said in my best pla-
cating tone. Weighers couldn't afford to take offense
easily.

I gestured permission to enter. Treesap stomped
over and leaned across the desk, glaring down at me.
He was a strikingly unattractive old coot. His brown-
and-white fur was thinning, one of his fangs had broken off, and his dilapidated darterhide beltpouch was
an insult to fashion. Despite this and his abrasive personality, he was a skilled doctor with a thriving
practice.

"There's no time to waste, Slasher!" he ranted. His
breath was making an unfavorable impression on my
nose. "I can't see any patients until we settle this!"

"Settle what?"

"You won't believe it until you smell and see it!
Come on!"

"Will you slow down, for Kraal's sake, and explain
what the problem is instead of blowing like a thunderfish?" I wondered what could be upsetting Treesap

so much. I had seen him with his fur up before, but never so high that he stopped making sense. Maybe senility was setting in.

I pointed to one of the chairs. "Why don't you sit down, take a deep breath, then tell me about it from the beginning?"

"I want you to come over to my stall," he said a bit less fiercely. But he made no move to sit down. "There's something there that . . . I don't understand. Not that I expect you to explain it to me. But it creates a *twilga* problem that's way beyond me."

"Something? Quit being so mysterious."

"Maybe you can put a name to it. But you won't be able to, until you get your tail out of that chair and come with me!"

I gave up. Sighing, I stood up and followed him out into the bright morning.

Treesap's stall was at the end of Doctor Street, near the docks. We cut across the challenge lawn and wove through the milling herd of adults, *tagnami* and the occasional wagon. Treesap ran on four legs, so I reluctantly did the same to keep up. Not only did it remind my legs how tired they were, but it was embarrassing. Civilized people walked upright in town except for emergencies. I made a mental note to add ten percent to his fee for discomfort. I said quick good mornings to friends in passing and wasn't there to hear their replies.

I was relieved to see that, even in his obsessed mood, Treesap didn't get too close to any adult. At his age, he couldn't outfight a half-starved cub.

His stall was small and plain compared to mine. The unadorned firebrick design was new and popular with savants, but to me it looked like an overgrown block with a shingled roof. A crowd in an ugly, snarling mood was gathered around the stall. As we carefully edged our way through, I found out the reason. Something was giving off a truly loathsome, dangerous smell. The fur on my back rose and my fangs bared uncontrollably. Protective instinct shoved rational judgment aside.

No one was getting too close to the stall. There was a lot of what-is-it chatter going on, but the snatches I heard didn't make any sense. Emerging from the crowd, I warily followed Treesap into the stall. The dangerous smell became stronger. Now I wasn't embarrassed about not being upright. Four legs for hunting, four legs for fighting.

The examination table and the other furnishings were as utilitarian as the stall itself; alcohol lamps hung from the ceiling to supplement the daylight when necessary. But I hardly noticed the deplorable decor. A couple of strides inside the stall I froze.

The source of the smell was lying on the smooth-stone floor.

It was some kind of animal, unlike any I had ever seen before. Almost as big as an adult, but thinner. It looked arboreal, with hindlegs that ended in lumpy silver paws, and spindly forelegs well suited to hanging onto branches. A slender neck supported a truly hideous head: kinky black fur on top, raw brown hide everywhere else. Its flat face included round eyes, stubby ears, a monstrous nose and plant-chewing teeth. Its frail body was wrapped in a loose, slick white hide, and it was decidedly hump-backed.

It was dead, of course. I assumed that the claw-slashes across its throat had been put there by Treesap. The dried blood was brown like a person's. "What happened?" I asked Treesap.

"I found it in here when I arrived this morning, so I killed it."

Perfectly understandable. With a scent like that you wouldn't want to take any chances. This sort of thing happened every now and then; the wall wasn't a perfect defense against wandering animals.

"It was quite a fight," Treesap bragged. "You can

smell how fearsome the beast was. But it trespassed on the wrong person's territory."

I looked around dubiously. No marks on Treesap, no visible damage to the stall, and the dead creature didn't look nearly as dangerous as it smelled. The "fight" must have taken place mostly in Treesap's mind. "But what was it doing here?" I wondered aloud. "If it was hunting for food, the breeder pens would have been a better place."

"Damnedest thing I ever saw," Treesap growled, scratching his snout. "It was rummaging through my medical tools, picking them up one at a time. Crazy."

I looked at the scalpels, bottles of bloodpuller worms, bandage rolls and so on arranged on his shelves. If the creature had been playing with them, it had also put them back where they belonged. Curious behavior for an animal.

I looked back at the carcass. It was a very odd creature. "I don't think that hide is hide at all. It looks like a covering of some sort. And that lump on its back could almost be a strange style of carrysack."

"So what?" Treesap demanded.

I hissed at his lack of imagination. "I've never heard or read of any animal like that. Here or anywhere else. Have you?"

Treesap shook his head.

"Have any of you?" I yelled out at the crowd, most of whom were eavesdropping shamelessly on our conversation.

"It could be a demon of the First or Second Circle," a priest suggested. Treesap looked even more pleased with himself at the notion.

"That evil . . . thing . . . is no servant of the god I worship," another priest disagreed. "Nor of any of the Ninety-Nine Gods for that matter."

"None of the Holy Writings mention anything like it," a third said to the first. "Only a witless priest of the god of swamp-muck could be so ignorant."

That set off a spirited theological discussion among the priests. Finding no help there, I turned to the savants. "Any of you recognize this carcass? Rubbertail, you study animals. Ever come across one like this?"

Rubbertail, a lean male with unkempt gray fur, looked up distractedly from staring at the creature. "Ur . . . no, Slasher. Nothing even close." The other savants nodded in agreement.

I turned back to Treesap. "So what do you want from me?" I asked him.

"Well, this carcass belongs to me, doesn't it?"

I thought. "No one has claimed ownership?"

"Are you joking! If this monster belongs to someone, I'll challenge the owner for unleashing it on me! It's ruining my business—no patients for sure until this place airs out!"

"Hmmm." It certainly wasn't an escapee from the breeder pens, or a work-beast like the miners' runlegs. It must have wandered in from the Wild. "Since no one has claimed it by now, I don't see any reason why you can't."

"Good. Rubbertail here wants to buy it from me to cut up and study. We haven't been able to agree on the *twilga*." Treesap gestured, and Rubbertail rushed into the stall, his *twilga* book out. His attention was still mostly on the creature.

Rubbertail was one of the top animal-science savants between the mountains and the sea. He specialized in breeding and territorial maintenance problems. If anyone could solve the mystery lying on the floor, it was he. "So the creature has piqued your curiosity, too?" I asked him.

"Ur . . . right, Slasher. This is big. A whole new species, maybe a whole new family."

"I would be interested in hearing anything you come up with."

"Of course. Always glad to talk shop."

Treesap growled. "Nobody is going to come up with anything, until I get my *twilga.*"

Business before intellectual curiosity. "Right," I said crisply. "Let's go over to my stall to negotiate. I can't think clearly in this reek. It makes me want to kill something."

"Sounds good to me," Treesap agreed. Rubbertail nodded reluctantly. He seemed afraid to leave the creature, as if it might get up and walk away in his absence.

We left the stall. The crowd was all but gone; most of the people had gotten tired of gawking and speculating and had returned to whatever they were doing before. Out here the breeze had cleared away much of the dangerous scent. I refilled my lungs with the relatively fresh air, then led the way back to my stall. Calmly and on two legs, like civilized adults.

On the way I tried to engage Treesap and Rubbertail in casual conversation. One trick of the Weigher trade was to get the clients in as relaxed a frame of mind as possible. I like to think of myself as a reasonably interesting conversationalist, but between Treesap's irascibility and Rubbertail's distraction, my efforts died as dead as the creature. I finally gave up. We walked the rest of the way in silence. It bothered me somewhat that this weighing, like most, was only going to deal with the petty issue of who owed whom when there were much larger questions to ask.

Arriving at my stall, I settled behind my desk and gestured Treesap and Rubbertail to chairs positioned at the other two points of an equilateral triangle. The Wary Triangle, it was called professionally.

"I take it you both want to hire me to weigh this matter for you?" I asked formally. A silly question under the circumstances, but attention to details was one of the things that had kept me alive so long.

"Yes," Rubbertail said quickly. He was eager to

make a deal, always a promising sign. Treesap growled his agreement.

"First things first. My standard fee for an in-stall weighing is sixteen *twil* per client per hundredth-day."

The time measure was a recent innovation in the profession. I liked it because it speeded up cases and generated more *twilga*.

They both nodded, although Treesap hissed, "Fang-and-claw marauding!" under his breath.

"Good. Now, Rubbertail, you want to buy the dead creature in Treesap's stall from him, right?"

"Yes."

"How much are you willing to pay for it?"

"I offered Treesap two hundred and fifty *twil*, which I consider a fair price."

I turned to Treesap. "I gather you rejected the offer. How much do you want?"

"Four hundred," he replied fiercely, his eyes jumping back and forth between Rubbertail and me.

The gap was rather wide and that wasn't a good sign. I was going to have to earn my fee on this one. "Okay, Rubbertail, justify your offer."

The savant was quiet for a few heartbeats, thinking. Then he said, "One. The dead creature cost Treesap nothing. Two. It's virtually worthless to everyone but me—he certainly wouldn't want to eat such bad-smelling meat."

"I could sell it to another savant," Treesap interrupted.

"Let Rubbertail have his say," I growled at him. "You'll get your turn." He bent his head in reluctant apology.

"I'm the only animal-science savant in town," Rubbertail pointed out, unperturbed. "By the time you could get it to Goodgame or Strongwood Thicket, the creature would have, ur . . . lost much of its value. Three. Two hundred and fifty *twil* is the standard price for a dead specimen of a rare species. Four. I'm not going to make much *twilga* on this—just what I can get for my dissertation from other savants."

It was a pleasure to deal with a precise mind. "Your turn, Treesap."

"The carcass isn't just rare—it's unique! Rubbertail said so himself!" Either the dispute or the *twilga* was stirring Treesap up. "It was on my territory! I risked my life to kill it! I'll take it home and use it for game-feed before I let anyone cheat me!"

Rubbertail looked shocked, but he didn't make any counterarguments. That put the problem squarely on my back.

I went over to a cabinet and brought the weighing index back to the desk. I could feel four impatient eyes glaring at me as I turned the thick parchment pages. Let them sweat it out. Speed wasn't nearly as important as being right. Petty issue or not, Coalgathering's existence depended on my ability to keep people from settling their disputes on the challenge lawn.

The category listings confirmed my memory and my fear: in all the weighings by all the Weighers since Coalgathering's founding, this situation had never come up. Sighing under my breath, I hunted for anything that might relate to it.

I jotted the page numbers of five possibles on a notesheet. Then I fetched the volumes containing the summaries, looked them up and skimmed them. The first two weighings confirmed Rubbertail's valuation of a dead rare-animal specimen. The third, about returning a lost religious relic to a priest, was a bit of a stretch. The fourth turned out to be a false trail. The last one, settling the ownership of a direbeast which had escaped from a breeder pen into a neighboring stall, offered a useful analysis of the rights involved.

Leaning back and closing my eyes, I cleared my mind of personal feelings. Weighers had to be able to think objectively. There were many factors to balance: the objective value of the dead creature, how much Rubbertail wanted it, the degree of Treesap's pride and greed, how to persuade and/or coerce concessions. No wonder they called it weighing.

Finally I opened my eyes and grinned at Treesap and Rubbertail. "A very challenging problem indeed. You both have made convincing arguments in your favor, therefore a compromise is in order. Each of you will leave here with more than you have now. I'm sure you can see the wisdom in that."

The old oil was having the desired effect on Rubbertail, but Treesap looked suspicious.

"The dead creature is undoubtedly an extraordinary specimen," I went on, "but how much that might increase its value is speculative. Rubbertail deserves most of the benefit from any additional value he discovers. Based on this, plus precedents from previous weighings, I judge that two hundred and ninety *twil* is a fair price for the dead creature."

Rubbertail winced at the amount; I knew that he wasn't a rich person. But Treesap bared his fangs and growled, "I told you I won't be cheated!"

Now it was my turn to get angry. "I stand by my weighing. Of course, if you aren't willing to accept it . . ." I glanced pointedly at the challenge lawn.

Treesap's fur stayed up for a few heartbeats. Then he thought better of it and subsided. "I accept your weighing," he muttered.

"So do I," Rubbertail said eagerly.

"Good. Two more satisfied clients. Let's wrap it up, shall we?"

We all got our *twilga* books and writingsticks out of our beltpouches and inscribed the transaction plus my fees. Then Treesap and Rubbertail hurried off to haul the dead creature over to the latter's stall on Savant Street.

As I started to write up the summary, my thoughts wandered back to the creature. I hoped I would get my curiosity-itch scratched.

# CHAPTER TWO

The rest of the morning was pretty dull. All my weighings were accepted. To survive as a Weigher, your negotiating skills had to improve as your fighting skills aged. I was still one tough predator, but not quite as tough as I used to be. Besides honing my ability to persuade others, I had earned a reputation for wisdom and honesty: a real life-saver when dealing with those adults who could outfight me.

A priest dragged in a worshipper who had fallen behind in his payments for religious instruction. A lovers' spat proved to be less convoluted and emotional than usual. The books yielded ready compensations for the loan of a tool, returning a strayed *tagnami*, letting a neighbor cross a territory, and so on.

Business slowed down to nothing after sunzenith. I idly watched a pack of *tagnami*, as they enjoyed some rare free time playing mock deathduel on the challenge lawn. A female with teasing eyes and a gray-pelted male were going at it while their friends cheered them on. I smiled at their nips and clawless batting, even as I instinctively analyzed their rudimentary fighting skills. Enjoy your play, little ones, I sighed to myself. I wish I were one of you again.

15

Enough of this. If I were going to laze away the afternoon, I could at least do it right. I closed up the stall and headed for Tavern Street. The fog had vanished from the west side of the river, and the sun was warmer than we usually got this late in the year. The breeze had died, allowing the townreek to thicken.

Snakeleg's Place was the biggest and most popular of the tavern stalls. Only the back room was roofed; the customer area was shaded by painted leather awnings. The half dozen tables well spaced across the planked floor were old but solid and functional. Drinks, not decor, were what counted at Snakeleg's Place.

"Ho, Slasher!" "How's the day treating you?" "Not another street-paving lecture, please!" "Going to be at Boulder's party tonight?" the regulars welcomed me, as I maneuvered through them to an empty table.

"Ho yourself, Loudroar. Not too badly, thank you. Why waste my breath. Wouldn't miss it," I answered cheerfully.

"Afternoon, Slasher." The Snake (as everybody called her) limped over on a hindleg and a wooden peg. A demonflier had gnawed the other hindleg; the replacement was Treesap's best work, as well as the inspiration for the tavern's name. "What will it be today?"

"The same as every other day, Snake."

"Coming right up." The Snake disappeared into the back room and emerged moments later carrying a steaming mug on a tray. She placed the mug in front of me with a flourish. We settled the *twilga*, then she hurried off to serve other customers.

The bubbling pink brew was fermented direbeast milk spiced with darter blood. Nobody else made it like the Snake. I took a sip, enjoying the warm glow reminiscent of the kill. I joined in the friendly word-batting of the regulars for a while, then concentrated on my drink.

A few sips later I smelled and heard someone coming toward my table. Looking up, I saw a young male stop at a respectful distance and smile at me. He was big and muscular with long legs, a lean waist and no flab anywhere to be seen. His fur, thick and well groomed, was reddish-brown except for a cute patch of white on his belly.

Irongut, that was his name. He was a clay-worker with a modest stall over on Goods Street. I knew him casually from a few weighings, and the little I could remember about him was favorable. But of course, his lower dominance ranking kept us from mixing socially.

"Good day, Slasher," he said. He had pretty good control for one so young, but I could smell that he was tense for some reason.

That piqued my curiosity. "Good day, Irongut. If you need a weighing, I'll be back in my stall in a hundredth-day or so."

"I wouldn't intrude on your free time with business," he said earnestly. "I was wondering if I might join you for a drink?"

"If you wish," I said in a neutral voice. I was curious about what he was up to, but I didn't plan to make it easier for him.

He sat lithely across the table from me, his shaggy tail sticking straight down from the chair's butthole. Another sign of tension.

The Snake limped over, took Irongut's order, and brought him a mug of spiked treeswinger blood. When the *twilga* was settled and the Snake went away, Irongut took a huge gulp of his drink.

"To what do I owe the honor of your company?" I asked him sharply. I was going to enjoy teasing this impudent cub.

"No particular reason," he lied. "I caught scent of you when I came in and thought I would say hello. I heard about the mysterious animal Treesap caught and

killed in his stall. I was too busy to go see it, but I
heard it wasn't something you would want to meet."

Okay, if he wanted to break the ice with small talk,
I would play along. "It certainly smelled dangerous."

"You saw it?"

"Treesap sold it to Rubbertail, the savant. They
came to me for a weighing."

"Was it as strange as everybody says?"

"Stranger." I gave him a brief description.

He was quiet for a few heartbeats, thinking. "I don't
like it. I think the animal's appearance is an omen. A
bad one."

The religious talk surprised me. Then I remembered that Irongut was unusually conservative for a
youngster. "I hope the creature was just a lone stray
from far away. Rubbertail will get to the bottom of
it."

The topic expired by unspoken mutual consent.

"I've always been interested in Weighing," Irongut
started a new one. It seemed to be a stride closer to
the real point; his scent was becoming very interesting
indeed. "I would like to learn more about your
profession."

"Really. Are you planning to challenge me for the
job?"

He flinched nicely. "No, of course not. I just
thought we might swap some stories."

"What makes you think I would care to hear about
the grubby details of making pots and jugs?"

He stiffened. "Clay-working is as honorable a trade
as any, I'll have you know."

"Of course it is," I said soothingly. I didn't want to
drive him away. "By all means, let's swap some stories.
Low gossip preferred."

"I think I can oblige you. Did you happen to notice
that Longfang hasn't been in town for the past few
days?"

Longfang was another clay-worker, a more successful

one than Irongut. I had a few of her prey sculptures at home. "As a matter of fact, I did. I suppose she's away on a business trip."

"Wrong. She's hiding out in her territory."

Longfang hiding? Longfang, who would spit in the eye of a direbeast. "I find that hard to believe."

"She was mixing a batch of glaze and must have had an accident. She spilled it all over herself. Damnable stuff—sticky as glue and you can't wash it out. I caught a glimpse of her as she ran for the North Gate. She looked like an afterbirth."

I almost spit brew as I howled in laughter. Heads turned briefly to see what was going on.

"Her fur will have to grow out and be clipped," Irongut went on. "We might not see her again until spring."

"I was wrong," I managed to admit as my laughter subsided. "Clay-working does have its moments."

I didn't have anything in my anecdote collection to top that, so I decided to use the old parent/*tagnami* gambit to reestablish my dominance. "Now it's my turn," I said. "What would you like to know about Weighing?"

"Everything. But for now I'll settle for the answer to one question. What does it feel like to be a Weigher?"

That was a deeper question than I had expected. Maybe Irongut's interest in Weighing was more than just a conversational ploy.

"Mainly, it makes me feel powerful," I replied, trying to be honest with myself as well as him. "Each weighing is a fight, a fight to bring two opposing points of view together. And I've won every one so far."

"Does it ever bother you to . . . interfere in people's lives?"

I nodded. "At times. But it has to be done—otherwise deathduels would depopulate the town. Besides, my clients pay me good *twilga* to interfere."

"We pay you what you're worth," Irongut said with

surprising intensity. "Coalgathering has never had a better Weigher. Nor has any other town."

I was finally getting a good read on his scent and I could hardly believe my nose. He was courting me! My first reaction was shocked amusement bordering on indignation. A young nobody like him had brass-plated balls to be stalking me.

My eyes wandered up the sleek fur of his chest to his powerful shoulders and the proud jut of his snout, and suddenly, I wasn't amused at all. The charming, mature professionals I usually ran with had been getting a bit staid lately. Maybe it was time for something different. Something fresh, young. Irongut was hardly an intellectual predator, but he was pleasant, aromatic and eager. I felt a delicious tingling between my hindlegs.

Control, I reminded myself. Don't let your rut-lust run amok. No Weigher worth her fur would make a snap decision on such an important matter. And if we did end up mating, I was going to be dominant. (In control, of course, not in position.)

"This has been a very interesting chat," I said sincerely. "I wish we could swap a few more stories. Unfortunately," I glanced at the tavern's new water clock, "I have to get back to work right now." I finished my drink and stood up.

Irongut smelled uncertain, which was exactly how I wanted him. "I enjoyed it too," he replied. Picking up his mug, he put on a good show of casualness.

"By the way," I said, "I'm going to Boulder's hunt party tonight. How about you?"

"I've been invited, but I haven't decided yet."

"Well, I hope I catch scent of you. We can continue our chat—swap more stories, or whatever."

Irongut grinned. He figured he had won a point, but he was too unsophisticated to feel my leash slipping around his neck. On that note I headed for the tavern's entrance.

Walking back to my stall, I noticed that my tail was wagging like a *tagnami*'s in her first cub-love. I quickly lowered it before anybody noticed.

But I still felt Kraal-blessed good.

No clients were waiting for me when I got back to my stall and none showed up the rest of the afternoon. I took advantage of the town's rare tranquility to catch up on my paperwork. I indexed the weighings from the past few days and read an article on territorial boundary disputes by the Weigher in Riverbend. I tried to keep my mind on business, but it kept wandering to sleek, reddish-brown fur and a firm, powerful body.

Finally the sun slanted down toward the hills beyond the river. Hearing the end-of-day town activity, I put the journal away and started to close up my stall. The sky and wind suggested a rainless night, so I left the upper-wall flaps rolled up again. I joined the flow of people and wagons on their way to the North Gate. The boats pulled away from the docks and headed upriver. The stalls and pens I passed were closed or closing.

There was the usual milling crowd having goodnight conversations in the clearing outside the gate. The noise from the people using the South Gate was like a distant echo of our own. Under the pelt of sociability lurked the real reason for the loitering: nobody wanted to leave their property until Coalgathering was empty.

The last person out closed the gate. The latch would stop any animal, even a wild adult. Townspeople, of course, stayed out of town at night except in emergencies. Travelers, wilders and marauders sometimes raided the town at night, and very occasionally a townsperson would sneak back to steal from somebody else's stall or pen. But not more than once. The thieves were identified and tracked by their spoor and circle-challenged. Their skulls adorned trophy poles in

front of stalls and pens around town, warnings to those
considering such dishonorable acts.

I wondered if the strange creature in Treesap's stall
had been smart enough to work the latch or had gotten into town by way of the river.

I looked around for Irongut (without looking like I
was looking), but he must have been at the other gate.
Rubbertail was deep in excited conversation with some
other savants. Treesap was nearby, but I had had quite
enough of him for one day.

We set out for our territories, spreading out in ragged groups on the commonland trails. The slower-
moving wagons rattled along behind. I glanced over
my shoulder. Coalgathering was silent and still, almost
part of the terrain.

I ran north with a pawful of my neighbors. We
loped along; age, tiring days, and the lack of any reason to hurry combined to set an easy pace. The
younger *tagnami* strained at their parents' choke
leashes. I chatted with Flatpaws and the other adults
as we climbed towards the gap between the God's
Fangs. We discussed the events of the day and the
strange creature was the main topic.

A sharp wind was coming up, but the smell of the
open was invigorating after a whole day of the town-
reek. Beyond the Fangs the meadowland soon became
a shadowed forest around us. Our group dwindled as
we came to territory after territory. Finally, reaching
mine, I also took my leave.

My territory. I felt happier, more secure, the
moment I entered it. My aching legs and pounding
heart didn't bother me as much. All my town-worries
went away. I was home.

The narrow side-trail ran west, toward the Muddy
River. Violet tangletree and fireclaw bush scented the
air over the seasonal rankness of mouldering leaves.
Birds cawed, screeched and flew away as my passage
disturbed them. Shafts of golden light slanted through

gaps in the trees; above the gaunt strongwood branches, the day was beginning to darken. I was ready for a light dinner, a nap, and then some serious partying at Boulder's.

A few hundred strides from the boundary of my territory, the trail dipped into a sheltered dell. A stream frothed through a lush meadow on its way from the Low Mountains to the river. My cabin straddled the stream near the middle of the meadow, surrounded by sad-looking flowerless flower beds. I approached the cabin warily from downwind, checking for uninvited guests. It smelled and looked right.

The old place hadn't changed much over the years since I had won it from my parent. The "log cabin" style was considered rustic if not downright out-of-date. But I had grown up here and I liked it the way it was. The strongwood logs, stripped of bark and glossy with weatherproofing, were laid out in a square lower-wall eight strides to a side. The bark had become the shingles on the wedge-shaped roof which sloped steeply to keep snow from collecting on it. The hearth's chimney was a brick tower on the side of the cabin next to the woodshed. The upper-wall flaps were rolled up so I could see that everything inside the cabin was as I had left it in the morning.

I glanced unhappily at several upkeep jobs that needed doing before the first snow. Then I lifted the old-fashioned doorway bars out of their notches and went in.

Now I was really home. The floor was strongwood planking covered with imported icestalker pelt rugs, except where the stream ran in a rock-lined trench. The inner halves of the logs had been planed, caulked and painted into lavender lower-walls. The furnishings were sturdy and well made, and had been in the cabin longer than I. Brass candleholders were mounted on the roof pillars. Every level surface was cluttered with books, dirty mugs, brushes, beltpouches, etc.—the spoor of my life. The cabin even smelled like me.

My hindpaws curled gratefully in the silky softness of the rugs. I lit the candles to fend off the fast-falling night, then dropped to four legs for a drink from the stream. The mountain-water was cold and wonderfully refreshing, especially after a long dusty run. I took no more than a sip. Hunting on a bloated bladder at my age was asking for indigestion.

I unbuckled my beltpouch and remembered to water the plants. Then my thoughts turned to dinner.

Nikniks were starting to chirp beyond the open upper-walls. The cool breeze out of the north carried faint, tantalizing promises of many tasty animals. There was no threat of rain or snow. Perfect hunting weather. Dropping to four legs, I loped out the doorway.

The night was complete under the forest canopy. I couldn't see much, even after my darksight adjusted. But this was my territory; I knew every tree, every rock, every fallen leaf. Besides, I had my nose and ears.

I followed the stream down toward the river. Sometimes a resource, like coal, made a territory valuable, but usually it was valued by the quantity and diversity of its game. By this traditional standard mine was a prime territory, one befitting a Weigher. The river nourished life, so that the territories along it were the richest in the region. Even in late autumn I wouldn't go hungry.

I moved as quickly and quietly as a stray moonbeam. The web of being, to which every animal and plant contributed a strand, intensified in the darkness. It cocooned and exhilarated me. At the same time it sensed and acknowledged my presence. I felt the heightened awareness, the fear, the movements.

I wasn't just the master of my territory; I was its caretaker. I defended it from outside predators, I pruned the sick and the old, I planted and fed, I undid the damage of storms/floods/fires, I controlled populations. I earned and held my place at the top of the food chain, and I claimed my due. But when I died the meanest creatures would have their turn with my carcass. I would give back what I had taken and go to Kraal with balanced *twilga*.

My reflective mood gave way to hunger and the thrill of the hunt. Just a snack to settle my stomach, actually, since I hopefully would be eating later. But a hunt was a hunt. My breathing quickened and deepened. My blood burned. I felt my extra-energy kick in, making me a predator-and-a-half for a short time and one mean bitch to boot.

I prowled along the river bank, then settled in behind a big millioneye shrub downwind of a favorite watering place for the local fauna. I caught no scent of poachers or other predators. Good. I waited for some tasty nocturnal animal to arrive for a "morning" drink.

I waited. A bug-itch behind my ear was driving me crazy since I couldn't move to scratch it. Finally I smelled and heard a family of lumpmeats waddle up to the bank.

I swallowed rising saliva. Lumpmeat was an acquired taste, but I had acquired it as a cub. The hard shell and stubby legs gave a lumpmeat the defensive posture of a rock. You had to pounce like lightning and decapitate it on the first swipe, before it could retreat into its shell.

Deciding to go after the bulbous head of the family, I leaped. The others hid in their shells, but I nailed papa. Out sprang my forepaw claws. Off went the nubbin head.

I finally got to scratch the maddening itch behind my ear. Then I dragged my dinner to a patch of groundplant a few strides away from the river bank, where I could dine comfortably and with fewer bugs for company. Rolling papa over, I sank my fangs into the soft belly. The cold-blooded meat was chewy but delicious. The surviving lumpmeats took advantage of my preoccupation to scuttle into the river and float away.

Leaving pretty much an empty bowl for the scavengers, I took a drink from the river and washed the blood off the fur around my mouth. My tail wagged contentedly.

I headed home, setting an easy pace for the sake of my digestion. Now that my hunger was satisfied, I remembered how tired I was. The music of the birds and the nikniks was like a soothing lullaby. I was yawning by the time the flickering yellow lights of my cabin emerged from the twilight to beckon me.

Everything inside was as it should have been. The breeze was turning brisk. If I had been staying in for the evening, I would have built a fire, but I would settle for a warm nap. I blew out the candles, climbed into my round snowyfeather bed, and pulled the furskin blanket over me.

# CHAPTER THREE

When I woke up, evening had given way to night. The sky beyond the open upper-walls was a black void in which hundreds of stars burned like tiny white candle flames. Sprinter was already near zenith, while Loper hung just above the southern horizon. Both of the moons were full, casting their soft, pale illumination over the dell and the forest.

I got up and stretched/creaked/yawned. A splash of cold stream water in my face finished the waking-up process. I let out a glad-to-be-alive howl that reminded every creature for hundreds of strides who was boss. I felt rested and refreshed, with a slight edge of hunger. Time to party.

After lighting the candles, I squatted in the downstream end of the trench. Then I washed up, shook dry, and brushed the mats out of my fur. I transferred my things into my new gem-studded formal beltpouch and put it on. I very much wanted to be at my best tonight. Irongut was going to be there.

It was time to go. I actually felt a bit nervous. I would be hunting two different types of quarry tonight, and I wasn't sure which would prove the more dangerous. I pushed the silly, juvenile feeling out of my mind.

I put the cabin in order, blew out the candles, and went into the night.

Entering the forest, I loped northwest along a different trail from the one which led to Coalgathering. It was less frequently used and more overgrown, but I still knew every stride of it, even in the darkness. The heavy, damp air was rich with the smells of growth and decay. As my leg muscles loosened, I picked up the pace until I was running at my best broken-country speed. Breathing easily and not even working up a sweat, I felt ready for anything.

I reached the boundary of my territory and emerged from the forest into more open ground that was commonland. I veered east onto the wide wheel-rutted trail to Stonebox Valley. The land rose gently with graystone outcrops jutting through the brush and groundplant. The interrupted ridges of the Low Mountains were towering shadow-cloaked presences a few thousand strides to each side.

The night world was a different world as the poets and songsmiths were always reminding us. Everything seemed to glow with its own subtle, secret light. The birds, bugs and scurrying creatures went about their business more quietly and cautiously. Only the frail white moonlight resisted the dominant black; all lesser colors were overwhelmed.

Stonebox Valley was rolling meadowland dotted with trees and shrubs, fed by energetic mountain streams. The groundplant was belly-high and almost as lush as the challenge lawn. Out-of-season groundflower stalks waved fitfully in the breeze. The game in these meadow territories tended to be low and fast: darters, direbeasts and so on. Nothing you would trade a river territory for, but a tasty change of pace. I licked my lips.

Although there was now a lot of sport involved, the

hunt party had evolved from two important customs. One was guest hunting: buying permission to hunt on another owner's territory because you were visiting or your territory was depleted. The other was group mating: a pack of people getting together so that everyone's pairing-off choices were improved, and so that the collective rut-scents whipped everyone into a frenzy. Direbeasts and Irongut. It was going to be quite a night.

I caught the scents of other partygoers who had passed this way ahead of me. The freshest one was a bit of a surprise; I hadn't thought that Rubbertail would be interested in this sort of tail-chase. But who was I to talk about going against type? I wanted to talk to him so I sped up to a flat-out sprint.

"Ho, Rubbertail!" I yelled as I heard his pounding paws up ahead. "Have mercy on an old predator! Slow up!"

The savant slowed his pace. When we were running easily side-by-side, he said, "Evening, Slasher. Heading for Boulder's party, I assume?"

"Where else? I'm glad I ran into you. Have you solved the mystery of Treesap's creature yet?"

"Well, I've completed the external examination and I've begun to dissect it. But everything I learn only increases the mystery." Rubbertail paused. "Is this interest of yours professional?"

I laughed. Rubbertail might be young, but he was no fool when it came to business. "No, just simple curiosity. Don't tell me any secrets I'll have to pay for."

"The things I can tell you for free are amazing enough." He seemed eager to talk about his research. "First, the lump on the animal's back did indeed turn out to be a strange kind of carrysack. It was filled with objects unlike anything I've ever seen before—I can't even guess at their origin, purpose or materials."

"You might think about selling them to other savants," I suggested. "They might be able to identify them."

"Good idea. Profitable for me in *twilga* as well as knowledge. And likely to be profitable for the Weigher, too."

"That never crossed my mind," I lied.

Rubbertail snorted. "The animal's 'skin' turned out to be an artificial covering, like a harsh weather garment but exotic in design and manufacture. As for the animal itself, what I've seen of its anatomy so far doesn't even come close to any known species. I almost wonder if the priests might not be right."

"You know what I think," I said. "I think it was a pack animal. Some traveler from distant parts was using it to carry his things, but it got away."

Rubbertail was quiet for a long time. "Maybe. But I doubt it. I don't think the answer is going to turn out to be that simple."

I wasn't particularly fond of the theory either, but it was the best one I could come up with.

Arriving at the boundary of Boulder's territory, Rubbertail and I stopped and howled for permission to enter. When we heard Boulder's welcoming howl, we set out on the side-trail across the meadows.

Boulder was a prosperous breeder of runlegs and direbeasts. We passed fenced-in pastures in which runlegs grazed and meandered stupidly; he raised them to sell as wagon-pullers and to feed to his direbeasts.

He had built his new cabin straddling a stream which wove through a broad meadow. It was mostly stonework, and big enough for him plus his pawful of *tagnami*. Behind it stood a tall barn, stacks of baled winter feed, and the stone walls of a direbeast pen. (You needed solid walls to hold direbeasts.) I hadn't visited him for a long time. The closer we got, the more impressed I was.

The party was already warming up. The meadow in

front of the cabin had been mowed to lawn-height for the occasion. Tables laden with liquid refreshments were set up between a pair of tangletrees. Lamps hanging from the branches added their illumination to the moonlight. About twenty of Coalgathering's leading citizens were drinking, chatting and milling about. Two of Boulder's *tagnami* were serving the guests; the rest were probably sleeping or keeping an eye on the territory.

"Welcome, Slasher! Welcome, Rubbertail! You honor me with your presence." Boulder popped out of the crowd as we approached, *twilga* book in paw. Boulder was the widest adult I had ever seen; he quivered when he moved. But under the fat he was as tough as weather-proofed strongwood. More than one challenger had misjudged him to their eternal regret.

"Evening, Boulder. Nice of you to invite me," I said and Rubbertail nodded his head in agreement. "So how much are tonight's festivities going to cost me?" I added.

"A mere sixty-five *twil* for the finest libations, stimulating company, great sport, and a rare culinary treat. I know, I know, you marvel that I can provide so much for so little."

I knew better than to haggle with Boulder. Sighing, I stood up, got out my own book, and we settled up. When he turned to Rubbertail, I said, "See you two later," and joined the party.

I knew most of the people here, so I circulated through the crowd, saying my hellos and making small talk. Passing the refreshment tables, I acquired a steaming mug of fermented direbeast milk that warmed the cool night. The breeze rustled the leaves on the trees and blew fallen ones across the meadow. The scent and the harsh sibilant cries from the stone-walled pen made my fangs ache; I smelled a similar excited edge in the other guests. There was some preliminary pairing-off sparring going on, but nobody's heart would really be in it until after the hunt.

We were waiting for the last few guests to straggle in. (Including Irongut.) Spotting Shrubfur the ironworker drinking by herself, I decided to put the time to good use. I wandered casually over to her. "Evening, Shrubfur," I said pleasantly.

"Evening, Slasher," she growled back. She was about my age, with rare orange-and-black striped fur. But her morose personality and the bulging muscles of her trade offset the effect of the beautiful pelt.

"Nice weather for a hunt, don't you think?" I asked.

"Uh huh."

"Looks like it's going to be a wet autumn though. And a miserable winter."

"Uh huh."

"I'm not looking forward to getting around town once the rains start. You remember what it was like last year? Streets turning into mud puddles, sinking knee-deep every step, mud-matted fur. Thoroughly uncomfortable."

Shrubfur fixed me with a long, unfriendly stare. "You never give up, do you?"

"Being persistent is part of my job."

"Persistence can be an annoying trait. Even a dangerous one."

"What do you have against improving our quality of life?" I asked soothingly. "Yours as well as ours?"

"I have a great deal against wasting *twilga*. I don't know why you want to throw yours away, but I work hard for mine."

"We all work hard. We work hard to make our lives better. Paving the streets is a stride in that direction."

Shrubfur snorted. "It's a stride toward self-indulgent weakness. We managed to get around town despite the mud last wet season. We'll manage it again this year, and next year, and all the years to come."

"Doesn't it mean anything to you that almost everybody else in town feels otherwise?"

"No. I don't let others do my thinking for me."

Irritated by her stubbornness, I growled, "If reason won't convince you, it might come to fangs and claws someday."

She didn't intimidate worth a damn. "The hunt-lust has your blood up, Slasher, so I'll ignore that threat. But if you really want to take the matter to the challenge lawn, I'll oblige you."

The argument might have escalated, but Boulder chose that moment to spring to the top of the direbeast pen next to its thick iron gate. "Ho, my friends!" he shouted over and over until he had everybody's attention.

"Now that everybody is here," he went on, "are you all ready to hunt?"

Our answering howls were loud and unanimously affirmative.

"Good, good. I have a direbeast in this pen for each of you. They're full-grown, with plenty of juicy meat on them. I'm counting on you fine folks to make meals of them, before they can reach my runleg pastures. Of course, they will do their best to be the diners rather than the dinners. Stubbytail and her medical equipment are set up in my barn to tend your wounds, if the matter isn't otherwise provided for. Good luck and good hunting, my friends!"

I thought he would never shut up. Draining my mug, I tossed it to a *tagnami*. My beltpouch joined the others on an empty table. In less than a hundredth-day all of us guests had formed a ragged line beside the direbeast pen, on four legs and in order by dominance. I was near the front, of course. Glancing back, I spotted Irongut; he looked very fit and ferocious. We exchanged smiles, then I got my mind back on business.

"Here we go!" Boulder yelled and pulled the gate open a crack.

A loud, angry direbeast thrashed and squeezed through the crack. It was a beauty: over three strides long. The long, low, maroon-scaled body looked too bulky to move fast, but the six wide-spread legs could run as fast as a person over short distances. The triangular head held twin rows of meat-tearing teeth; the jaws could unhinge and take a whole darter in one bite. The powerful tail with its sharp scales was equally dangerous.

For a moment I saw it. Then it was a dark blur speeding across the meadow, its loud sibilant cry echoing from the distant ridges.

"That's mine!" Blacksnout the miner yelled. Letting out a fierce hunting howl, he ran after it. We shouted encouragement in his wake.

One by one the penned direbeasts escaped. One by one my fellow guests took off after them. The night rang with cries and howls, and reeked of hunt-lust. Soon it was my turn.

I caught a quick scent of my direbeast as it struggled through the gate. Then it was off. I took off after it at a dead run.

It headed instinctively for the cover of the tall groundplant. I was about thirty strides back when it reached the unmowed meadow. It disappeared except for a fast-moving path of disturbed groundplant and its cries stopped. I plowed in after it.

The groundplant whipped my legs and belly and made treacherous footing for my driving paws. My mouth hung open so I could suck in huge, quick gasps of air. I throbbed with extra-energy. I ached with the need to sink my fangs into a red-scaled throat. Gone was the sophisticated, rational professional. I was an animal. A hunting animal.

Wild howls erupted unbidden from my throat. No need for stealth, not yet. I heard other hunting howls in the distance. The direbeasts were spreading out. They were lone predators, too.

Suddenly the groundplant up ahead stopped moving, and the footfalls and rustling died. I skidded to a stop and froze. The breeze hissed across the meadow, nikniks chirped, and faint sounds marked the progress of other hunts; otherwise the night was still. The wind was blowing left to right, revealing neither one of us to the other.

Direbeasts were as smart as animals got. The blind instinct which had driven mine to flee the pen had dissipated. It knew it had only one pursuer, and it was hungry. Now it was stalking me.

I licked my lips.

It would be moving toward me now, slowly, more quietly than I could manage in the tall groundplant. I wouldn't hear it until it pounced. Which would be too late.

I slunk to the right. If I could get downwind of it, the breeze would tell me where it was. I moved as cautiously and silently as I could, all senses straining. The groundplant was waving gently, innocently, but I knew that at any moment those murderous jaws could spring out of it. The fur along my spine rose. I wasn't afraid, of course, just very alert.

I came to a dry stream bed running in roughly the right direction. I could travel more quietly on dirt and keep below my direbeast's line of sight. I crept down into the shallow trench and followed it, almost crawling on my belly.

It was a good idea. It almost worked.

I had gone about fifteen strides when I caught the faintest scent of direbeast. It thickened fast. Too fast. I leaped sideways.

A long, dark shape scuttled down the bank faster than a stooping demonflier. A sibilant cry cut through the night. Jaws snapped shut and teeth gnashed where I had been a bare moment before.

My direbeast scrambled around to face me. I sprang for the momentarily exposed throat, but its massive tail batted me aside like a cub's playball. Hide tore and blood flowed where the scales raked my left flank. I howled in pain.

A rough landing knocked the wind out of me, but I managed to roll to my paws. Just in time to see my direbeast leap at me.

Dodging to the right, I unsheathed my foreclaws and ripped its belly for at least a stride. The sensation of sinking my claws into a deadly enemy was almost as good as mating. I enjoyed its maddened cries as it scuttled around to face me.

Panting and trembling, we glared at each other for a moment. Its slanted eyes were lenses focusing hate and hunger and primordial cunning. Our combined hunt-lust was making a reek that smothered all other scents.

It spun and tried to cut me in half with its tail. But this time I was ready. I ducked, caught the tip in my fangs, and bit it off. Hot, sweet blood sprayed my face. My direbeast shrieked, scrambled up the bank and was gone.

The ugly gash in my flank burned like demonfire and I was leaking blood faster than I liked. But Stubbytail would have to wait. This wasn't finished yet. I jumped out of the stream bed and sprinted after my direbeast.

Again I found myself chasing a patch of disturbed groundplant. My direbeast had lost interest in everything but escape. I couldn't make my best speed; a weakening numbness was spreading from my wounded flank. I was gasping for breath and I knew I was leaving a wake of blood. I couldn't keep this up for long.

Fortunately, my direbeast was slowed down even more by its damage. Its pained cries were getting louder, the splashes of its blood fresher. I was slowly, agonizingly closing the gap between us. I reached deep inside myself for my last extra-energy reserves.

Now my howls were a challenge to my prey, to the world.

When I was just a pawful of strides behind my dire-beast, it realized that it wasn't going to get away. It stopped and turned. I warily matched its action. Panting, dripping sweat and blood, we glared at each other across a narrow gap of groundplant.

We each read the same message in the snarling face of the other. Let's finish this.

It sprang low. I sprang high and came down squarely on its back facing the tail. I planted my claws as best I could in the scaled hide. We hit the ground hard.

Its tail swung up to smash me. With a lightning move I caught the damaged end in my fangs. Shrieking, it tried to pull the tail free and shake me off its back. I fought to hang on.

It rolled sideways. The ground slammed into me, then five hundred rock-weights of direbeast squashed me flat. Agony exploded in my flank, searing me. My thoughts turned fuzzy. We writhed and thrashed through the groundplant. The gaping triangular head darted at my right hindleg, the knife-sharp teeth gnashed on fur.

Retracting my claws, I let go of the tail and scrambled around towards its front.

And frantically arched my back to avoid the darting head.

But the dangerous gamble had paid off. I saw a flash of pink unscaled flesh: my direbeast's throat. I slashed with my right foreclaws.

Blood splashed across my chest. The tail hit me, but without its former strength. The long body spasmed twice. Then it lay still, belly up, on a death-bed of crushed groundplant. The slanted eyes stared without seeing.

I looked up at the moons and let out a lung-empty-ing howl of triumph.

I licked my wounds until the bleeding stopped. The pain subsided but didn't go away. My panting gradu-ally slowed to normal breathing and most of my strength returned. Along with my appetite.

I smelled grinners and lesser scavengers slinking into the meadow, attracted by my kill. My warning howl stopped them. They would just have to wait their turn.

I sank my fangs into the tender belly and ate until I was comfortably full. Then I kept eating until I was gorged. The warm, bloody meat was perfect, neither gamey nor overfed. An all-too-rare gourmet's delight.

Bloated, I lurched over to a nearby stream. After drinking my fill, I washed the blood and dirt off my fur, and licked myself into presentability. Not a very good job without a comb or mirror, but under the circumstances it would do.

I started back to Boulder's cabin, walking upright and slowly to aid digestion. I passed other guests din-ing and, of course, gave them a wide berth. I heard and smelled scavengers picking at other carcasses.

The party was going strong again by the time I arrived. About two-thirds of the guests were milling around the lawn, drinking and bragging about their kills. Bandages had replaced some fur. Some of the guests looked more chewed on than me, but not many. Irongut didn't have a scratch, curse him.

I yelled (and received) congratulations, as I retrieved my beltpouch and gave myself a quick comb-ing. Then I headed for the barn.

Stubbytail had set up shop amid the wagons and tools. The hide-partitioned cubicle looked like a minia-ture version of Treesap's stall. Stubbytail happened to be my regular doctor as well as Boulder's. Blinking at me through the glasses which made her look like a nightwing, she said, "Evening, Slasher. That's a nasty-looking slash in your flank."

"My direbeast looks a lot worse," I growled. I was sore and irritable. "But I may be getting too slow for this sort of tail-chase. How did it go?"

"Vinetail needed a wagon ride home, and Shadow's *tagnami* isn't a *tagnami* anymore."

Poor old Shadow; I was going to miss him. But it wasn't the worst way to go.

Stubbytail went to work. She cleaned my wounds with treenut alcohol which overwhelmed my nose and made me whimper. Then she bandaged them and gave me an energy drink.

"If you can stay out of trouble for a day or two, you'll be fine," she said reassuringly.

"Thanks, Doc." I left the cubicle, passing some other guests waiting their turns, and rejoined the party.

Things were heating up. One of Boulder's *tagnami* was playing sweet, sultry music on a tuskhorn. All of the guests were back (except Vinetail and Shadow) and the crowd was sorting into quietly talking couples. The air was thick with rut-scents.

Keeping control, I wandered over to the tables for another mug of fermented direbeast milk. The steaming brew eased my aches and pains. Rockpaws the gem-worker approached me, radiating the kind of sophisticated charm I usually appreciated. But he quickly smelled my lack of interest and moved on. I spotted Irongut drinking alone, but I avoided eye contact. I wasn't sure in my own mind what I wanted, but I certainly wasn't about to throw myself at him.

One couple dropped to four legs and loped toward a nearby thicket. I didn't bother to identify them; the pairings would be gossipped all over town tomorrow. As other couples left to mate, I went to the edge of the lawn to admire the moons and stars, and to breathe less stimulating air.

"Evening, Slasher."

Irongut's voice startled me and sent tingles along my spine. But I was under control again when I turned to face him. "Evening to you, too," I said casually. "Enjoying the party?"

"Absolutely." He grinned, pleased with himself. I had to admit that he looked and smelled great. The mighty hunter fresh from his kill. "You look like you had a bit of trouble, though," he went on. "I hope you're okay?"

"Nothing I couldn't handle," I growled. His pairing gambit had two fangs: reminding me of the advantages of youth and challenging me to prove my good health. Both fangs bit deep. "The bandages are mainly for effect—I wouldn't want folks to look at me and wonder if my direbeast had died of old age."

Irongut laughed. Well he might, too; it had been a pretty weak comeback. Why did he have to be so attractive and so annoying at the same time.

Irongut's rut-scent was emerging from the pack, closing around me like ghostly jaws. My eyes involuntarily raked him from hindpaws to crest, and my breath caught. He noticed both slips, curse him.

"Lovely night for a party," he said with poorly simulated innocence. "We won't have many more this nice before the wet season starts, I imagine."

"Uh huh."

"A lovely night for hunting, for socializing, for . . . whatever."

"Uh huh."

"Particularly for whatever." He locked eyes with me and his grin widened. "I bet I can beat you to those nice, secluded fuzzyfruit trees over there."

"And what does the winner get?" I asked coyly.

"The winner gets to be on top."

It was an old joke, but I couldn't help laughing as I replied, "A lot of good that would do me."

"So?" he asked eagerly, with endearing earnestness.

"So your offer is very flattering. But it's late, I'm tired, and the morning isn't far off. The only run I'm interested in is to home and bed. I'm sure you won't be lonely long—Sharpbite has been circling you like a hungry demonflier. Good night."

Leaving a stunned, slack-jawed Irongut staring at me, I turned and walked away. I crossed the lawn and said good-night to Boulder and the few remaining guests. My mind was seething with conflicting emotions. I felt leaden and empty, and the tingling anticipation between my hindlegs turned to aching. But I would be damned to demonfire before I let him dominate me. No matter what it cost me.

So I told my lusting body to shut up and set out for home.

# CHAPTER FOUR

The smells and sounds of sunrise roused me from a fitful sleep. I vaguely remembered dreams in which Irongut and the direbeast had figured disturbingly. The bedding was a wadded tangle, most of it on the floor. My body ached all over and burned under the bandages. The hangover didn't help, either.

Sleeping in was tempting but not feasible. Too much to do.

I struggled out of bed, stretched and yawned amid a creaking of middle-aged bones. Swaying on four legs, I rubbed sore spots with my tail. Desperate measures were called for. I staggered over to the stream trench and plunged my head in all the way.

I came up howling and shaking off frigid water, wide awake. Filling my favorite cup from the trench, I took a short but refreshing drink. Then I went over to the wall mirror and combed out my fur, one hundred strokes from snout to tail, carefully avoiding the wounds.

I paused a moment to shamelessly admire myself in the mirror. Still a classic specimen of femininity. Thick, glossy black cub-fur. Gleaming white fangs in a boldly jutting snout. Just the right amount of arch to the back. Stomach firm with no middle-aged droop. Stubbytail's patch job added a distinguished air. The old scars across my left shoulder and flank were healing nicely. They reminded me to check my trap before heading to town.

I made the bed and tidied up the cabin. Picking out a beltpouch, I filled it and put it on. After a last sniff around to make sure that everything was as it should be, I went outside.

The sky was gray from horizon to horizon, threatening rain. Thick, dark clouds rode a howling northwest wind. Treetops and branches whipped, shedding many of their remaining leaves. The air was chill and misty, and it smelled as fresh as if it had been newly made. The day promised to be an uncomfortable one, but even so, its extra-energy invigorated me. I let out an it's-good-to-be-alive howl.

The wind brought me the day's first news of my territory. No crawler, demonflier or other hostile scents. It was safe to leave the cabin unattended. On the other paw, I didn't smell any breakfast nearby. My appetite was waking up. Last night's direbeast was just a pleasant memory; today I would have to settle for more mundane fare.

But first things first. I unrolled the upper-wall flaps and hooked them in place, sealing the cabin against the coming rain. Then, dropping to four legs, I loped across the dew-slick meadow and under the eaves of the forest. My muscles warmed up, stopped aching; I lengthened and quickened my stride until I was running easily. Trunks and underbrush blurred past.

The trail took me over a ridge, across a small stream, and through more woods. Finally I came to the southeast corner of my territory.

The flora and fauna were no different beyond the invisible boundary. But a territory wasn't a physical thing; it was a challenge to all comers. This is my land.

Trespass and die. The form of the challenge was older than history.

I ran the bounds at top speed: west to the river, north along the bank, east to the commonland, then back to where I started. I didn't come across any suspicious spoor. I squatted in the usual places and set my warnoffs. Thanks to the party, I had no trouble fulfilling my obligation. I didn't meet any of my neighbors since I was running late. But I could smell that they had already set theirs.

Now I was really ready for breakfast. Lurking at the edge of a stream-nourished meadow where I hadn't hunted lately, I asked Kraal to send me a big juicy darter. What I got, about a hundredth-day later, was a grinner. The wiry scavenger slunk nervously toward the stream.

I sprang at it. It fled across the thick groundplant, but I was faster. I brought it down near a stand of strongwood saplings. Eating my fill of the tough, almost flavorless meat, I left the rest of the steaming carcass for other scavengers. Such was the fellowship of their kind. I took a long drink of water from the stream and cleaned up.

I took a detour on my way to Coalgathering to check my trap. I had dug it along a game trail near the eastern boundary of my territory, where cubs sometimes wandered in from the Wild to hunt. Game tended to be more plentiful in the territories because we had settled the best land to begin with, and then purged it of all predators but ourselves.

The trap was elegantly simple: a sheer-walled pit with a camouflaged cover of twigs and leaves and a tethered slitherer for bait. Approaching from downwind, I smelled that the trap was unsprung before I saw it. I veered away, so my spoor wouldn't scare off any cub, and headed for town.

I loped on to the commonland trail to town, then picked up my pace. No rain yet. I hoped it would hold off until I reached town so I wouldn't regret leaving my stall's flaps up last night.

Nobody was in scent or sight on the trail. I wasn't surprised; I was making being late to town a way of life. But today I didn't miss my neighbors' company. A solitary morning run was a good time to get some thinking done, and I had a lot to think about.

Two things, actually. One of which I wasn't so eager to reflect on, so I turned first to the subject of the mysterious creature.

I certainly wasn't a traveler. But I had heard my share of traveler's tales, and I had what I considered to be a good layperson's knowledge of animal-science. West to the ocean, east to the Great Mountains, north to the frozen land, and south to the swamps and deserts, the fauna were well known. Nothing even remotely like the creature had ever been reported.

But that left a lot of the world where legend, rumor and imagination ran wild. In the frozen land there were said to be people with shaggy white fur who hunted incredible monsters. Beyond the swamps and deserts the climate supposedly became liveable again, but the seasons were reversed. Farther to the east legends put people/plants/animals like us, yet different, and another ocean. There were even tales of sailors crossing the oceans and discovering other lands.

In a world like this, where we really knew so little, why should one more mystery bother me? But it did. I hoped that Rubbertail would have more information today. I might even buy it if it was that sort and reasonably priced.

The subject exhausted itself. I was passing between God's Fangs, panting hard, feeling some soreness from my wounds but not too much. The cold wind felt good on my face.

Only one subject left. Irongut.

In retrospect I wasn't so sure that my dominance ploy last night had been the best way to go. It wasn't that I still felt my non-coital depression. Well, not just that. I was worried that in my determination to establish control of the relationship, I might have killed it in the womb. Irongut was unusually proud for his age. I might have put him off my scent for good.

I hoped that my charms and his persistence would prevent that. He would still have to come to me; I had my own pride to consider. But when he did (if he did), there were ways to make myself not utterly unavailable. I had used them very effectively when I was younger and I still remembered them.

As I approached the North Gate, I slowed to a walk and stood up. I didn't want the folks up ahead to see me gasping and dragging my tail. The usual townreek was almost non-existent thanks to the wind, for which my nose was grateful. The streets were as crowded and noisy as usual, but with most business being conducted behind upper-wall flaps, the town seemed half deserted. The seasonal change from bright and exciting to drab and dull had begun. I didn't like it, but there was nothing I could do about it except survive until spring.

A light drizzle started to fall just as I arrived at my stall. Congratulating myself on my weather prediction, I ran the bounds for hostile spoor, then quickly pulled down the stall's flaps. The notion of spending the day in an airless cave didn't appeal to me, so I only used the flaps on the windward side. Deciding that it wasn't quite cold enough for a fire, I finished my opening-up routine.

Most of my morning weighings involved, not surprisingly, last night's hunt party. A couple of disgruntled guests who hadn't made their kills also failed to make their cases against Boulder. Sanddigger, a typically pompous coal territory owner, objected unreasonably to Stubbytail's medical care. A mating failure-to-perform complaint provided some juicy gossip.

Around sunzenith I slogged through the rain and

mud to Savant Street. Rubbertail's stall was a firebrick box like Treesap's, but farther from those of his neighbors to protect them (and therefore him) from its rotting-carcass reek. The flaps were down, but I smelled that Rubbertail wasn't and hadn't been in today. Probably studying the mysterious creature at his cabin, where he did his more antisocial research. Wet, muddy and disappointed, I returned to my stall.

The rain stopped about mid-afternoon and sunlight began to appear through gaps in the thinning cloud cover. The wind calmed down to a gusty breeze. Drying and rolling up my flaps, I saw other stall owners doing the same. Coalgathering came fully to life. Soon the mud and puddles were the only reminders of the storm.

I had planned to skip my usual pilgrimmage to Snakeleg's Place; sharing a flap-sealed tavern with a pack of wet, smelly adults didn't appeal to me. Now, with no clients in scent, I changed my mind and strolled over to Tavern Street.

The flaps were up when I arrived at Snakeleg's Place. The regulars were installed at their tables. The Snake grunted her usual monosyllabic permission in reply to my entry request, then added, "Don't forget to wipe your paws, Slasher. I run a clean establishment."

"If we had paved streets in this town, we wouldn't have to," I complained. Ignoring the chorus of hisses, I used the doormat, then wove through the tables to an empty upwind one.

The Snake finished serving a tray of mugs, then stomped over to my table. "What will it be today, Slasher?"

"The usual—hot and bloody. Time to turn this miserable day around."

"You got that one right. My trade would have to pick up some to be lousy."

The Snake headed for the back room and soon emerged carrying my mug. After we settled the *twilga*, she said conversationally, "I gather from the bandaging that you had a hot time at Boulder's tail-chase last night."

"Indeed." The Snake's wooden leg kept her from hunting anything fast these days, but she used to be one hell of a predator and she liked to keep her paw in. "A stimulating evening."

"So I hear. Did you make your kill?"

My back fur rose at the impertinent question. I wasn't *that* old. "Of course," I said stiffly.

"Don't fluff your fur," the Snake soothed. "How did it go?"

I told her about my direbeast. The drink helped me warm to my subject and I went on at some length. The Snake and the regulars were an appreciative audience, contributing their own reminiscences of old hunts.

"All well and good," the Snake congratulated me when I finished. Then, lowering her voice so that only I could hear it, she added, "But I hear that the bigger prey got away."

"I beg your pardon?"

"Rockpaws was in earlier. He mentioned that you had a discreet post-hunt chat with young Irongut and that it ended rather abruptly with you leaving the party—alone. The same Irongut who was drinking with you here yesterday."

As usual, the rumormongers seemed to know more about what was going on than the principals. At least this principal. My back fur rose indignantly. "My conversations are my own business," I growled.

"Clawed a sore spot, did I," the Snake chuckled. "I thought as much—judging from what Rockpaws told me Irongut did later."

I got a grip on myself to keep scent or sight from revealing my interest. I would have given a fang to know how Irongut had spent the rest of the party. But only a cub-wit would have yielded to such an obvious dominance ploy.

"I hope he enjoyed himself," I replied casually, refusing to buy gossip with gossip.

"He did, or so—" The Snake paused, glanced behind me, and grinned. "But maybe he'll tell you about it himself." With that she limped away and started clearing tables.

I smelled Irongut coming up behind me. I turned and looked up at him. "Good day, Irongut," I said as calmly as I could.

"Likewise, Slasher." Irongut smiled broadly. Then he winced. His eyes were scarlet slits and he moved with a hint of gingerness. His fur was dull and flat.

I felt a nip of worry. "You look like webwing bait. Are you okay?"

"Never better," he replied proudly.

I nodded to the table's other chair. "Care to join me?" I felt eyes around the tavern watching and heard whispered conversations. I ignored them.

In answer to my invitation, Irongut settled into the chair with somewhat less than his usual litheness. "Can't stay long—I've got a big pot in the kiln. Just stopped by to find out how you're keeping."

"Not too badly for an old bag of fur."

"How are your wounds doing?"

"Healing nicely, thank you." Since he had raised the subject of Boulder's party, I could try to find out what the Snake had been hinting at. "Did you stay long after I left last night?"

"Until the liquid refreshments ran out."

That would explain his fragile condition. He didn't seem the sort to overindulge, so it must have been a reaction to my rejection. But why was he admitting his weakness to me?

"Then I took your advice." A self-satisfied tone

crept into Irongut's voice. "I sought out Sharpbite, and we had quite a romp."

So that was his ploy! Shock me into revealing jealous anger and thereby lay a heavy dominance paw on me. Well, he was due for a disappointment and an education. Feeling and revealing were two entirely different things. Keeping rigid control, I spoke with outward casualness. "I'm glad for you. She's an attractive young female and undoubtedly has a fine future ahead of her."

My indifference blunted his self-satisfaction; the reminder of Sharpbite's low dominance ranking finished it off. Fortunately for him the Snake chose that moment to come over and take his order. The mug of spiked treeswinger blood arrived and he lapped at it thoughtfully.

Don't drive him away now, I reminded myself. Looking him in the eye and smiling slightly, I said, "I didn't so much as cross your spoor this morning. Have you been hiding from me?"

I watched while Irongut tried to decide whether to act offended or amused. Finally he gave it all up. His soft growl was sweetly bashful in such a fierce looking young male. I let my gaze wander down his firm, powerful body, and imagined . . .

Taking a deep breath, I managed to maintain my dignity. Irongut had to come to me. It wouldn't be fitting for one of my years and dominance ranking to howl for him as if he were my first cublove.

He pulled himself together. "I wasn't sure you would want my company again. After last night."

"Don't try to fool a Weigher. You were hoping I would come to you. But you must understand that my pride is older and stronger than yours."

"I know that now," he said softly, "which is why I'm here."

I smiled. While we were batting at each other with words, we were both struggling to keep our rut-scents from rising and revealing. But neither of us was being very successful, more of an embarrassment to me than him. If things got any more out of control, the people at the nearby tables would notice.

So I tried to push the images and sensations into the back of my mind and said, "Your pot might crack if you don't get back to it."

Irongut's expression turned rigid. "You're right. Maybe we'll catch scent of each other again soon."

"Maybe we will." If he had a nose worthy of the name, he wouldn't need more of an answer.

He finished his drink and trotted off stiffly, trying to look unconcerned. I waited a few thousandth-days, for propriety's sake as well as to calm down. Then I headed back to my stall.

The rest of the afternoon's weighings were dry, dull business disputes. I spent most of the time researching old cases and making calculations. Happily all of my decisions were accepted without objections. A rain-slicked challenge lawn made victory as dependent on luck as on skill, and I wasn't particularly eager to die over the price of a keg of nails.

My mind kept wandering to thoughts of Irongut and the mysterious creature. I hadn't made any progress today toward resolving either situation. That bothered me; impatience was one of my few character flaws.

The sun dropped beyond the river and the town emptied out. As I ran home with my neighbors, I enjoyed the beauty of the rain-scrubbed world. Streams flowed with new vigor, drops fell from glistening leaves, even the air smelled fresher. Our chatter consisted mostly of complaints about how the storm had disrupted our days.

My cabin was musty from being flapped, but none of the rain had gotten inside and everything else was as it should be. I rolled up all the flaps to let the evening breeze in. Some bulbbugs had sought shelter from the wet meadow on my floor; I licked them up as an appetizer. Then I went out into the gathering darkness to hunt some dinner.

I crept through the shadowy shapes of tangletrees and fireclaw bushes. The rain had driven mudworms out of the ground and birds were feeding on them. Coming upon a flock of landed fanwings, I managed to pounce on two big meaty ones before their sharp ears could warn them. I ate everything except the feathers.

I walked slowly back to the cabin, lit the candles, and stretched out on the bed to relax and digest. Stars and both moons peeked through gaps in the non-threatening clouds. Nikniks chirped noisily. It was a bit chilly, but not uncomfortably so. I didn't plan to use the hearth until snow covered the ground.

How to put my evening to the best use? I owed a few letters to friends in nearby towns or I could play my new tuskhorn. There was the half-read book of Skyeyes' poems.

I yawned as drowsiness began to claim me. Maybe the best thing would be to turn in early.

Howling snapped me out of it. Faint howling from the southeast boundary of my territory. I sat up and cocked my ears.

Not a danger warning or a challenge or even an entry request from a visiting friend. It was a lusty mating howl. I recognized Irongut's deep baritone.

Suddenly I wasn't the least bit sleepy. Should I tighten his leash even more? No, he had learned his lesson. There was an earnest sincerity in his howls. Moreover, my own self-control wasn't nearly as legendary as I sometimes liked to think. My body moaned for him. Enjoy, it said. You won't excite the young males much longer.

I sprang to my hindpaws and howled back my invitation. Hurrying over to the mirror, I ran a quick comb through my fur. Then I waited by the door and pretended to be calm.

Then, nearer, I heard him howl again. I instinctively dropped to four legs. A blood challenge! What in the great world womb could he be fighting here on my territory? Most of the large predators had learned better the hard way. Maybe a wild adult had wandered over the mountains, hungry or sick enough to have ignored my warnoffs.

Trespass on my territory! I raced out the doorway, across the meadow, and crashed into the woods, bulling a straight path toward Irongut. Meanwhile his howls subsided into fighting growls. Something screamed, a high-pitched shriek that I didn't recognize. Then came silence, except for the cautiously returning nocturnal sounds.

I tore through dense, tangled underbrush. Branches lashed my face and forelegs. I ran flat out, calling up my extra-energy. Concern for Irongut fanned my burning rage.

Bursting into a moons-lit meadow, I found Irongut poised a few strides upwind of his kill.

I caught a whiff of the carcass and quickly joined him upwind.

He was breathing hard, but he seemed to be intact. "I offer you *twilga* for hunting on your territory," he said apologetically.

That was just a formality, of course. No one could have done anything except attack such an obvious enemy, no matter where it was encountered. I wasn't the type to worry about technicalities. "It was a trespasser, not part of my game stock. And it sure as death doesn't smell edible. No value, no *twilga*."

We both stared at the dead creature sprawled on the groundplant.

"What is it?" Irongut wondered aloud. "I've never smelled or seen anything like it."

"I have—the creature that was killed in town yesterday.

It's something new for the animal-science texts. Even Rubbertail couldn't put a name to it."

It was definitely the same species of puny, furless monster. My fangs bared. I edged closer for a careful sniff; all I could stand. "Something is wrong here," I said sharply.

"Huh?"

"This creature smells like the other one."

"So? Probably a herd of them are migrating over the mountains. Believe me, they're no fighters. This one hardly put up a struggle. If any more of them trespass, we'll slaughter them."

"I mean they smell *exactly* alike. Not like the same species or even the same pack—like the *same creature*. But that's impossible. The other one is dead, probably cut up and in jars of alcohol by now."

Irongut shrugged. "One more riddle for the savants."

I noticed a small box lying on the groundplant next to the carcass. It was white and slick like varnished wood, but the material didn't look familiar. It had tiny odd features on one side and a rectangular opening. "Is that yours?" I asked.

"No. The creature was playing with it when I came into the clearing."

"Playing?"

"Taking bits of plants, bugs and so on, shoving them into the hole in the box, then jabbing at those little bumps on the side."

I was inclined to laugh, but I didn't want to hurt Irongut's feelings and ruin the night. "How do you think it came by the box?"

"Probably stole it from someone's cabin during the day. If so, we'll most likely hear about it tomorrow."

I took his forepaw in mine. "Let's leave the carcass for the crawlers. I'm in no mood for mysteries tonight." But I decided to return in a few nights, when the dangerous scent would be blown to the winds, to have a better look at the box.

"I'm glad you invited me in," Irongut said softly.

"I'm glad you came."

Our scents were definitely communicating now. I was very aware of my hindthighs rubbing together as I moved.

Without further words and with poorly concealed haste, we loped toward my cabin.

# CHAPTER FIVE

I woke up slowly, allowing myself the luxury of a pawful of sleepy lazing. I stretched until my bones creaked, then pulled the furskin blanket back over me to keep out the brisk morning air. I felt wonderful.

Irongut had left shortly before moonset. No owner would willingly spend the whole night away from his or her own territory, but I couldn't help wishing that I might roll over and find him lying beside me. My body still felt him. I remembered the frame of the bed straining almost to the breaking point, his paws raking my back, the buds of pleasure blossoming one after another.

High as my expectations had been, Irongut had managed to exceed them. I could hardly wait for our next romp.

Enough reminiscing. I kicked the blanket aside and rolled out of bed, getting all four legs under me before landing. Pretty frisky for a mature lady, especially after such a night. I should have felt like I had been squeezed through a knothole; instead I was exhilarated.

It was a fine morning, with a heady blend of wood-land scents drifting in through the upper-walls and the doorway. The cloudless sky was beginning to brighten. All in all, an excellent beginning to the day.

I tried to speed up my morning routine, to regain the time lost to self-indulgence. I washed and finished waking up at the stream trench. While combing the mats out of my fur, I examined myself in the mirror. Irongut had marked me (and vice versa, I recalled pleasantly) with the usual assortment of bruises and bites, but he had demonstrated unexpected maturity by not drawing blood. I found my beltpouch where I had thrown it in last night's haste. Leaving the tidying up of the cabin for later, I went outside.

The air was cool and fresh, with an autumn tang of mouldering leaves. The lavender sky was streaked with crimson over the eastern horizon. The groundplant felt dew-slick underpaw. I didn't smell anything dangerous nearby, so I barred the doorway and set out across the meadow.

Curiously, considering how active I had been last night, I wasn't very hungry. I loped toward the river until I came to a stand of roundnut trees which had rained ripe nuts on the ground. Crouching, I imitated a boulder. Finally a nutcheek scampered down a trunk after the nuts. I pounced, pinned it under a forepaw, then ate it in two bites.

I washed down my light breakfast at a nearby stream. Then I ran the bounds of my territory and set my warnoffs. I picked up some time by going at my best pace, risking indigestion. When that was done, I headed for the eastern boundary to check my trap.

As I approached the trap, I could smell a cub in it. My heart fluttered at the thought of impending parenthood. The bond of parental love seemed to be stronger in the gender which bore cubs; males tended to see *tagnami* primarily as a source of free labor. Their loss.

The camouflaged cover of the trap had fallen in and the slitherer bait was gone. I went to the edge and peered down into the two-stride-deep pit. Amid the leaves and twigs which covered the floor was a healthy looking little furball about seven or eight years old. Perfect. Younger than that they weren't mature enough to handle *tagnami* education. And older, if still wild, they were unteachable. But this one would do just fine.

It stood on its hindlegs, trying to claw its way out of the pit. It was about a stride tall with a flat snout and rather ordinary gray and white striped fur. A glance between the hindthighs told me that it . . . he was male. He eyed me warily and he stank of fear. I wondered if he could have been one of mine. I had gone into the Wild four times to drop cubs. But no, the timing wasn't right for any of them.

Some discipline and education and this cub would make a fine replacement for my last *tagnami*, Keen-eyes. Too bad it hadn't been Keenbrain. He had been a bit too greedy and a bit too slow: a fatal combination. He had posted his challenge before reaching his fighting peak, convinced that the old lady had aged enough to be taken. He had been wrong, barely. That had been a few ten-days ago and the wounds were almost healed.

So now I needed a new *tagnami*. To love. To raise to worthy adulthood. To do the scut work around my territory. And to maybe someday take my job and territory and life away from me, just as I had taken them from my parent, Bigbite.

Daydreaming again. A sure sign that senility was creeping up on me. I jabbed a forepaw down into the pit, managing to avoid the young claws, and got the cub by the scruff of the neck. Up and out I yanked him.

I held him out in front of me to admire him. He was a little beauty. Lean, but not half-starved as wild cubs too often were. No visible scars. Big green eyes. He was bleating and squirming, trying to escape, so I administered my first parental lesson. I cuffed him unconscious. Slinging the limp body across my back, I set out for town.

Acquiring a new *tagnami* had put me back behind schedule, and his added weight slowed my running pace. I arrived in town even later than usual. I was going to have to do something about this. Tardiness wasn't an admired trait, especially in a professional. There was already a joke in circulation referring to me as "the late Weigher."

Coalgathering was unusually busy, noisy and smelly. The streets, still muddy in places from yesterday's rain, were crowded with artisans and wagonloads of building materials. Owners were taking advantage of the dry weather to fix up their cabins for the coming snow season. The activity reminded me that I had some similar chores to do before it was too late. But first things first. I headed for School Street.

My cargo attracted some comments from those I passed.

"Ho, Slasher! Is that thing on your back a cub or a kill?"

"Cute *tagnami*! Looks just like you!"

"Is that the next Weigher?"

I responded in kind to the friendly jibes as I maneuvered through the bustle and the mud. Let them cackle. My *tagnami* was going to do well, even better than his parent.

Turning onto School Street, I went straight to old Bentback's stall. It was smaller and more basic than the schools around it; Bentback didn't believe in frills. Pole-supported runleg hide awnings were the only covering. Four cubs about the same age as mine were squirming restlessly on two log benches, chained to them by the hindlegs to prevent wandering. The only other furnishings were a decrepit, weatherworn desk, chair, chalkboard and cabinet. The floor was unfinished strongwood planking dappled with cub dung.

Bentback was, as usual, at the chalkboard trying to beat some sense into his students. The deformity which had earned him his name made him stand leaning forward. His patchy brown fur was long and matted, and his fangs were worn flat. But his grin and his bright eyes were those of a youngster.

"I hunt!" he growled, his forepaw slashing at an imaginary foe.

"I hunt!" three of the cubs repeated in their high, squeaky voices.

Bentback hurried over to the other cub, who was occupied with licking his fur. Bentback gave the cub a sharp flick with his short rawhide whip. The cub yelped and glared up at Bentback.

"I hunt!" Bentback growled, slashing again.

"I hunt!" the cub bleated quickly, eyeing the whip.

Noticing me, Bentback came over. "Morning, Slasher," he said cheerfully.

"Morning, Bentback. Doesn't look like anything has changed since I sat on that back log wishing I could claw your heart out."

Bentback's laugh sounded more like a cough. He took the cub off of my back and looked the furball over with a skilled eye. He casually avoided the tiny claws; the cub was waking up. "Going to try again, eh?"

"You know how it is. Can't live with them or without them."

"The real trick is outliving them. Got a name for this one?"

I hadn't thought about it, so I did now. The cub was a bit small for his age. "How about Runt?"

"With a name like that, he'll either grow up into a great fighter or die young."

"That's the general idea."

"I take it you want to enroll him in my school. Well, you're in luck. As you can see, I'm just starting a new class."

We brought out our *twilga* books. "What's your current rate?" I asked.

"Six *twil* per day for as long as it takes."

"That's pretty steep. I can do better down the street."

"You get what you pay for. I limit my class size so I can give every student individual attention."

I was only arguing because Bentback would have been disappointed in me if I hadn't shown a proper regard for *twilga*. He had educated me and all of my previous *tagnami*. He was the best teacher in Coalgathering, and I wasn't about to entrust Runt to anybody else. "So be it," I said at last.

We checked our books and found a balance in my favor from a weighing last month. We subtracted a day's fee and entered the new balance. My job gave me *twilga* with almost everybody in town, so I rarely had to play around with third-party balances.

Bentback fetched a pair of short chains from the cabinet. Then he took Runt over to an empty spot at the end of the back log and installed him. My old seat, I noted warmly.

"See you at dusk," Bentback said over his shoulder as he returned to the chalkboard.

"Goodbye." I patted Runt's fuzzy little head. "Be good, *shirwa*," I said softly. Then I left.

I hurried along Breeder Street toward my stall. The aromas raised saliva even though I had just eaten. Roars, snarls, cackles, honks, peeps and haggling created an ear-curdling din. I admired the pens filled with direbeasts, lumpmeats, darters: literally every kind of local game animal.

My territory was pretty well stocked at the moment. But come the end of winter it would need restocking. At that time I would reluctantly make the necessary purchases. Reluctantly, because nobody liked doing business with breeders. They were an odd, less-than-

respectable lot, suspected of "stalking" meals in their
pens and other dark deeds.

Arriving at my stall, I was relieved to find no crowd
of angry clients waiting for me. But my sniffing around
for trespassers told me that a few had been there and
left. I opened up for business as quickly as I could.
There was a cold wind coming out of the north, so I
shoveled some coal into the hearth and lit my first fire
of the season.

Business was brisk, reflecting the unusual amount
of pre-snow season activity around town. The cold
weather frayed tempers. It took every bit of my skill
to keep petty disputes from growing into deathduels.
Even so, two of my minor weighings were rejected
and went to the challenge lawn for non-lethal fights.
An entertaining morning for the spectating townsfolk,
but not a very successful or profitable one for the
Weigher.

The glow from Irongut's visit and my new *tagnami*
managed to survive the business setbacks. News of
Runt had spread quickly. There was more ribbing and
I swapped *tagnami* stories with my friendlier clients.

The flurry of weighings tapered off around sunzenith and I took advantage of the lull to relax. Leaning
back in my chair, I put my hindlegs up on the desk.
Orange flames danced cheerfully in the hearth, wrap-
ping me in their warmth. I was too comfortable to get
up and drag my tail over to Snakeleg's Place. I wished
that a mug of fermented direbeast milk would appear
on my desk in a bolt of sorcerous lightning.

I had been too busy to think about either of last
night's visitors. Now Irongut came first and vividly to
mind. I hadn't caught scent of him this morning,
which didn't surprise me. Neither of us wanted to be
too obvious about our relationship in town; no point
in giving the rumormongers more to talk about. But
I hoped I would cross his path this afternoon. Just to

smell him. And my heart beat faster when I thought about tonight.

Then there was the matter of the less pleasant of the two visitors: the dead whatever-it-was. Eventually I would bestir myself to go look up Rubbertail, if he was in town. He would be interested in the appearance of another, identical-smelling creature. Maybe even enough to pay good *twilga* for it. At the least, he might have some more information to impart.

Identical-smelling? The more I thought about it, the harder it was to accept. My nose wasn't the keenest in Coalgathering, but it wasn't the dullest, either. There were *always* differences in the scents of individual animals, even two smallwings hatched from the same egg. Some people might have suggested that my memory was at fault, but one thing I never forgot was a hostile scent. Shrugging, I added it to the list of mysteries concerning the creatures.

Peripherally I noticed that something was happening outside. People from all around town were converging on the challenge lawn. They were in a hurry; some were even running on four legs. There was a growing volume of excited conversations.

What in Kraal's name was going on? I didn't smell, see or hear anything to get excited about. The usual explanation would have been a challenge, but no ordinary fight would have attracted such a big crowd. Besides, everybody seemed to be looking up at the sky.

Flatpaws' *tagnami* was scampering by. "Hold it!" I yelled.

The *tagnami*, a cute female just shy of adulthood, plainly wanted to keep going. But she saw who was yelling at her and skidded to a stop. "Yes, ma'am!"

"What's going on?"

"Something is falling out of the sky!"

Her words didn't make any sense. A bird would land, not fall, and it wouldn't attract much attention either way. A meteorite wouldn't still be falling, and if one big enough to see in daytime had landed in the challenge lawn, I surely would have heard it. "What do you mean by 'something'?" I demanded.

"I don't know, ma'am! I've never seen anything like it!"

That was what you got for asking a *tagnami* a serious question. I dismissed her with a gesture and she disappeared into the growing crowd around the challenge lawn.

Curiosity got the better of comfort. I got up and went outside.

Long, wispy clouds were streaming fast overhead, highlighted against the pale blue sky. The wind was scattering the plumes of dark smoke from dozens of hearth fires. Flocks of birds were wheeling above the treetops. But that wasn't what everybody was staring at.

Something was falling out of the sky. I had never seen anything like it.

It wasn't really falling, but floating down slowly, like a swampflower's seed sac. But this—thing—was round, white and huge! Bigger than a demonflier. A smaller object was dangling underneath it, attached by long ropes.

It was moving south with the wind as it descended and its course became clear. It was going to come down in the middle of the challenge lawn.

About half the town was gathered in a ragged ring around the challenge lawn, as closely packed as propriety would allow. The adults with the highest dominance ranking were on the inside, of course, while the *tagnami* on the outside jostled each other for better viewing. The scent of curiosity and excitement was overpowering.

As I worked my way to the inside of the ring, I caught scraps of conversations.

"—that size can't possibly fly—"

"—a demon of the Sixth Circle—"

"—seems to be coming here on purpose—"

"—the only open space big enough for it *to* land—"

I reached the edge of the challenge lawn. The losers of the morning's festivities had long since left to visit their doctors. A napping traveler hastily vacated his "bed", and the entire circle was empty.

The smaller object settled onto the lush crimson groundplant. Somehow I wasn't surprised to see that it was yet another of the mysterious creatures which suddenly seemed determined to plague my life. Standing erect on its hindlegs, it touched its chest with a forepaw, and the ropes pulled free. The huge white ball rose sharply, taking the ropes along. In a few heartbeats the ball and ropes disappeared into the clouds.

Finally a live one! The outlandishness of the creature's arrival had shredded my theory as to its origin and sharpened my curiosity. This time I intended to get some answers.

# CHAPTER SIX

The creature was wearing a glass bowl over its head; otherwise it looked exactly like the other two. Its scent hadn't reached me yet, but I would have taken any wager that it smelled the same, too.

Everyone seemed to be enjoying the unique entertainment. The creature turned slowly, staring at all of us. We stared back at it.

"Witness a divine coming!" one of the priests announced loudly. "Hengar, the god of storms, wielder of lightning, has come down from his high territory to bless the faithful and punish the worshippers of false gods!"

"Grinner dung!" another priest objected. "How can you possibly claim that this puny, tailless, evil creature hails from Godhome?"

"It's a demon, I tell you!" a third contributed. "Come to avenge its fallen fellow!"

Other priests expressed their opinions. The theological discussions grew heated, promising several challenges at a more convenient time. I found the chatter more amusing than informative. I liked to think that I was as devout as any rational person, but this time I figured the true explanation lay elsewhere.

The creature lifted the glass bowl from its head. It

was facing roughly in my direction, still staring silently at us. Long heartbeats passed. Then, slowly, it raised its odd right forepaw in the air, the pad facing front and all five claw-tips sticking up.

Savants were arguing eagerly among themselves. The upshot of one debate near me was that this must certainly be an intelligent being, maybe even as intelligent as a person. The ball-and-ropes could have been some sort of monstrous, unknown animal. But the slick white hide of Treesap's corpse had turned out to be a manufactured garment, like harsh-weather cloaks, though exotic in material and design. Under it, Rubbertail had found more of the hideous brown flesh. This hide looked the same. And the carrysack was also the same—the carrysack that had turned out to be filled with items which were mostly total mysteries.

The priests, meanwhile, were still stirring themselves up with talk of demons and ill omens.

The mention of Rubbertail made me wonder if he were here. He would claw himself ragged if he missed this. Glancing around, I spotted his excited face behind the inner ring of spectators. He plainly wished for a better view, but his professional curiosity didn't extend to committing suicide.

The situation was definitely novel. Everybody seemed to be waiting for somebody to take the initiative in doing something about it. There wasn't any time to hold a town meeting. The creature's terrible scent was beginning to spread. I could smell and see that some of our more notorious hotheads—notably Farrunner the carpenter—were baring their fangs. With hopeful grins, many in the ring of spectators were awaiting a unique battle.

I remembered the box I had seen last night and I was prepared to go along with the idea that the creature might be intelligent. Not very, though, or it wouldn't have come so docilely to its dying place. But the questions the savants were asking each other were also bouncing around inside my skull. What was it? Where did it come from? How many more of them were there? Why were they popping up all of a sudden?

But it didn't look like Rubbertail and the other savants would get the chance to put their questions to the creature. Farrunner took three strides toward it, then turned to face us.

He was big and powerfully built and managed a sinewy quickness despite his size. His black-and-gray striped pelt showed the scars of previous deathduels. "I post a challenge!" he growled. "This beast is obviously evil and dangerous—you can all smell that! Do any of you want to interfere?"

The priests looked pleased with this development. Some of the other hotheads were upset at being excluded from the fun, but Farrunner had a well-deserved reputation as a fighter. No one challenged his posting. He grinned smugly at the savants who were muttering under their breaths but didn't dare object aloud. Savants were rarely great fighters.

Rubbertail looked like he was going to claw himself ragged after all. His gaze jumped back and forth between intense scrutiny of the creature and enraged glaring at Farrunner. Noticing me, he shot me a beseeching look.

Farrunner turned back to the creature. "I doubt you have the wit to understand me, but you're shaped like a person, so I'll treat you like one! I challenge you to a deathduel!"

The creature didn't react.

Howls were coming from all around the ring. The mood was definitely for blood. I felt the rage, too, but fought to control it. Weighers were supposed to look beyond obvious answers and to exercise self-discipline while doing so. Killing these creatures every time one turned up wouldn't solve any of the riddles.

I stepped forward. "Wait up a moment, Farrunner.

This is something that has never happened before. It may be more complicated than it seems."

"No complications, Slasher. I'll just let its blood out."

"I think you should let Rubbertail here or another animal-science savant have it. I'll work out a fair *twilga* compensation."

"There isn't enough *twilga* in Rubbertail's book to snatch this unique prey out from under my claws," Farrunner growled.

"If not, installment payments can be arranged. Give your Weigher a chance."

"I'll be very glad to sell Rubbertail the carcass— it'll be available in a few thousandth-days. Now quit interfering, you old bitch!"

That did it. I had tried to be polite. I had tried to be reasonable. But the young punk had a venom-soaked tongue. I wasn't sure that I could take him, but life without pride was a cold thing anyway. Moreover, I had a hunch that the answers to my questions might be too important—and not just to the savants—to let them bleed to death on the challenge lawn.

"According to Irongut these creatures don't provide much sport," I growled. "Perhaps I can tempt you with something better."

"I'm listening."

"Only blood can wash away the stain you've placed on my honor. I challenge you to a deathduel."

Farrunner grinned at the thought of dramatically improving his dominance ranking. "Challenge accepted!"

So much for the formalities. We tossed aside our beltpouches. Then Farrunner dropped to four legs, and so did I. The nearest spectators moved back. The creature continued to watch in patient silence.

Farrunner and I circled each other warily. He knew my reputation, too. We hissed at each other, but spoke no more words.

Excitement at this unexpected but greatly appreciated

bonus spread around the ring. Shouts of encouragement and advice were aimed at both of us, while writingsticks scribbled wagers in *twilga* books. Farrunner seemed to be getting the better odds. Not a promising sign.

We edged closer. His back fur was up, his fangs were bared, and his eyes were red-rimmed slits. His hunt-lust smothered the scents of the spectators. I was in pretty much the same state. Extra-energy coursed through my body. I was wound tight, ready to act or react.

Suddenly, Farrunner sprang forward and slashed with a forepaw at my snout. Foreplay rather than a serious attack. I dropped back on my haunches and the claws missed by the width of a mudworm.

I didn't respond. There was a science to fighting and you learned it if you survived enough challenges. I wanted to dissect Farrunner's style so I could better dissect him.

He sprang and slashed again. And again. And again. Basic gut and gulp, with no flair, but backed by the strength and ferocity of young adulthood. I ducked, dodged and fell back. He came after me, his confidence growing. Some of the know-nothings among the spectators hissed.

Finally, I was ready. I dropped a shoulder out of the path of his slashing attack, then raked his chest with my foreclaws. Startled and angry, he jumped back. Bright red blood dripped from the shallow wound.

I didn't give him time to recover. Springing at him, I slashed left-paw-then-right-paw at his throat. He managed to bat both paws aside, and almost got my left foreleg between his jaws for good measure.

He charged. Sidestepping, I tripped him with my tail. But he was back on his paws before I could take advantage of it.

I faked a pounce, then slashed low at his forelegs.

It was one of my best moves and I had high hopes for it.

A split-heartbeat later, I yanked back a fang-grooved foreleg. Kraal, he was fast!

By mutual unspoken consent, we paused to assess the situation. Backing up a few strides, we panted and glared at each other. Instinctively I licked my wound. It wasn't serious, but the tiredness I felt so early in the proceedings was. The spectators, even the creature, were only vague presences in the background. Every sense I owned was focused on Farrunner.

He tried to catch me napping with a flat-pawed lunge, and the fight was on again.

Rolling onto my back, I let him come down straddling me. His slavering jaws sought my throat. I got a foreleg under his neck just in time, and his fangs snapped a thousandth-stride from their goal. Hot saliva dripped on me. His breath was thick and fetid.

I brought my hindlegs up and tried a flurry of belly kicks, but there wasn't enough room between us. We were caught in a straining, trembling tableau.

I yanked one of Farrunner's hindlegs out from under him with my tail. He sagged to my right, and I scrambled on top of him. Clawing at each other's backs, fangs struggling to get at exposed throats, we rolled across the springy groundplant. The slashes along my spine burned like hellfire, and we left a wide crimson trail. I bit off a howl of pain.

Squirming like a slitherer, I managed to sink my fangs into Farrunner's haunch. I tore out a mouthful of fur as he jerked away. Blood spurted in my eyes.

I was only blinded for a heartbeat, but that was all a skilled fighter needed. He caught my right foreleg in his jaws and started chewing.

I couldn't help howling this time. It *hurt*! But I also hooked a claw into his privates. He had to disengage before I could ruin him.

We crouched low, a pawful of strides apart, watching

each other warily through slitted eyes. I tried to lick away the blood and agony from my foreleg, but it was barely holding me up. A red haze blurred my vision and my extra-energy was exhausted. I was just about all in.

Farrunner, meanwhile, looked a bit frayed but basically intact. And eager for more.

Strategy, I told myself. Strategy. He was strong, fast and mean enough for a whole town of adults, and his reflexes were almost demonic. So what did I have in my favor? Experience, maybe. I would have to teach him a trick he had never seen before.

An old one came to mind. If he guessed wrong, it would work. Unfortunately it was an all-or-nothing proposition.

I slunk forward to within a couple of strides of Farrunner. Pouncing range. A wary veteran would have looked over all the angles before reacting, but he wasn't noted for his patience.

He sprang at me, a furry blur almost too quick to be seen. Long, needle-sharp claws slashed at my throat.

But my countermove, using up all of my remaining strength, was also a blur. Not a sideways lunge. That was the traditional and, therefore, the expected reaction. His sideways-raking forepaw covered too wide an arc for me to have avoided. Instead, I dropped under the claws.

Crouching as low on my haunches as possible, I felt a spine-chilling breeze as the claws parted the fur on the top of my head. Then I uncoiled and hurtled at Farrunner.

My timing had to be perfect. It was. There was his unprotected neck right in front of me.

His claws tore desperately at my back. I lost some more fur and hide, and my howl sounded more like a whimper. But my fangs bit deeply into his tough neck muscle. Arterial blood spurted. My jaws clamped shut and ripped.

I spat out a mouthful of fur and warm meat; cannibalism was considered in very bad taste. With a bubbling sigh Farrunner dropped limply to the lawn. His life poured out onto the groundplant, at first swiftly, then sluggishly, then no more.

Straddling my fallen prey, I let out a victory howl.

Cheering erupted around the ring from my supporters and those who enjoyed a good fight. Wagers were settled up. Stubbytail came toward me with her patch kit under one foreleg and a *twilga* gleam in her eye.

I growled her back. Time enough for that later. Victory was a powerful stimulant; I felt well enough to keep going without help, at least temporarily. The blood staining the fur on my back and haunch wasn't too wide a stream, and the pain was no worse than I had known and endured many times before.

The creature was still standing near the middle of the lawn. It had watched the fight silently but attentively, and now it was staring at me.

I now owned everything that had been Farrunner's. I didn't want any of it—his territory wasn't nearly as nice as mine—so I would probably sell it to his *tagnami*. But at the moment I had a more urgent matter to worry about.

"I'm claiming the challenge-right for this creature!" I shouted to the spectators. "Anybody feel luckier than Farrunner?"

Several other hotheads smelled and looked inclined to take me up on my invitation. The general mood was definitely getting ugly. I felt the same unreasoning hatred of the creature distorting my own judgment. Any moment now we would all fall upon it in a slaughtering frenzy, despite my challenge-right. How could something so puny and helpless have such a dangerous scent?

It was as simple as that.

"Rubbertail!" I shouted at a nearby cluster of chattering savants. "Do you have any jars of alcohol in your stall?"

He turned to face me, looking wounded. "A tragedy is about to happen here! This is no time for guzzling!"

"You overeducated idiot! If you want to save this creature for science, run like a cub and bring me a big jar of alcohol!"

Rubbertail reflected for a moment, then smiled broadly. "I see! A brilliant notion—it just might work!"

"Not if you keep biting air until it's too late!" I growled.

Rubbertail spun and charged away from the ring like a hungry watersnorter. I watched the rising tide of hunt-lust, trying to hold it at bay by sheer force of will. Time crawled by.

Finally Rubbertail returned, carrying a sizeable ceramic jar. "Here you are, Slasher!" he panted.

I took it. "We'll settle the *twilga* for this later! Stand back!"

"Good luck," Rubbertail said as he retreated.

He had fetched the alcohol just in time. Some of the spectators had dropped to four legs and were slinking toward the creature, fangs bared. I shouted, "Wait, my friends! Please! A moment for your Weigher! I think I can end the danger!"

There were growls of protest, but the slinkers paused.

Taking a deep breath and holding it, I walked toward the creature. What would it do? If it tried to bolt, we were both out of luck.

The creature stood still. It watched me closely, though, as I removed the jar's lid. Slowly, carefully I poured the contents over the creature's head and shoulders.

The creature flinched, but it didn't try to avoid the stinging alcohol. Maybe it understood.

I breathed as shallowly as possible. The alcohol murdered my nose, but the scent of the creature was completely drowned. I found that I could now deal with the situation with a Weigher's proper dispassion.

The creature stood as if it never dropped to four legs. The forepaws were slender and frail-looking, but well shaped for working with tools. The lack of a tail made it seem unbalanced.

I could feel the hunt-lust seeping out of the spectators. The prospects for a unique deathduel were fading fast; some people were already drifting back to whatever they had been doing. The attitude of the rest was subsiding into curiosity.

The creature reached back into its carrysack and pulled out a small gray box with two short strings dangling from it. The strings ended in a pair of black half-bulbs. The creature stuck one of them to its forehead, then held out the other one to me. It twisted its mouth in some kind of expression.

I thought I knew what it wanted me to do, but I wasn't sure that I wanted to oblige. The act could have been a harmless friendship ritual . . . or something else. Something dangerous.

Rubbertail and some of the other savants were edging up behind me, chattering among themselves like redwings in mating season. A few priests came with them.

"Any idea what that thing is?" I asked Rubbertail over my shoulder.

"No. But I suggest you take it. It could be important, and I'm sure it's safe."

I growled at Rubbertail; in his zeal he had come dangerously close to implying that I was afraid. Then I turned back to face the creature. To the Netherworld with it! I grabbed the half-bulb out of the strange paw and stuck the flat side to my forehead.

The creature touched a green square on the box.

I stood as stiff as a petrified treetrunk for a pawful of heartbeats. Then I ripped the half-bulb from my forehead and howled like a wounded cub.

Images had stampeded through my mind like a herd of spooked bigmeats. Hundreds. Hundreds of hundreds. Much too fast to be seen, but I sensed that some of them were my own memories. Others were . . . from somewhere else. I shivered; I had no desire to see those more clearly.

The creature put the demon-box back in its carrysack. "Can you understand me?" it asked.

The words coming from the oddly flat muzzle sounded more like treeswinger squawking than anything else, but they were barely understandable. I managed to keep my shock from smelling or showing.

"Yes," I replied with all the steadiness I could muster, "if you speak very slowly."

"That's good. My name is Ralphayers."

"I'm called Slasher. What did you just do to me?"

"The translator is a tool for learning languages fast. It isn't harmful."

I didn't believe in magic. But if the box was a product of science, this ugly monster knew things of which our savants only dreamed. "We can settle the *twilga* for that later, Ralphayers, and for my other service."

"Other service?"

"Keeping you alive. So far, at least."

"I see. Where I come from we have different customs. But I'll be glad to follow yours, as soon as I learn what they are."

The hundred questions I wanted to ask all tried to come out of my mouth at the same time, unsuccessfully. Getting control, I started with the most important one. "What in Kraal's name are you? Where do you come from?"

The creature paused before answering. "The stars are faraway suns and they have worlds, too. I'm from one of them called Earth."

That was a mighty big bite to get down. Still, the sky-science did match certain radical theories. And nothing even remotely like the creature was known to our animal-science—or demon-lore, for that matter. So accept it as a working hypothesis. "How did you come here? And why?"

"My people built a . . . a skyboat. It sailed here on a voyage that took many years, crewed only by machines, and now it's circling your world. When the machines found that our kind of people could live here, they . . . grew three of me. We landed one by one to study your world. My two brothers didn't last long."

Rubbertail and the rest of the savants were taking all this in avidly, as were the pawful of others who remained. I understood maybe a third of what the creature had said, but I went on doggedly. "What do you do with the information you gather?"

"The skyboat . . . sees and hears everything that happens to me, and it sends reports back to my world. Unfortunately they will take years to get there, so I can't talk with my people."

So that was why the other creature had been putting bugs and plants into its box. It had been doing some kind of research. Fascinating. Obviously this was a venture involving more participants and *twilga* than I had ever imagined possible. What incredible Weighers they must have!

"Why are you doing this?" I asked. "What could possibly repay such a huge effort?"

"Pure knowledge. We're a very curious people. Plus we've found that indulging our hunger for knowledge can be profitable in practical terms. I hope to live among you, to learn more about you."

"That won't be easy," I pointed out. "You know nothing of our customs, and your first mistake will most likely be your last. You can't even come near us without being doused in something with an overpowering smell."

"Now I see why your people killed my brothers," the creature replied. "Some kind of scent hostility-trigger—rather primitive for an intelligent species. So I smell like an enemy, do I?"

I growled yes. What a prize this creature would be, if I could handle the opportunity properly. It plainly knew things that many people would pay through the snout to learn. And it would need a guide, a broker: someone with the imagination to exploit its knowledge for everyone's good, as well as the skill to keep it alive. Who better than a Weigher? Who else would have the wisdom to work for the benefit of the town as well as herself? Who else would be able to unravel the unique *twilga* involved?

The gods don't like to hear us praise our abilities too highly, even in our thoughts. While I dreamed, my common sense slept. And I saw a blurred motion behind the creature.

I had forgotten that there was one person who would hold a grudge against the creature not based on scent. One to whom the honor won by finishing her parent's last task would justify the deadly risk of offending me by usurping my challenge-right.

Before I could react, there was a crack like a tree branch breaking. The creature sagged loosely to the lawn. Its head was almost detached from its scrawny neck. Bright red blood formed a spreading puddle under it. In the sudden shocked silence of the onlookers, I glared across the carcass at Farrunner's *tagnami*.

She was a petite beauty with pale white, almost silvery fur and thoughtful aquamarine eyes. Her fastidious grooming and the erect way she held herself bespoke a maturity beyond her years. It was a wonder to me how some *tagnami* turned out so differently from their parents. Blood like ours dripped from her foreclaws.

A more impetuous person would have challenged her for her audacity. But I was a Weigher, and anyway, I admired her loyalty. An all-too-rare trait in today's youth.

"I offer *twilga* in apology for violating your challenge-right," she said formally. She looked like one who expected to die, which was a reasonable expectation under the circumstances.

I stared down at the dead creature, feeling a sadness greater than I understood. So many things we might have learned.

To Farrunner's heir—*tagnami* no longer—I said, "I accept your offer. Wait for me. We'll go to my stall and settle the amount."

"Yes, ma'am."

Those who had been hoping for a last bit of blood from us headed back to their business. Some friends came over to congratulate me on taking Farrunner. The savants and priests closed in to gawk at the creature's carcass. I made a quick deal with Rubbertail for the carcass and carrysack; oversupply drove the price way down. Farrunner's corpse would stay where it was until his heir and I settled its ownership. Then she would haul it to her new territory for burial.

Now that the excitement was over, the weakness and red haze were coming back. I wobbled over to Stubbytail. "I'm all yours, Doc."

"One of these days you'll wait too long," Stubbytail complained. She did what she could with the patch kit. Then she guided my less-than-steady legs toward her stall for a more thorough job.

Farrunner's heir followed me dutifully. I intended to punish her insolence with a *twilga* settlement she would be years repaying.

# CHAPTER SEVEN

I settled back in my chair and watched Sweetscent—Farrunner's heir—leave my stall. My stern expression dissolved into a grin. She had conducted her end of the settlement negotiations like an honorable adult and had accepted my terms without a whimper. Her back was arched with the pride of a new territory owner rather than crushed under her enormous *twilga* burden. Her tail wagged jauntily. Those just above her in the dominance ranking had better sharpen their claws.

There were no clients waiting outside for which I was grateful. I felt like somebody's well-chewed meal.

Stubbytail had worked on me long, well and expensively. After using one of her foul-smelling concoctions to clean my wounds, she had closed and anaesthetized them with rows of stingbug pincers. Bandages were wrapped around my back and foreleg like chokevines. A mugful of another concoction had cleared away the red haze and put some strength back in my limbs. A big dinner kill and a good night of sleep would continue the healing process.

Emotionally, I was bouncing back and forth between euphoria and a sense of loss. The euphoria came from beating Farrunner and surviving to enjoy it. I was still one tough bitch. The sense of loss came from thinking about what the dead creature that had called itself Ralphayers might have meant to my career.

I gradually realized that I wanted—make that needed— a drink. Since one wouldn't come to me, I got up and wobbled over to Snakeleg's.

The regulars looked up from their mugs as I entered. Sometimes I wondered if they ever spent any time tending to their businesses or territories.

"Ho, Slasher! Hell of a fight!"

"I'm going to remember that ground-skimming move of yours!"

"Five *twil* I won, though you did have me regretting my wager there for a few beats!"

"You must be making your doctor rich!"

Responding in kind, I headed for an empty table and dropped gratefully into a chair. The Snake came over to take my order. She plainly wanted to hear about the fight, but after yesterday's failed dominance gambit it would have cost her too much to ask.

I savored the steaming mug of fermented direbeast milk as if it were the last one I would ever have, because I had just been reminded that it might be. Halfway to the bottom of the mug I caught scent of Rubbertail. Turning, I saw him approaching the table.

"May I join you?" he asked. He smelled and looked like a runleg with a burr in its paw.

"Be my guest."

He sat down across from me and ordered a mug of water. Savants.

"Let me guess," I said. "You're upset because your live specimen turned into a dead one."

"If only that ... that ignoramous Farrunner had been willing to listen to reason!" Rubbertail erupted in uncharacteristic rage. "I wish I believed in hell, so I could imagine him roasting there! And how could you have let that mere snip of a *tagnami* catch you asleep on your paws?"

My back fur rose a bit, but I couldn't take offense at the truth. "It wasn't one of my best moments," I admitted.

"Such a terrible loss to science," Rubbertail said mostly to himself.

I finished off my mug. "I regret the creature's death as much as you do, believe me. Did you hear what it said to me?"

"Every word."

"What do you think of its story?"

"That it was a visitor from another world?" The young savant paused. "Well, my study of the first specimen is still very preliminary, but I can almost guarantee that it isn't part of our web of being. And of course the priests' claim that it was some kind of demon is ridiculous. In short, I'm inclined to believe it."

"That makes two of us," I agreed. "It's the least unbelieveable explanation."

"A visitor from another world." Rubbertail sighed. "Just think about the knowledge we might have bought from it."

"I have," I assured him. "But at least you have a couple of carcasses to cut up."

Rubbertail glared at my lack of understanding. "That's like having a lumpmeat's shell when you're hungry for lumpmeat."

"Did the creature's talk of skyboats and being grown by machines and talking to another world make any sense to you?"

Rubbertail paused again. "Well, I believe that eventually science will show us how to do everything. Maybe the creatures—a misleading term to describe them, by the way, but I don't know a better one—are much more scientifically advanced than we are."

I bristled. "Surely you aren't claiming that those puny, helpless things are smarter than us?"

"When you figure out a way to float down from the sky, we'll debate the point."

"I would be more impressed with their intelligence if they didn't keep getting themselves killed."

"There is that," Rubbertail admitted. Then getting up, he added, "My friend Snowpelt, the sky-science savant, will be very interested in the creature's story. I think I'll go write him a letter, see how much he'll pay. Thanks for an enjoyable chat—I feel somewhat better than when I sat down."

"I admire your dedication to your profession," I said dryly. "Lesser townsfolk have been congratulating me on my victory over Farrunner."

"Huh? Oh, yes, congratulations. Goodbye."

He left, and about a hundredth-day later, I did the same. Business picked up after I returned to my stall, mostly wager disputes arising from my fight with Farrunner. They generated the usual amount of excitement and armchair expertise, but no blood. My weighings were all accepted, which was fortunate for me considering the shape I was in to defend them.

At sunset I went over to School Street and retrieved Runt. Any progress he had made toward adulthood was too subtle for me to detect. During the run home, I fell well behind my neighbors as I wrestled with my energetic/hostile/tricky little furball.

My territory and cabin were as I had left them that morning. Getting one of Keeneyes' old leashes, I chained Runt to a pillar. He took to the collar about as well as you would expect. When he calmed down, I put a runleg-hide mat under him. "Mess off the mat and I'll make you wear it," I said affectionately, patting his fuzzy head.

He tried to bite my forepaw off.

Hunting wasn't very good that night. I had to settle for a couple of darters. I ate mine, then brought the smaller one back for Runt. I talked to him while he "stalked" his dead meal; it was supposed to help him with his language skills. When he finished eating, he curled up in a ball and started snoring.

I sat by an open upper-wall, where the cool breeze brought me the tale of the night. A solid pelt of clouds cut off the moons light. I smelled dampness in the air; it would be raining by sunrise, I figured unhappily. Nothing dangerous intruded on the normal scents and sounds.

The cabin was warm and homey in the flickering yellow candlelight. Runt's scent was spreading. Soon it would permeate the cabin, clinging to every part, marking it as his territory as much as mine. But I didn't mind. Quite the opposite; the place had seemed empty since Keeneyes' demise.

Tired and sore, I was considering turning in early when I heard Irongut's distant howling for permission to enter.

Even though I had been expecting him, I was surprised. A lot had happened since last night. I was in no shape for a romp, especially not the paces he would put me through. My spirit was definitely willing, but my body had done about all it was going to do today.

Still, Irongut deserved better than a warnoff howl. I would explain it to him personally, so I could be sure he would return when I was myself again. I howled permission to enter.

I combed the parts of my pelt that weren't bandaged and was waiting by the doorway when Irongut arrived.

"Evening, Slasher," he said pleasantly. He smelled good, with a reassuring amount of lust and a touching concern.

"Evening to you, too. It's nice of you to come calling." I guided him to a chair and we both sat down.

Irongut looked at the still-sleeping Runt. "I see you caught yourself a fine *tagnami*."

"Allow me to present Runt, my new pride and joy."

"He's a lucky cub to have you for a parent."

"You flatter me," I said coyly.

Irongut's mood turned serious. "You've had an eventful day, I hear."

"Indeed." I had admired his maturity in not rushing to me in town to see if I was well. I would have been a long time living that down.

"Farrunner was a fearsome fighter. Congratulations on beating him."

"Thanks. As you can see, it wasn't easy."

"You look like you'll live," he said gruffly, but his scent of concern strengthened.

"Stubbytail will be glad to hear you agree with her diagnosis."

Irongut relaxed. "I've heard a pawful of versions of your amazing encounter. If you aren't tired of talking about it, would you care to tell me what really happened?"

"I rarely tire of talking about myself." So I told him the whole story of Ralphayers' brief visit to town. He listened thoughtfully, without interrupting.

At the end I asked, "So what do you think? Was it a visitor from another world or a demon?"

His answer surprised me. "Maybe it was both."

"Huh?" I replied brilliantly.

"It was different from us and it could do things we can't. That made it dangerous. I'm glad it's dead."

"That's a rather narrow attitude, don't you think?"

"No. The gods made our world and our ways. Something from Outside could only be an emissary of evil sent to harm us."

There was no point in arguing theology with the devout, especially when you weren't too sure of your side. "Well, it's a moot point now."

But even as I spoke, I wondered if it was.

Irongut got up and came over to me. "I've been thinking about last night all day," he whispered throatily. "Remembering it very fondly."

"So that's why you were so concerned about my health," I teased him.

The air was getting thick with rut-lust. Surprisingly, some of it was mine. An aftereffect of the fight.

I caressed the incredibly soft fur of his cheek. "I'm sorry to have to disappoint both of us, *gorwana*, but I'm all in. Blame Farrunner."

He took my paw and licked it. My breath caught.

"Patience," I gasped. "When I'm healed and rested, your virtue will be rewarded."

"You underestimate yourself," Irongut breathed. His tail was playing with mine, and my treacherous appendage was playing back.

"Unless, of course," he added, "it takes longer to recover at your age . . . ?"

Damn him! "If you open my wounds, I'll open your throat!"

"I'll be gentle," he promised.

We moved as one toward my bed.

Ten-days passed. The first snows came, draping the forests and meadows with a thin pelt of lacy whiteness. The days became shorter; the nights colder. The web of being slowed. People spent less time in town and more time laired in their territories, living on scarce game and winter-fat.

Life settled back to normal except for the speculations about the Ralphayers creatures, now growing into epic legends. Travelers carried the stories up and down the river, and over the mountains. Since my victory over Farrunner was part of the tale, I wasn't entirely displeased.

Winter or not, Weighers were expected to be available to settle disputes as many days as possible. So it was that on one cold morning I was sitting in my stall, warming my forepaws over a small hearthfire. The upper-wall flaps were in place to keep the heat from fleeing.

I had just settled an intricate debt problem without any challenges and I was feeling indecently pleased with myself. Longfur had been dragged in by a pawful of townsfolk to whom he had been tardy in paying his *twilga*. Had he been a real deadbeat, I would have given him the usual options of settling up at once or fighting his creditors in a circle challenge. But he was a responsible person whose fermented milk trade had temporarily slumped; the dryeye plague last summer had savaged his herds. So I worked out late payment penalties and installment plans which satisfied everybody.

My relaxed mood was interrupted when somebody outside shouted, "More demons! Come and see, everybody! Pray to Olowa, the all-powerful god of volcanos, to deliver us from danger! More demons are descending upon us!"

My ears cocked. Demons? Could it possibly mean that, by some miracle, I was going to get a second chance?

I hurried out into the windless but still biting chill. The wan blue sky was streaked with wispy clouds, a muted winter canopy. I shivered from the sudden temperature drop and I could see my breath. Sounds carried sharply in the heavy air.

A priest was standing at the edge of the challenge lawn, pointing almost straight up. I looked. Everybody else within hearing looked, too. But most of the others, having seen this trick before, paid no further attention and went on about their business.

Still, a pawful of priests, savants (but no Rubbertail) and curious *tagnami* joined me in running over to the edge of the challenge lawn.

Not one, but two creatures were falling from the sky.

The pair of enormous ball-and-ropes still looked like animals, although Rubbertail had told me that the first one was most likely a made thing. Like the paper toys that floated away after you held them over a fire. The creatures were touching their chests with their fore-paws in a way which seemed to affect the speed and direction of their descent.

They landed in the middle of the challenge lawn, as close together as the size of the balls would allow. The pair of ball-and-ropes climbed back into the sky. The creatures removed the clear bowls from their heads.

One was another exact copy of Ralphayers. The other was different. It was shorter, a bit thinner and curiously curved. Its face was narrow and pinkish white. It had a long, wavy golden mane.

I stepped forward. The other adults and *tagnami* stayed at the edge of the lawn and watched silently, honoring my outstanding challenge-right.

"Welcome to Coalgathering!" I shouted at the creatures. They wouldn't understand me, of course, but the proprieties should be observed at all times. Especially between soon-to-be business associates.

"It's good to see you again, Slasher," the Ralphayers copy replied.

I flinched as if from an attacking enemy, while behind me the spectators erupted into excited conversations. How could it speak our language without hooking me up to a "translator" first? Even worse, how could it know my name?

"Are you trying to make me believe in ghosts?" I asked the Ralphayers copy. "The others like you are all dead."

"I . . . remember everything my brothers did. So I feel I know you." It and the other creature started to walk toward me.

"Stay where you are," I warned them quickly, "unless you want to be turned into memories, too. Stay where we can't smell you."

Their faces twisted. The smaller creature spoke in a higher-pitched voice. "I think we'll be safe from that danger, at least."

I realized two startling facts just as shouts from some of the savants announced them. First, both of the creatures were speaking our language just as naturally as any person. Second and more important, their scents were totally unlike the evil, dangerous smell of the others.

They smelled like . . . like groundflowers! Pleasant, harmless groundflowers. There were no growls coming from those gathered behind me. If anything, there were a few purrs.

"Are you like the nightslitherer that can change its scent?" I asked them.

"No," the Ralphayers copy replied. "When the machines aboard the skyboat grew us after my last brother died, they made some changes so that we can survive here. We can even eat your plants and animals."

Roots and leaves? I shuddered.

"We're here to learn as much as possible about you and your world," the smaller creature added. "This will be a long-term study, one we hope our, uh, *tagnami*, will continue after we die. They will have to, since the machines aboard the skyboat can't grow any more of us."

Here it was—my oft-dreamed-of second chance to become rich and famous by brokering the incredible alien knowledge. If I could manage to keep these two creatures alive. "You're going to have to learn our customs very quickly. You obviously aren't fighters, so you must learn how to avoid offending people."

The Ralphayers copy paused. "We're more dangerous fighters than you can imagine. But we came here to make friends and to learn. Like my brothers, we would rather die than fight you. We like staying alive as much as you do, but we believe in what we're doing even more."

I would attempt to figure that out later. Right now I had the greatest *twilga* transaction in history to arrange. It would be the stuff of legends among

Weighers and would, of course, compensate me handsomely.

"You'll need someone to teach you our customs," I began my pitch, "and to vouch for you with fang and claw until the town accepts you."

The smaller creature said, "We have a great store of scientific and technological information aboard the skyboat, which we can summon through our machines. Some of it should be of use to you. We'll give it to you as a token of our friendship."

The fur on my back rose and I stifled a growl. Fortunately no one else had been close enough to make out its soft words. "*Never* offer to give an adult anything!" I said sharply. "It could prove to be fatal."

"Why?"

They had so much to learn. What kind of crazy customs did they live by? "To suggest that an adult needs help, as if she were a *tagnami*, is the worst possible kind of insult. You must *sell* your knowledge for a good price, and thereby establish your worth."

The two creatures squawked at each other in what I assumed was their alien language, going on for some time. Finally the smaller one turned back to me and asked, "Would it be possible for us to hire the services of someone who can teach us what we need to know?"

"Of course, and I recommend myself for the job. I'm the town Weigher, an excellent haggler, well educated—and a fierce fighter, to deal with any challenges that might come your way."

"What's a Weigher?" the Ralphayers copy asked.

"We balance the values of goods, services and violations of custom, so people can interact more constructively and less violently."

"You . . . run the town?"

"I don't understand your question. Adults run their own territories, *tagnami* and town affairs."

The creatures squawked at each other some more. Then the Ralphayers copy said to me, "We accept your offer and trust you to set a fair price for your services. How do we begin?"

No negotiating? No checking my credentials? No looking elsewhere for a better deal? This was almost too easy. Fortunately for them I was an honorable professional; I could think of one or two of my colleagues who would have taken the maximum advantage of their naivete.

I wasn't about to make the Sweetscent mistake twice. Saving the self-congratulation for later, I got my mind back on business. I thought about the creature's question. How *do* we begin? This wasn't the sort of situation I could look up in my books.

You begin with the most basic need. "First we have to get you a territory. Let me think what's available . . . ah, the Coldcrag place. No one will challenge you for it, and I'm sure I can get it for you cheaply. The game stock is lousy."

"No problem there," the Ralphayers copy replied. "There's enough edible vegetation around here for us to get by, even this time of year."

"Good." I hid my real reaction to their diet. "I'll get you settled, start your education in our customs, and smooth the trail for you here in town."

That last part didn't look as though it would be too difficult. The priests and savants were gathered around, hanging on every word. But not too close. They had heard my commitment to handle challenges for the creatures; that claw slashed both ways.

"The free entertainment is over, my friends," I told them. "Go back to whatever you were doing. You will all have the chance to quench your curiosity later, for a very modest amount of *twilga*."

The townsfolk drifted away reluctantly. The two creatures and I were soon alone on the challenge lawn. "Are you ready to go buy your territory?" I asked them.

"A moment, please," the smaller creature replied.

Both of them put their head bowls in their carrysacks.
"Now we're ready."

"One thing before we get started—I strongly suggest that you say and do nothing unless I tell you to."

"Sound medical advice," the Ralphayers copy agreed.

I set out for Broker Street and they followed behind me like a pair of well-trained *tagnami*.

# CHAPTER EIGHT

"Don't walk within two strides of any adult!" I warned the creatures urgently, as we maneuvered through the crowd. "That would be considered a challenge, with unfortunate consequences."

"Point noted," the Ralphayers copy replied.

Their flimsy white garments seemed poor protection from the breath-misting chill, but the creatures looked more comfortable than I felt in my fur. We slogged through the mud and slush which used to be streets. Curse Shrubfur and the rest of the holdouts!

All noses were sniffing out the creatures, naturally. Passers-by stared. Shoppers stopped shopping and tradespeople came out of their stalls. A growing herd of *tagnami* was following us at a safe distance. The creatures didn't seem to mind; they were staring at the town just as raptly. I basked proudly in the reflected attention.

"I should complete our introductions," the Ralphayers copy said to me. "I'm Ralphayers Delta and this is Pamayers Alpha, but Ralphayers and Pamayers will do. Our kind of people are called humans."

"Welcome to the town of Coalgathering, Ralphayers, Pamayers," I replied formally. "My name, as you know, is Slasher."

One of Ralphayers' odd forepaws darted toward me. I growled instinctively, and he yanked it back.

"In case you're wondering," Pamayers added, "we're a duo-sexual species, like yours. I'm an adult female and Ralph is an adult male."

A breeding pair. Rubbertail would undoubtedly find the topic of alien sex fascinating, but to me it was faintly repulsive.

Broker Street was an unkempt collection of used goods and adults haggling over them. Jeweleyes' neat stall stood like an oasis amid the clutter, because he dealt in territories. He came to the doorway to meet us. Sleek and well groomed, he looked every bit the successful broker that he was. I would have to be sharp.

"Good day, Slasher," he said to me absently, staring at the creatures. He plainly didn't know whether to treat them as adults, *tagnami*, or animals.

I wasn't so sure myself, but as their broker, I was obligated to give them the benefit of the doubt. "Good day, Jeweleyes. Allow me to present the savants from another world, Ralphayers and Pamayers."

"We're pleased to meet you," Pamayers said. Jeweleyes' jaw dropped.

I took quick advantage of his discomfiture. "I'm representing them, since they aren't familiar with our customs. They want to buy the Coldcrag territory. But if we have to stand out here in the cold for another heartbeat, we'll take our business elsewhere."

The chance to unload the worst territory in the region brushed aside all lesser matters. "Come in, friends! Please!"

We followed Jeweleyes inside. His decor was a bit on the gaudy side for my taste, but I appreciated the warm hearthfire. He and I sat down to talk business.

The humans were looking at the big territory map strung between two pillars.

"Ah, yes, the Coldcrag territory," Jeweleyes began. "You show your usual excellent judgment in choosing a territory as distinguished as these savants."

"Distinguished? The Coldcrag place?" I laughed. "All the game in that rock garden wouldn't fill one of the Snake's mugs."

We went at each other like that for a couple of hundredth-days until I beat the smooth carrion-eater down to a reasonable price.

When we got out our *twilga* books, Ralphayers came over to join us. "Are you going to pay for the territory?" he asked me.

"Yes, as your broker. We'll make the *twilga* good between us later." Not too much later, I hoped; the cost of even a lousy territory was going to be a sore blow to my *twilga* balance.

"We can pay for the territory ourselves."

"With what? You don't even have a *twilga* book, let alone anything to put in it."

"The machines aboard our skyboat have . . . studied the land around Coalgathering," Pamayers said, still looking at the map. "Would the location of an undeveloped coal deposit bigger than those being mined be of value?"

A blur of motion, and Jeweleyes was standing beside the female human. "Pamayers, most welcome of savants, if the location was, ur, exclusive information, it would be of some minor value."

The humans looked at me. I smiled. "Jeweleyes," I said, "why don't you come back here, and we'll discuss it."

A hundredth-day later the humans and I left Jeweleyes' stall. They were the new owners of the Coldcrag territory, and a substantial *twilga* balance as well; all duly noted in my book. Joint ownership by two adults was a novel concept, but my Weigher's expertise had enabled me to grasp it and properly craft the transaction.

I took the humans to my stall. They eagerly looked over my weighing books while I closed up. Fortunately there were no irate clients to explain my prolonged absence to. Then we went over to School Street so I could collect Runt. The humans were charmed by the little furball with his pawful of vocabulary. Pamayers tried to pet him before I could warn her, and almost lost a forepaw.

Coldcrag was about three thousand strides east of town, beyond (and above) the coal territories. I led my strange herd out the South Gate and onto a commonland trail. Runt frolicked at my tail, glad to see me and grateful for the early escape from Bentback. The humans followed well behind Runt.

I set out across the snow-covered groundplant at an easy pace. A few heartbeats later I heard Pamayer's faint yell. "Hold up . . . Slasher! Please!"

Stopping and turning, I saw the humans about fifty strides back. Their upright, bouncing, slow-motion version of running almost made me laugh.

"Look funny," Runt bleated.

"Hush," I whispered. "It's not polite to make fun of people, even when they are funny."

The humans finally caught up. They were both gasping for breath and Pamayers' face had turned bright red. "What's the matter?" I asked.

"We can't run as fast as you," she gasped. "Or for more than a few hundred strides with so much weight on our backs."

"You're joking," I replied incredulously. "It must take you forever to travel long distances."

"Not really. We use powered vehicles like our skyboat."

"Do you have a couple of them in your carrysacks?"

"Unfortunately, no."

So we walked. The trail climbed through gaunt

woods and white meadows that gradually gave way to
a rocky slope. The frozen streams with their icicle-
hung waterfalls were beautiful, but I spent most of
my time answering questions about every plant and
animal we passed.

Finally we reached a high plain carved out of the
mountains by some god. No tall strongwood trees
here, just patches of wind-deformed tangletrees and
fireclaw bushes. The lesser vegetation ranged from
sparse to non-existent. Boulders and rock outcrops
dominated the terrain. As for game, my nose and eyes
had little to report. The panoramic view of the river
valley was the only good thing to be said of Coldcrag.

"This is your territory," I told the humans, bracing
for their anger.

"All this land is ours?" Ralphayers asked.

"I'm afraid so." I led them over to a stride-tall pile
of rocks. "This is one of the cairns that mark the
boundaries of your territory. Don't trespass on adjoin-
ing territories. There's just enough daylight left for
you to run . . . well, walk the bounds and set your
warnoffs."

"What are warnoffs and how do we set them?"

I told him.

He made a long noise like a watersnorter belching,
while Pamayers' face turned red again. The humans
squawked at each other for quite awhile. Finally Pamayers spoke to me. "Slasher, would you please turn
around."

As I turned my back and Runt's to her, I noticed
that Ralphayers was doing the same. Aliens. "Save
some for the other places," I said over my shoulder.

We hiked around the cub-sized territory. The humans
alternated warnoffs: a practice sure to confuse any
potential trespasser. The sun had set and a dark night
under one crescent moon was gathering when we
reached the clearing which held the cabin.

The ruins of a cabin, actually. A bolt of lightning

must have hit it since Shadow's demise. The roof was gone; the pillars and lower-walls were burned almost to the foundation. My fangs bared. "Jeweleyes!" I howled. "I'll have your skull on a pole for this!"

"What's the matter?" Ralphayers asked.

"The grinner dung neglected to mention that the cabin had burned down."

"That's okay—we would have had to practically rebuild it anyway. We have camping gear for the time being."

"This is a very nice territory," Pamayers added. "I've spotted quite a few plants we can eat."

The humans took off their carrysacks, opened them, and pulled out a pair of short silver rods. They squeezed them. Twin beams of brilliant light turned the area around the cabin day-time bright. I squinted for a few heartbeats, until my eyes adjusted. Lamps, I supposed, but Kraal's own lamps.

"The cabin is firewood, all right," Ralphayers said, "but the foundation looks usable."

"What are those things for?" I demanded, pointing at the rods.

"We call them flashlights. Our darksight isn't as good as yours, so we need artificial help."

Runt was getting restless for dinner and I was beginning to wonder what had happened to my territory since breakfast. "Time for me to leave," I told them. "Anything else you need before I go?"

"Can't think of a thing," Ralphayers replied.

"Try to stay out of trouble until morning—refer any challengers to me. I'll be by shortly after sunrise. Do you have entry calls where you come from?"

"Not like you mean."

I let out a howl. "That means somebody wants permission to enter your territory." Another howl. "That's how you give permission. Try it."

Ralphayers made a miserable little squawk that wouldn't have carried a hundred strides. I sighed. "We'll work on it. Good night."

"Good night to you, too," Ralphayers replied. "It has been one hell of a day for all of us."

"Thanks for all your help," Pamayers added.

I looked at the two puny, defenseless humans huddled close together in the darkness of the clearing like spooked bigmeats. I should have felt disgust. Instead, I found myself wondering how I would do as a visitor on their crazy world. Would I even have the courage to try it? There were many kinds of bravery.

"There isn't enough game up here to attract predators," I said gently, "and nobody is going to violate my challenge-right. If you can keep from freezing to death, you will be fine."

Runt and I stretched our legs running home, to warm up and to get there quicker. My territory and cabin were as they should have been. I brought down a stickleg nibbling on redberry leaves and used the carcass to give Runt a pouncing lesson before we devoured it. Soon we were settled in the cabin around a blazing hearthfire. I half-expected a visit from Irongut, but he didn't come calling. We turned in early.

Morning dawned as clear and cold as the day before. After a meager breakfast of nutcheeks, I took Runt to town and school. Then I headed out to Coldcrag.

At the boundary I noted with approval that the humans had remembered to set fresh warnoffs. I howled for permission to enter. By listening as hard as I could, I managed to hear the answering squawk. I loped across the rocky terrain to the cabin clearing.

A bright red, three-stride-tall half-egg sat in a patch of snow-cleared ground, near the ruins of the cabin. It was made of the same kind of stuff as their garments. It had a doorway-like slit in one side and I guessed that it was some kind of portable shelter in which the humans had spent the night. It looked grimly claustrophobic; I wondered how one, let alone two people, could spend any length of time in it.

The humans had managed to get a campfire going in front of the half-egg. A tripod held a pot of boiling water over the fire, while the humans stood around it, warming their hands.

"Good morning, Slasher," they harmonized.

"Morning, Ralphayers, Pamayers." I joined them by the crackling, sharp-smelling blaze. "I see you have your own ways of doing things. How do you like our world so far?"

"It's wonderful," Pamayers replied.

"It'll be even more wonderful come spring," Ralphayers added. "You've arrived at an opportune moment. Our supplies will be landing soon—should be quite a show."

I politely kept myself from saying that it was a show I had already seen twice.

They were looking up at the pale blue sky, so I did too. Another ball-and-ropes was coming down, with a round-ended white cylinder dangling under it. Instead of descending toward the clearing, though, it was riding the stiff wind west.

"Something must be wrong with the guidance system," Pamayers said.

"Your whatever-it-is is heading for Blacksnout's territory," I replied. "You better stop it."

"We can't."

"That's bad. Very bad. Come on." I ran for the western boundary, following the cylinder slowly enough for the humans to keep up. Trespassing was bad enough, but it had to be Blacksnout's territory—an arched-back, arrogant, *twilga*-loving miner's territory.

The cylinder landed on a snowy slope about fifty strides beyond the boundary. I stopped at the edge of the humans' territory and stared at it. It looked like metal, six strides tall and three wide. The ball didn't fly away this time; it whipped in the wind like a demonflier.

"Let's go get it," Ralphayers said.

I tried to keep the shock out of my scent and voice. "Trespass is a challenge offense. It's one of the most immoral acts an adult can commit."

"But we aren't going to damage or steal anything. We're just getting our own property."

"That doesn't matter."

"Blacksnout won't even know we were there."

I wondered how humans managed to survive without noses, ears or common sense. "He would smell your spoor the next time he ran his bounds. But he won't have to—here he comes now."

Blacksnout was running up the slope, flanked by two of his *tagnami*. Stopping a pawful of strides from the cylinder, he glared at it.

Like most miners, he was a huge slab of muscle. His brown-and-white striped pelt bore the scars of past fights and mining accidents. He was living proof that you didn't have to be smart to be rich, just stubborn and bad-tempered. The notion of accepting a challenge from him didn't enthuse me.

"Morning, Blacksnout!" I called out cheerfully.

The glare swung around toward us. "What in Zagal's name is that thing?" he growled.

Pamayers opened her mouth to speak. I growled at her sharply, and she closed it.

Strategy, I reminded myself. I turned back to Blacksnout. "Have you met my two friends and clients, the distinguished savants from another world, Ralphayers and Pamayers?"

"I heard about them in town. Do they have something to do with that thing being on my territory?"

"It's part of their skyboat," I explained. "It accidently fell out of the sky. They intended no trespass, and they offer *twilga* for any harm done."

"Harm?" Blacksnout scratched his head.

"Of course, I don't see that it's doing any harm just lying there," I said innocently.

"The harm is that it's on my territory!"

"A truly unique addition—wreckage from another world. You might even owe the humans *twilga*, since they have inadvertently increased the worth of your territory."

Blacksnout's fangs bared and an angry scent drifted across the border. "I want that trash off my land!"

"If the humans remove it, will that balance the *twilga* for it falling there in the first place?"

"Yes, yes!" Blacksnout growled. "Just get rid of it!"

"Very well." I gestured to the humans. "Go get your trash."

The humans walked nervously to the cylinder, giving Blacksnout and his *tagnami* a wide berth. They went to the ends and picked it up. The floating ball seemed to make it much lighter than it should have been. They carried it back across the boundary.

Dampness had appeared on their faces.

"No more trash better fall on my territory!" Blacksnout growled after them. Without another word, he and his *tagnami* started back down the slope.

The humans kept going with their prize toward the cabin clearing. They progressed slowly, amid much gasping and groaning and with many rest stops. I followed along, enjoying the entertainment. They finally dropped the cylinder beside the red half-egg. Ralphayers did something to it which caused the ball-and-ropes to fly away.

The humans leaned against it, wiping the dampness from their faces. "That was beautiful," Ralphayers gasped at me.

"What?"

"The trick you pulled on Blacksnout."

I bristled. "I didn't say anything to him that wasn't true."

"Of course. That's the best way to lie."

Apparently he was familiar with that trick of the Weigher trade. "Are you going to unpack your supplies now?" I asked, curious to see more of the strange alien things.

"Not until we get the cabin rebuilt," Pamayers replied.

"For that you will need a lot more than Jeweleyes' *twilga*," I pointed out. "Shall we go to town and earn some?"

"That would be the best place to begin our research, too."

So we took a leisurely stroll to town. I used the time to give the humans a lesson in town customs. I would be glad when it was safe to let them wander about unattended. I didn't have enough life left to waste any of it.

Rubbertail was the obvious first choice for a customer. Selling him some of the humans' knowledge would be like stalking game in a breeder's pen. Passing through the South Gate, we headed for Savant Street.

The humans attracted less attention today. The novelty had worn off and most townsfolk were tending to their business.

Approaching Rubbertail's stall, I saw that he was inside. We stopped at the doorway. He was doing something to something on a table; the carrion reek kept him from smelling us.

"Morning, Rubbertail," I said.

"Morning, Slasher," he replied absently, not looking up from his work.

"I thought you would want to meet the aliens," I said dryly. "My mistake—we won't bother you any further."

Rubbertail straightened, turned and stared. His mouth opened. The knife-like instrument in his forepaw clattered to the smoothstone floor. "Please . . . don't go!"

"Rubbertail," I said formally, "may I present the savants from Earth, Ralphayers, Pamayers. Ralphayers,

Pamayers, the distinguished animal-science savant, Rubbertail."

Rubbertail brushed past me in a way that would have cost him dearly with a less understanding adult. "Welcome, welcome!" he gasped at the humans. "Please come in!"

We followed him inside. I assumed that I was included in the invitation although he seemed to have forgotten that I existed.

The smells of fresh blood, rotting meat and alcohol were overpowering. It was cold, too, with the hearth unlit. The interior was a messy clutter of specimens, jars, books, instruments and wall-mounted anatomical charts. The place made my fangs ache, but the humans seemed fascinated.

"We're pleased to meet you," Pamayers told Rubbertail. "Your work looks very impressive."

"Ah . . . thank you." Rubbertail was trying to stare at every part of both humans at once.

"We want to learn everything we can about your world's animal-science. Slasher suggested that you would be an excellent source of information."

"I want to know everything about your web of being, too. Since our desires are similar, why don't we exchange information?"

I spoke up before the humans could do something stupid like agree. "That would be the proper thing to do, Rubbertail, if the value of both contributions were the same. But as you yourself pointed out to me, the humans come from a much more advanced civilization. Therefore, their knowledge is broader, deeper and more valuable than yours. You should pay a modest bonus to the humans."

"How modest?" Rubbertail demanded impatiently.

There wasn't anything in my books about this sort of transaction. I quickly and roughly balanced the humans' need for *twilga*, Rubbertail's eagerness, and the likely use he would make of the knowledge. "Twenty-five *twil* per every hundredth-day of discussion."

Rubbertail's back fur rose. "You can't be serious!"

"If you aren't interested, maybe one of your colleagues will be."

Rubbertail trembled, hamstrung between eagerness and shock. Finally he calmed down. "Very well," he sighed. "I'll pay."

"A very wise decision."

Having accepted the heavy blow to his *twilga* balance, Rubbertail's excitement returned. "Can we begin now?"

I looked at the humans. "Fine by us," Ralphayers said.

"Then I'll leave you to your discussion. Can you find my stall when you're done, and avoid being killed on the way?"

"We're not *tagnami*."

"Of course not. But until you're more familiar with our ways, you should pretend you are."

"We'll be careful," Pamayers said.

Still, as I left the stall, I prayed to Kraal that he would return the humans to me intact.

While I was avoiding my Weigher duties, I decided on one more detour. Irongut's stall. I figured he would be interested in hearing about the humans and that gave me an excuse to see him. Tail high, feeling generally pleased with the world, I headed for Artisan Street.

Passing a couple of priests enmeshed in a theological discussion, I bid them a cheerful good morning. Instead of responding in kind as they were wont to do, they glared at me. Then they pointedly turned their tails to me and resumed their conversation.

I was shocked. I couldn't think of anything I had done to offend them. Going back to question them was out; their low dominance ranking would have made that embarrassing. As for challenging them, only a hothead like Farrunner would have picked a fight over a minor insult. So, angry and puzzled, I kept going.

Irongut's stall was built in the traditional style, with no modern improvements. The lower-walls and pillars were unfinished strongwood, with clear weatherproofing, and the shingles were bark. The combination kiln and hearth had no chimney. Dark smoke rose from the hole in the roof's peak indicating that Irongut was in and at work. I went up the smoothstone steps to the doorway.

The inside was neat but spartan. The kiln dominated the middle of the planked floor, while shelves along the walls held blocks of clay, working tools, glazes, brushes and finished products. The colorful pots, bowls, jugs and so on testified to Irongut's skill. My lover was seated at his pottery wheel, kicking the heavy stone lower-wheel to keep it turning, and shaping a lump of wet clay on the upper-wheel. He smelled wonderful.

"Morning, Irongut."

He stopped working, wiped his forepaws on a rag, and came over. "Morning, Slasher. Come in."

I followed him to the chairs where he haggled with customers and we sat down. His scent and tone bothered me. They seemed more reserved than necessary to protect our reputations.

"I hear that two more of the strange creatures dropped out of the sky yesterday," Irongut said, "and that you've taken charge of them."

"I'm acting as their guide and broker," I corrected him. "Considering how much more than us they must know, selling their knowledge should make me a very rich Weigher."

"I was afraid you had something like that in mind."

I remembered his hostile reaction to the first Ralphayers and decided a change of subject might be a good idea. "A strange thing happened to me on the way over."

"What was that?"

"Loudhowl and Sapling showed me their tails, for no reason that I can think of."

Irongut was silent for a pawful of heartbeats. Then he said, "You can't?"

Something about his words got my back fur up. "If you want to tell me something, don't be so dung-eating cryptic."

"Very well. Not everyone in town is as pleased as you are about the creatures being among us."

"Are the priests still going on about that demon nonsense?" I asked incredulously.

"Just because you don't believe it, doesn't mean it isn't true."

"The *humans* are just as mortal as you or I. They're people from another world."

"You only have their word for that."

"As opposed to priestly babbling?"

Irongut stiffened. "You should show the priests more respect. Besides, they aren't the only ones who are concerned. There are some others who worry about what the creatures' knowledge might do to our ways."

"Hidebound traditionalists who want every day to be exactly like the day before," I snorted. "If it were up to them, we would still be walking on four legs in the Wild."

"It's possible to believe in the rightness of our ways, and not want them poisoned by evil notions from Outside."

"Only if you're an ignorant, short-sighted fool."

Okay, it wasn't the most tactful way to make my point. Irongut sprang to four legs. "You no longer have my permission to be here!"

Thrown out like a naughty *tagnami!* By him! My scent of rage matched his in strength. "Then I'll leave!" I growled and stormed out of the stall.

# CHAPTER NINE

The next few ten-days were as hectic as any that I could recall. As well as tending to my territory, my *tagnami* and my Weighing, I had the two humans to look after. And in many ways they were as helpless as Runt.

Artisans were hired to rebuild the Coldcrag cabin. Constructed to the humans' specifications, it devoured *twilga* the way a herd of bigmeats did prairie groundplant, and turned out to be a truly bizarre structure. Other artisans scratched behind their ears in wonderment, then produced fixtures and furniture unlike any that had ever been before. From the white cylinder came personal items, more strange garments, plus many machines which remained inexplicable despite the humans' efforts to explain them.

I was right about their ineptness as hunters. But by stocking Coldcrag generously from the breeder pens and using a cheat called a bow, they managed to bring down some game. They also gathered and ate a disgusting variety of fruits, nuts, berries, leaves and roots; they even planned to grow more come spring.

As soon as the humans were settled in their territory, they turned more of their attention to the research they had come to do. They talked to everybody in town who would talk to them. They went shopping: books, maps, artwork, jewelry, musical instruments and more. They hiked into the Wild to study the flora, fauna and the land itself.

Coming up with the *twilga* for all this didn't prove to be a problem. The humans were able to supply valuable knowledge on just about any subject. Savants, artisans, miners, people in almost every field—the trickle of customers became a rushing stream, then a broad and powerful river, thanks, in no small part, to my brokering. The humans rejected some of the requests because the knowledge was either too advanced to be of use or might have been dangerous. But that still left more than enough business.

As I came to know the humans better, I found that I liked them. Pamayers had a reserved dignity which commanded respect, while Ralphayers' cynicism made him interesting company. But I couldn't claim that I had acquired a better understanding of them. Their oddest trait was how they acted like a single person in many ways. They conducted business together, owned everything together, even lived in the cabin together. Just thinking about so much togetherness made my fangs ache.

Teaching the humans civilized behavior was the hardest part of my job and, for the first few ten-days, I had all I could handle keeping them alive. Some of the priests and the more conservative townsfolk still clung to the evil demon theory and muttered against the humans. The hidebound ignorance had cost me a fine romance; I hadn't caught scent of Irongut since our spat. But most of the townsfolk accepted the presence of the humans or, at least, tolerated it. The humans gradually achieved a rudimentary grasp of our customs and a precarious place at the bottom of the dominance ranking. By the time the days reached their shortest, the humans were an established part of

Coalgathering and my life was getting back to normal at last.

Which meant, among other things, resuming my campaign to get the streets paved. Soon the snow and ground would thaw and we would be mud-wading again. Unfortunately, the holdouts were still holding out. When I thought about the fantastic things the humans had accomplished because of their ability to cooperate, and how hard it was for us to agree on even the simplest group action, it raised my back fur. Then I had my brainstorm.

Why not consult the humans?

As usual, I was puffing for breath by the time I reached the boundary of the humans' territory. Coldcrag was about as far from town as you could get before finding yourself in the Wild. My burning muscles and creaking joints reminded me of my years, as if I needed reminding.

A sullen overcast robbed sunzenith of much of its light and a freezing wind blew fat flakes in my face. The scrawny woods and meadows of the high plains looked even scrawnier buried in snow. The pricklytrees had lost their leaves and the redberry bushes looked positively anemic. A droopwing perched on a bare branch, cawing mournfully.

Winter had its place in the web of being, but that didn't mean I had to like it.

I howled for permission to enter the humans' territory. Moments later I heard a distant tuskhorn blare out its reasonable imitation of a permission-to-enter call. The humans simply didn't have the lung power for long-distance communication, so they had come up with another of their cheats.

Drawn by the chimney plume and its promise of warmth, I hurried along the trail toward the cabin clearing.

The cabin was at least four times the size of mine,

which seemed an excessive amount of floorspace for just two people. Some of its innovations—like the frame construction, the double walls for insulation, and the leakless tar roof—had earned the humans a sizeable amount of *twilga*. But its most bizarre feature was that it was sealed tight. The walls went all the way up to the roof. There were a few holes which the humans called windows, but they were filled with glass panes. A hinged piece of wall closed the doorway when nobody was using it. The claustrophobic design trapped the hearth's warmth, which was good, but it also trapped the smells, which should have been intolerable. But the humans had no noses to speak of.

Ralphayers was standing in the open doorway, framed by the warm yellow light from inside. One forepaw gripped a curved, gleaming tuskhorn. "Welcome, Slasher!" he yelled over the wind. "Shake the snow off your pelt and come on in!"

I hesitated. Flower smell or not, their pent-up reek in the cabin always made my fangs ache. But I was the guest, and I knew that the humans found snow and below-freezing cold even less comfortable than I did. Their hearthfire still beckoned me. "Very well," I replied reluctantly.

The cabin was as bizarre on the inside as it was on the outside. More walls divided it into parts dedicated to different uses. Ceiling-hung alcohol lamps provided bright light. Complicated arrangements of pipes, bowls and wooden supports replaced the stream for drinking and sanitary purposes. There were machines for burning, freezing and otherwise ruining food. It was like entering another world which, under the circumstances, was an accurate simile.

Ralphayers led me into the part of the cabin which the humans called a living room. There was a warm, cheery blaze going in the oddly shaped firebrick wall hearth (another of their highly profitable innovations). Pamayers was seated at a table reading a book aloud.

The humans had a fantastic appetite for our books; recent purchases were stacked all around the floor. A speaking-box with its glowing lights sat in front of her. (Unlike the earlier Ralphayers who were somehow linked to the skyboat, these two had to use their boxes to communicate with it. The former method only worked for a short time.)

Pamayers put down the book. "Hello, Slasher," she said, showing me the human version of a smile. "It's nice of you to drop by on such a miserable day."

My visit had an ulterior purpose: to find out if the humans' advanced knowledge included some way to get Shrubfur and the other holdouts to contribute *twilga* to the street paving project. I didn't know how talking the problem over with the humans could help; it wasn't the sort of thing they had been doing. But they were full of surprises and I was out of options except the challenge lawn, which wasn't justified by the need.

It wouldn't do to just jump into a business discussion. Politeness dictated some small talk first. "How is your research coming?" I asked.

"Incredibly well," Pamayers replied. Ralphayers sat in the chair next to her while I stretched out on a rug by the hearth. "There's so much data to collect, digest and relay to the skyboat for transmission to Earth. We're beginning to unravel a few of the tough questions about your people."

"Such as?"

"Such as why are you intelligent?"

They were always raising the sort of topics which gave me headaches. "What do you mean?"

Ralphayers took up the explanation. "Our religion, like yours, teaches that intelligence is a divine gift. But according to our science, intelligence evolved as a survival trait, like strength or speed. The most effective survival trait, in fact, since the species with the highest intelligence dominates on each of our worlds."

I was vaguely familiar with the savants' theory of evolution. It was easier to believe that Kraal and the rest of the gods had conjured our world and us out of nothingness. On the other paw, it was difficult to dispute the knowledge of people who could travel from star to star.

"You can see why humans had to evolve intelligence to survive," Ralphayers went on. "We're weak and slow, we have no natural weapons or armor, and we can't even hide in trees like our ancestors. So we use our minds and hands to make artificial substitutes. But you? You're big, strong, fast, and equipped with fangs and claws. With all those survival traits going for you, why did you need to be intelligent, too?"

I thought about it for a few heartbeats, then gave up. "I hope you're not looking to me for an answer. You should take the matter up with young Rubbertail and the other savants."

"We have," Pamayers replied. The way they alternated one end of a conversation was eerie. "Our working hypothesis is that you evolved intelligence as a defense against a danger greater than starvation or hostile predators."

My back fur rose instinctively. "What danger?" I asked sharply.

"Yourselves."

My fur subsided, but I felt another confusion-generated headache coming on. "I don't understand."

"With your territorial instinct and year-round breeding, there must have always been tremendous population pressure and competition for the best land. Smarter people fought better and figured out ways to avoid more fights. They tended to be the survivors and the breeders."

That made a vague kind of sense. "One of our earliest legends tells of people fighting over territories to the verge of total extinction, until the hero brings peace by establishing a primitive version of our present customs."

"It's probably pretty accurate," Ralphayers commented, "except that the 'hero' was more likely a long and difficult process of socialization. From basic live-and-let-live at watering holes to your towns, territories and *twilga*."

There was a lull in the conversation. The crackling of the fire and the howling wind outside filled the silence.

Ralphayers was looking at me closely. "You didn't come here for a scholarly discussion," he said at last. "Out with it, Slasher."

"Okay. But first we have to settle the *twilga* I'll owe you for your advice."

"Forget it. It's the least we can do, after everything you've—" Ralphayers caught himself, helped by Pamayers' frown and my low growl. "Sorry. The standard consultation fee will be fine by us. What's your problem?"

"You walk in it evey time you go to town, or rather you wade in it. The dirt streets. I've been trying for years to get all the adults to pledge the *twilga* to get them paved."

"You put the bite on us a couple of ten-days ago, remember?"

"Of course. Unfortunately, not everybody is as sensible as you are."

"I'm surprised," Pamayers said. "Your sales pitch was very persuasive. Surely the whole town would want to chip in for something like that."

I laughed bitterly. "You couldn't get everybody to agree that the sun rises in the east. I've whittled the holdouts down to four, but them I can't budge. Any suggestions?"

The humans squawked at each other in their own language, then turned back to me. "Unfortunately, your problem is inherent in the nature of your species," Ralphayers said.

"What do you mean?"

"You're lone predators. You don't need each other to survive—you're more likely to see other adults as competitors or enemies. So you don't cooperate well."

"How do you manage it?"

"It comes naturally for us because we're herd animals."

He said it as if he wasn't ashamed. I shuddered.

"Our research indicates that our two species are equally intelligent," Pamayers said, "and that yours is a bit older than ours. But the difficulty you have in cooperating has slowed your progress in fields requiring group effort."

"Of that I'm already painfully aware. When I think of Earth as you describe it—thousands of thousands of people working together to create wonders like your journey here—our inability to get our streets paved burns like slitherer venom!"

"It shouldn't. Our species are different, with different strengths and weaknesses. We envy your independence and individualism."

"We aren't animals—we can think and learn! *I* can see the value of cooperation! Why can't Shrubfur and . . . the other hidebound traditionalists?" I had been about to add Irongut to the list, but hadn't. I wondered how much of my anger was philosophical and how much of it was personal.

"Your profession gives you a perspective on cooperation which is uncommon among your people."

"So what you're telling me is that human-style cooperation won't work for us. Very well, we need our own style. Can you help me, or can't you?"

"Don't you have any customs for resolving such impasses?"

"If the need were great enough, I could challenge

the holdouts. But it isn't. All that leaves is persuasion which isn't working."

The humans squawked at each other some more. They seemed to be arguing, with Ralphayers getting the better of it. Finally he spoke to me. "I have a possible way to persuade the holdouts. It stretches your ethical structure a bit, but I don't think it's an outright break."

"I'm listening."

"Check our *twilga* book and see if we have balances with the holdouts."

I got out their book which I carried as their broker. "Yes. Quite large ones."

"Good. My notion is to use them as a lever. Since you do our shopping, suppose you decided to use all of our *twilga* with the holdouts right now? What would happen?"

"They couldn't possibly honor that much additional debt. They would have to scramble to arrange extensions and the value of their *twilga* would go way down. It would hurt."

"Suppose you pointed out this possibility to them, but at the same time you offered not to do it—*if* they chip in on the street paving?"

The notion whirled around under my skull, making me dizzy. I didn't know how to react to it. It could work. But was it right?

"What . . . what would the *twilga* balance be?" I wondered aloud. "You supply your *twilga* . . ."

"Actually, I don't see that we have any *twilga* interest in this at all," Ralphayers replied. "We get our debts paid either way. The only *twilga* transaction is between you, acting on behalf of the town, and the holdouts. The town gets its streets paved, the holdouts pay their share, and their paws stay unmuddy, too."

I felt like I had drunk too much fermented dire-beast milk. By Kraal, it just might be the answer! A whole herd of possibilities for town improvements

stampeded past my mind's eye. Ralphayers' analysis of
the *twilga* balance was imaginative and convincing; my
doubt disappeared.

"I'll give it a try," I told him.

"Good luck," he replied. Pamayers continued her
curious silence.

We settled the *twilga* for the advice. We talked a
bit longer, but my heart wasn't in it. I was eager to get
back to town to try out Ralphayers' scheme. Finally I
wished the humans well with their research and left.

I decided to test the scheme first on the most
intractable of the holdouts—Shrubfur. In my eagerness I ran like a cub through the snowstorm. I planned
what I was going to say, then rehearsed it mentally to
a fine polish.

Coalgathering was half-deserted, as the less hardy
laired up in their territories. But I expected that
Shrubfur would be at work. I headed straight for her
stall.

Metalworker's Street ran a close second to Coal
Street as the ugliest part of town. The stalls were stone
and firebrick blocks surrounded by piles of ores and
scrap metal. Fat columns of smoke rose from the over-
sized furnace chimneys. The reek of burning coal and
the din of hammers banging on anvils assaulted my
senses. Shrubfur's stall was the biggest and ugliest,
both testimony to her single-mindedness.

I stopped at the steps. Big as the stall was, the
smelting furnace filled most of it. A *tagnami* was shov-
eling coke into the red-hot maw, while another
pumped the bellows. An anvil, a water trough and
other iron-working tools surrounded the furnace. The
lower-wall shelves held wagon hitches, knife blades,
clock springs, hammerheads, bowls of nails and so on.
It was an efficient-looking workplace, but not aestheti-
cally pleasing. The blast of hot air from the furnace
thawed me out.

Shrubfur, wearing gloves and a leather apron, was

cracking a mold. Smelling me, she put down her tools and came over to the doorway. Her hostile scent arrived first.

"Afternoon, Shrubfur," I said pleasantly. "I would like to discuss something with you, if you have a moment."

I didn't expect an invitation inside from her and I wasn't disappointed. "Afternoon, Slasher," she rumbled. "Are you here to order some iron or to harangue me about the street paving again?"

"The latter, I'm afraid."

"Look, I tell you and I tell you, I can't afford it. And even if I could, why should I waste my hard-earned *twilga* on a useless luxury? A bit of mud never hurt anybody."

"That's a rather narrow point of view."

She let out a low growl. "Are you insulting me?"

"No, of course not," I replied quickly. "But ... Shrubfur, my friend, you have a problem. I'm here to help you with it, if I can."

"What problem?"

"You've run up quite a large debt to the humans for that information about the metal they call steel. I hope you can honor it—all of it—since I'm going shopping for them today."

Shrubfur bared her fangs nervously. "I ... I assumed ... with so many others owing them too ..."

"That's true, of course. I could use other adults' *twilga* today. The choice is mine."

It took a few heartbeats for the implication to penetrate the dense stuff between her ears. Then she tensed, as if she was about to attack. I tensed, too. But she managed to get control of herself. "I suppose the humans won't accept installment payments with a late penalty?" she growled.

"You suppose correctly."

"I could challenge them over this!"

"I stand in their place," I reminded her. "It's part of my job."

"I know. I believe I can take you, Slasher."

"You and what god? But even if you did, you would be branded as someone who doesn't honor her *twilga*. Who would sell to you or buy from you then?"

Shrubfur just stood there, looking like she wanted to howl in rage. Or pain. I knew the feeling well; the humans had a knack for stirring it.

Finally she growled, "I agree to pay a share for the street paving."

I felt a thrill almost like that of a kill. But gloating would have been an unwise tactic, so I hid it. "You will think well of your decision when you don't have to mudwade on rainy days."

Shrubfur gave me a coldly ferocious look. "It wasn't my decision; I'll *never* think well of it. This doesn't end the matter. You're doing a bad thing, Slasher. Very bad!"

# CHAPTER TEN

Shrubfur showed me her tail and returned to her work. Under the circumstances it would have been small-minded of me to take offense. Besides, I was glad to be out of range of the reek of her hatred.

Whistling a cheery tune, I headed for Priest Street. I hardly noticed the snow and freezing wind.

I visited Greeneyes, Gulper and Longfang—the three remaining holdouts—in turn. Being the same sort as Shrubfur, they were all at work. Their reactions to my proposition were the same, too. But they all eventually pledged their *twilga* shares for the street paving. Their anger didn't worry me, any more than Shrubfur's had. These things passed.

I returned to my stall and opened up for business. I was glowing with triumph, as I handled the rest of the day's weighings. Tomorrow I would hire the best artisans for the paving job, calculate the *twilga* shares (including my modest fee), and begin the laborious task of redeeming the pledges. I spent much of the afternoon lost in thought, planning the details.

Which might explain why I didn't notice—at the time—the paucity of clients, the groups of people who stopped talking when I passed, the silent reception at Snakeleg's, and the whispers at my tail.

At sundown I closed up my stall, fetched Runt from school, and set out for home.

I was still trying to decide whether traditional firebrick or the human innovation asphalt would be better for the paving, and which artisans did the best work for the least *twilga*. I didn't miss the usual friendly goodnights or the running company.

We reached the cabin as darkness closed around it. A flap strap had broken, letting some snow inside. After I finished giving Runt a lesson in swearing, I fixed the flap, cleaned up, and managed to get a hearthfire lit.

Runt was learning fast. He followed me around, trying to imitate what I was doing. I let him help when he could and cuffed him when he got underpaw. Meanwhile, I told him about my street paving triumph while he struggled with his meager vocabulary to tell me about school.

"Good job, Runt," I said when we finished, scratching behind his ears. "Mommy loves you."

"Runt loves Mommy!"

"That's nice to hear. Are you hungry?"

Runt jumped up and down and let out a high-pitched howl.

"Me, too. Let's go hunt up something tasty for dinner. Be good or we'll both go to bed hungry."

"Okay!"

The hunting was long, cold and frustrating. The storm had subsided to flurries, but the snow was so deep in the open that I made better time on my hindlegs. Runt followed my tail. We moved silently through the shadowed woods, like spirits from a ghost legend.

I was on the verge of giving up and telling my stomach to be patient until morning, when I sniffed out a borer burrow. I showed Runt how to dig it open, then we ate our fill. Not the most delicious of dinners, but during the snow season you couldn't be choosy.

We hurried back to the warmth of the cabin. Runt curled up on his little bed by the fire; soon he was batting at dream-prey in his sleep. Lighting the candles on my writing table, I set out to answer a letter from my colleague in Goodgame.

I was almost done when a well-remembered entry cry cut through the night noises. My heart jumped up into my throat. Irongut!

I had almost given up hope. Time had only hardened his hostility toward the humans; according to the rumormongers, he was becoming a leading voice among the hidebound traditionalists. I didn't see why a mere philosophical difference should kill a wonderful relationship, but Irongut was young, with all the zealousness of youth. He hadn't been able to face me and, of course, I couldn't go to him.

But now he was here.

If he was here for romance, he would find me ready, willing and able. After an appropriate apology for throwing me out of his stall, of course. I howled permission for him to enter. Then I tidied up the desk, ran a quick comb through my fur, and went to the doorway to welcome him.

He emerged from the darkness looking better than ever. But the moment he entered the cabin, I smelled trouble. Be careful, I told myself. Something is up.

"Evening, Irongut," I said pleasantly.

"It's good to see you, Slasher." Irongut went over to the hearth, where the strongwood logs were blazing and crackling. "I haven't caught scent of you lately. You've been too busy with your creatures. I've missed you."

"They call themselves humans, *gorwana*." Lovewords still came naturally, at least for me. "I've missed you, too. How have you been?"

"Fine, thank you."

So it was going to be like that.

"How's business?" I asked, keeping the conversation alive until he was ready to get to the meat.

"Lousy. The new kilning techniques that the humans sold to the other clay-workers have almost made me obsolete."

"You can buy the techniques from them, too."

His scent turned hostile. "I don't want any unnatural knowledge, not a bit of it. Even if I never sell another pot." He paused, then made what he probably thought was a convincing show of passion. "But I didn't come here to argue morality, *gorwana*. I came to be with you." He moved close to me, and started licking behind my left ear.

I backed away. "Okay, it's truth time. What are you trying to accomplish?"

"I don't understand."

"Do you think I'm a fresh-caught *tagnami* that you can trick? You insult me. You aren't in a romantic mood—anybody with a nose worthy of the name could tell that. So why did you really come here?"

"I . . . wanted to talk to you."

"About what?"

"About . . . ur . . . Weighing. You know that I'm interested in your profession. I thought we might—"

"Irongut, *gorwana*, you don't get enough practice to be a convincing liar. You're here for some other reason, one you aren't willing to admit to. I don't appreciate being treated this way."

Irongut just stood there silently, smelling and looking very uncomfortable.

Suddenly I thought of the one subject about which Irongut might feel the need to lie to me. "It's something to do with the humans, isn't it?"

More silence.

"Kraal curse it, Irongut, go home! You no longer have permission to be on my territory. I'm going out to Coldcrag, to make sure the humans are all right."

Irongut moved to block the doorway. "No, you aren't. That's why I came here tonight—to keep you out of it."

Dictating to me in my own cabin! A challenge almost exploded from my lips. Only the fact that it was Irongut, and that I knew he wasn't really opposing me, enabled me to keep my anger under control. "Out of what?" I demanded.

He didn't answer.

"If you aren't going to talk to me, then get out! You won't fight me. But if you don't move, I'll have to walk over or right through you."

He couldn't outglare me and finally stepped aside. "Please stay here tonight," he begged. "With me or without me. You can't help the humans."

You could have sliced iron with my anger. "You know about my duty to them. I'm going. If you tell me what I'm walking into, it might help me avoid trouble."

He thought that through, then spoke in a low growl. "Word spread quickly about the immoral trick you used to put over the street paving. Some of us feel the humans are the source of this evil, and many others. So Shrubfur and a pawful of other right-thinking townsfolk are going to visit Coldcrag tonight. For a circle challenge."

Overkill, I thought. Any one adult could kill both humans without much effort. I didn't see the need for multiple challenges, except maybe to provide moral support for such drastic action. "Violating my challenge-right! Skulking behind my back! You thought I would ignore this shame, if I didn't have a chance to prevent it! No! I'll buy my honor back with blood, if it comes to that!"

"I—"

"Go home, Irongut!" My voice softened. "I forgive you for your part in this. Your heart was in the right place, though Kraal knows where your brain was."

"What are you going to do?" He asked stiffly.

"My job."

Irongut backed out of the doorway, reeking worry and sorrow. "The humans are dangerous and very bad luck. I hope you survive the night, *gorwana.*" Then he was gone.

I rushed around the cabin, filling my carrysack with the things I figured I would need. I had enough imagination to see the only two possible outcomes of what I had to do. Neither of them was good. I looked around the cabin as I packed, locking the memory in my heart.

I would have felt sick but for the heat of my rage which burned away all lesser emotions.

Runt had slept the sleep of the innocent through Irongut's visit. I went over to his blanket and gently stroked his back fur. "Sleep well, my little furball. Tomorrow it's back to the Wild for you, unless the new owner needs a *tagnami.*"

I put out the fire and the candles, as if I were just going out for a visit. Part of me wanted to burn the cabin to the ground so nobody else could make it their home. But most of me wanted to be able to pretend that it would always be waiting for me to return, just as it was now.

I was down the steps and just starting across the meadow when I heard a faint but urgent bleat from behind. "Mommy!"

I stopped and turned. Runt was standing in the doorway, rubbing the sleep from his eyes.

Claws ripped through my heart. I went back to him and knelt so I could talk to him eye-to-eye. "Runt, *shirwa,* Mommy has to go away. Go back to sleep."

"When Mommy come back?"

I had to wipe dampness from my eyes and clear my throat before I could speak. "Mommy won't be coming back."

Runt stared at me, round-eyed. "Why?"

How could I explain it to him? I only half-understood it myself. "I just have to."

"Runt go with!" he bleated.

I tried to tell him that he couldn't, but the words wouldn't leave my mouth. He was so helpless. Too civilized to survive in the Wild, not civilized enough to make a place for himself in town. His fate might not be much better with me. But he was my *tagnami*, my responsibility while I still lived. And I loved him.

"Run fast or be left behind," I told him sternly. I set out again across the meadow and Runt followed close.

We followed a game trail toward the eastern boundary of my territory. I set the best pace that I figured Runt could manage over a distance. The storm had moved on beyond the Low Mountains, but the night was still breath-misting cold. The rolling fields were pale white in the moonlight, but the thickets were grave-black.

The tears stayed in my eyes as my territory passed around me for the last time. Even in the heart of winter, there was an austere beauty to the discerning observer. Nightfliers cawed in gaunt strongwood branches. Millioneye shrubs wore their berries like festive decorations. A family of grinners tore at a lump-meat carcass. The breeze told a tale of hardy life struggling to survive and dormant life awaiting rebirth.

I couldn't imagine what a landless life would be like. Of course, depending on what Kraal had in store for me tonight, the issue might not arise.

Crossing the boundary was a wrenching experience. I wiped the last tears from my eyes, yelled at Runt to keep up, and turned onto the commonland trail.

I had only a vague, quickly thrown together plan for what I would do when I got to Coldcrag. Now I took the opportunity to fill in the details. Everything depended on me getting there first. Shrubfur was probably organizing the circle challenge and her

territory was farther from Coldcrag than mine. Moreover, circle challenges usually required a lot of preliminary negotiation to settle the individual rights. I had
a reasonable chance.

"Are you getting tired?" I asked Runt.

"No tired. Runt like run."

"That's good."

I wasn't really stretching my stride, but the snow
dragged at my legs and each breath felt like icicle
knives in my lungs. Before long, my muscles were
burning and I was panting. Kraal, I *was* getting old!

I kept checking the breeze for person-scents and
paused every so often to put my ear to the ground.
We seemed to be alone in the night. The territories
we passed were quiet. Was I early, or too late?

We reached the boundary of Coldcrag, still without
any sign of the circle challengers. Even in an emer-
gency like this we couldn't enter the humans' territory
without permission—*we* weren't here to issue a challenge. We stopped and I howled an entry cry.

Thousandth-days passed. If the deed was already
done, I would return home. In the morning I would
set out to identify the challengers and regain my
honor. I wouldn't last long enough to attend to all of
them, but my effort would become a legend of the
town. Then I would be able to sleep soundly.

But that wouldn't bring the humans back to life.
They were still my key to wealth and fame, and I
was beginning to realize that they might be equally
important to my world. Besides, I was also beginning
to think of them as friends. I would mourn and miss
them.

The tuskhorn finally sounded its imitation permission to enter. I must have roused the humans from
sleep. Good news, at least for the moment.

"Come along," I told Runt. "Watch out for ice
patches."

"Runt like slide."

I sighed. Youth.

We ran across the broken, treacherous ground. Coldcrag at night in the heart of winter could have passed for Netherworld. Sprinter had set, but Loper was still high and bright among the stars. We scrambled over jagged rock formations and under bare branches that moved with the wind like threatening claws. I set a recklessly fast pace, as though demons were on our trail.

They probably were.

Ralphayers was standing in the doorway of the cabin, shivering from the cold. Pamayers stood behind him. She was using one of their lamp-rods to illuminate the area around them; otherwise the cabin was dark. They were both wearing the baggy garments they called pajamas.

Runt and I skidded to a stop in front of them, panting and trembling.

"Welcome, Slasher, Runt," Pamayers said. "It's rather late for a social call. Is something wrong?"

"Very wrong. I strongly recommend that you put on your traveling garments, and pack your camping gear, quick. We have to get away from here."

"Huh? Why?" Ralphayers stifled a yawn.

"A group of townsfolk is coming here to kill you two. They might be closing in right now."

Pamayers' face changed color from pink to white. "You're . . . you're sure about this?"

"Yes, yes, yes! But don't believe me—stick around and smell them for yourself. You'll get to participate in one of our quaint rituals called a circle challenge. You won't enjoy it."

"Why? What have we done?"

"You didn't do it—I did. I listened to you instead of my common sense. But we haven't time to get into that now. Are you coming or staying?"

The humans squawked at each other in their own language while I popped my claws nervously. Finally

Ralphayers said to me, "We'll trust your judgment and do as you advise. But we'll need a better explanation later."

"You'll get it, if there is a later for us. Now hurry, please!"

They ducked back inside the cabin. I stayed outside so I could keep sniffing and listening for the circle challengers. Runt was making snowballs and throwing them at a tree stump. I didn't think he quite grasped the seriousness of the situation.

I glanced through the open doorway. The humans had emerged from what they called the bedroom, wearing their bulky traveling garments. They had the carrysacks filled with camping gear which they used on their research trips into the Wild; they were frantically stuffing food and other items into them. Meanwhile, they chattered at each other in low but intense voices. When they finished packing, they slung the carrysacks on their backs and hurried outside.

Pamayers closed the doorway barrier behind her, but the humans didn't seem very concerned about losing their territory. They seemed to be more afraid of dying. Such improprieties no longer surprised or outraged me. Different worlds, different ways.

"Runt," I growled softly, "come here."

He scampered over. "Mommy?"

"If Mommy is killed, you run away. Stay away from people. Hunt, grow, be happy, and remember me."

"Mommy not die!"

"I hope you're right. But remember what I said."

Pamayers patted Runt's head. Their relationship was improving; he growled, but didn't bite.

The humans were peering nervously at the shadowed outcrops and vegetation. "How long do we have before they show up?" Ralphayers asked me.

"They are here."

The wind was flowing down out of the mountains, while the challengers were coming from the opposite direction, so I heard them before I could smell them. They were on the humans' territory, spread out to prevent escape, and closing in on the cabin. At least seven. I couldn't see any of them, of course; a broken twig here, a scuff there told me where they were. They weren't being particularly stealthy since they didn't expect much opposition from the humans.

Time to enlighten them. I howled the traditional trespass challenge. The humans backed away from me and held each other. Runt tried to imitate my cry, but I shushed him.

Silence gripped the night. None of the challengers responded; they were probably reevaluating their plan based on my presence. The nocturnal animals were wisely hiding.

"Yes, Slasher is here!" I shouted. "I'm here to accept any and all challenges of Ralphayers and Pamayers! You already owe them *twilga* for trespassing! I suggest you turn around and slink away before your debt becomes too large for you to survive it!"

I admired my bravado. I might possibly win the first two or three deathduels, but even my ego couldn't pretend that I would live to complete the circle.

They knew it, too. Shrubfur's voice came from the black forest eaves. "Return to your territory, Slasher, while you can! You've been seduced by these evil creatures! But when their influence is gone, you'll be one of us again!'

"I'm more respectable than any of you!" I yelled back. "I'm not afraid of new ideas or in need of a skulking pack when an *adult* would hunt alone!"

My insult put an end to the futile discussion. Fierce howling cut through the night from all directions, a few ten-strides away but moving closer. The din sent all the nocturnal animals scurrying or flying to safety. The humans crowded behind me, trembling like lureflower petals. Runt howled back, full of the fearlessness and ignorance of youth.

"Ready to go?" I yelled to the humans over the howling.

"Yes!" Ralphayers replied. "But what can we do? They are all around us! We can't fight them—wouldn't even if we could! And we can't run fast enough to escape!"

"But you can!" Pamayers added. "Take Runt and get away!"

My nerves were a bit frayed. Forgetting that she didn't know any better, I glared down at her. "*Never* tell me to betray my honor!"

"I'm . . . sorry!" she gulped.

Getting control, I answered Ralphayers' question. "Remember those Earth animals you told me about, horses? Well, pretend I'm one! Both of you straddle my back and grab onto my fur!"

"You're strong, but not that strong!" Ralphayers objected.

"You better hope I am! Get on!"

They did, awkwardly. Ralphayers sat in front of my carrysack, Pamayers behind it. My legs almost buckled. The humans were heavier than they looked. But I figured that I could still make better speed than their pitiful excuse for running.

"Hang on tight!" I told the humans. "It's going to be a rough trip. Runt, follow my tail! Don't wander!"

"Okay, Mommy!"

"Here we go!" I sprang across the white-crusted ground of the clearing, away from Coalgathering and my territory, toward the Wild. The howling died. It was time for fangs and claws.

"Where are we going?" Pamayers shouted over the drum rhythm of my driving legs and the shrieking wind.

"Away from the hunters!" I gasped. "If we manage that . . . we'll see!"

I could have tried to dart between two of the slower challengers. But such a show of cowardice would make us legitimate prey; they would hunt us to the death. Besides, I was mad from snout to tail. If I had to abandon everything I owned except my honor, I would go with style and at least a small victory.

I ran straight at Shrubfur.

She loped out of the underbrush in front of me, a vague shadowy shape. I would have approached a fight with her cautiously under the best of circumstances; with the burden on my back it was downright crazy. Well, so was I, a little bit.

"Stay right there!" I shouted at her. "I'm coming with a red welcome for you!" My scent of rage and fight-lust was so strong that even I could smell it.

The other challengers kept their distance. This was between Shrubfur and me now. She held her ground, bracing to defend herself and counterattack. She didn't smell afraid. But . . . maybe . . . a bit uncertain.

The gap between us was closing fast. My back ached. The humans were shouting questions that I didn't bother to hear, and Runt was howling his own high-pitched challenges. Shrubfur had become my entire universe. If she didn't step aside, I was going to claw a path right through her. Or go down trying.

I understood her uncertainty. In fact, the still rational part of my mind was counting on it. She wasn't sure she could beat me and her reason for trying wasn't very strong; her grievance was against the humans. And they were abandoning their territory under challenge. It rarely happened, but it was as effective a banishment as death.

Shrubfur's snarling face loomed in front of me. I readied my fangs to rip out her throat and wondered where her claws would rake me.

At the last possible heartbeat, she leaped aside. She was just out of clawing range to my right, reeking of hatred, growling virulently, as I hurtled by her.

The scrawny woods wrapped darkness around me and the snow under my paws became slippery frozen ground and thick drifts. The humans were still shouting questions. Runt's howls turned triumphant.

Just as I thought we were going to get away clean, Shrubfur must have regretted her indecisiveness. Her pursuit howl was promptly echoed by the rest of the challengers. Running legs pounded the ground behind us. The hunt was up.

My rage began to cool, allowing me to concentrate fully on the agony that each stride wrung from my breaking back.

"Are you all right?" I shouted to the humans.

"Yes!" Ralphayers answered. "What happened back there? Were you going to fight that person?"

"Later . . . !" I gasped. "The challengers are on . . . our trail! Have to . . . outrun them! Need . . . all my strength!"

"You can't possibly outrun them, not while carrying us!"

That deserved and got no answer. Of course I couldn't, but there was no honorable alternative to trying.

I was scrambling upslope, heading east for the Sunrise Pass which led over the mountains and into the Wild. The stunted trees and underbrush became sparser, giving way to snow-covered graystone. I gasped with each stride. My pace was becoming ragged. I could smell and hear the hunters, on both sides as well as behind, closing in on us fast.

I hadn't expected to be pursued and had no clever scheme to escape. But I kept at it doggedly, ignoring more questions from the humans. An anxious tone crept into Runt's howls.

The summit of the pass was just ahead now. If I could make it through, at least I would be running downhill.

The hunters were within a ten-stride or two of bringing us down. My back hurt so much that I almost looked forward to it.

Suddenly and dramatically in the wan moonslight, the white trail curved downward. I saw the Wild below, tree-tops and rivers and broad plains reaching to the horizon. I didn't like the smell or look of it. I didn't belong there.

But my choices had been whittled down to two, and I liked the other even less. I started down, staggering, hindknees buckling.

It took me several heartbeats to realize that the humans, Runt and I were alone on the downward trail. The hunters had stopped at the summit. I could feel their eyes even though I was beyond their view: a barrier of hate and warning at my tail.

It seemed I would live a bit longer.

# CHAPTER ELEVEN

I pulled up slowly on trembling legs. My back felt like a couple of watersnorters had taken the humans' place. "Off!" I yelled.

The humans scrambled onto their own hindlegs. "Why did they stop?" Pamayers asked. "Are we safe now?"

"Safe from the challengers, yes. It seems they're willing to settle for just running us out. But we're in the Wild now. There are quite a few dangerous creatures about, large and small, ones we've purged from our territories, so keep a sharp lookout."

I continued down the trail: a rough path blazed by travelers as well as mothers-to-be. Runt was right behind me and the humans brought up the rear of my odd herd. I set an easy walking pace. Relieved of most of my burden, I felt light enough to float. But my back and legs still ached.

The wooded slopes and dales were much like those on the other side of the Low Mountains, but there were subtle differences. White-barked firetrees, flowervines and spinebushes competed with the more familiar species. Mysterious animal-scents tantalized my nose. Less rain and snow fell here, so the vegetation

was sparser. The scarcity of game explained why it
hadn't been claimed for territories.

"Why?" Pamayers asked so softly that I might have
thought she was talking to herself, except that she
wasn't using her own strange language.

"Why what?" I responded.

"Why all of this? What did we do wrong, to be
driven out like this? I thought your fellow townsfolk
were beginning to accept us."

"Most of them do," I agreed. "But some of our
more conservative ones believe that your alien notion
of cooperation is a threat to our ways. When I tried
your scheme on Shrubfur and the rest of the holdouts,
they smelled it as proof and decided to kill you, or at
least drive you away. The rest is recent history."

"But . . . but cooperation is what makes civilization
work," Ralphayers objected. "Even the challengers
proved that when they got together to deal with us.
Your hyper-individualism has held back your growth.
There's so much you just can't *do* without group
effort."

I let out a low growl. "For a savant you aren't very
quick on the uptake. We may not have the herd
instinct of your kind, but we do cooperate. We do it
in our own way. As for growth . . ."

I stopped. All the times I had cursed the short-
sighted conservatism of my fellow adults, and here I
was babbling their cant like Shrubfur or Irongut. Was
my loss turning me against my own beliefs? And
against the humans?

They were quiet for a pawful of heartbeats. Then
Pamayers said something to Ralphayers in their own
language. I was beginning to grasp their alien emotions; her tone suggested that a challenge might be
imminent. My ears cocked. But Ralphayers' reply was
mild and the mysterious tension faded.

"You're right," Pamayers said to me, "and we were

wrong to suggest what we did. We're here to study your mores, not change them."

"I was the one who bought your scheme and tried it. A Weigher should have known better. I was . . . tempted. And I've been properly punished. So let's not talk about this any more tonight."

"Runt sleepy!" my *tagnami* yawned. "We sleep soon?"

"Very soon," I promised. "Just a little farther, *shirwa*, then we'll stop."

"You've told us what we're escaping from," Ralphayers said. "What are we escaping to?"

I paused. "Our immediate need is for a safe place to camp for the night. I don't know the Wild well, but I remember a spot nearby which should do."

"But what's going to happen to us tomorrow?" Pamayers asked.

"I don't know!" I snapped, short-tempered from my pain and loss. "This is a new experience for me, too. So far I've been concentrating on keeping us alive tonight."

"Is there any hope that we'll ever be able to return to Coalgathering?"

"No. The circle challenge still stands. No matter how long we waited, if we showed our snouts in town, I would have to fight for you. I can't beat seven or eight adults in a row."

"And we wouldn't want you to fight anyone on our behalf," Pamayers said firmly. "Could we negotiate with the challengers, work out a less drastic solution to the problem?"

I laughed. "Maybe. How good are you at negotiating with your throat slashed from ear to ear?"

"Point taken," Ralphayers replied. "So what are our options?"

There were four possible trails to take; two I hated and two I hated even more. I decided to sour the humans on the latter, then sell them the former. "Well, we could turn traveler or wilder."

"Traveling might suit us," Pamayers said. "We could learn more about your world that way. But I'm not sure we understand the concept completely. I gather that travelers are savants, tradespeople, performers and so on who wander from town to town. But how do they fit into your social and economic systems?"

"Travelers are considered a disreputable lot since they don't have territories like decent folks. They earn a bit of *twilga* in a town, buy what they need, then move on. They live in the Wild with all its dangers. Frankly, I don't think you two would last long. But if that's your choice, I'll help you as much as I can."

The humans squawked at each other. I looked up past bare branches at the cold stars and felt empty. I was no traveler. I had to have land of my own under my paws, a fixed place in the universe. But my territory would belong to someone else tomorrow.

"You're right," Pamayers said to me. "We wouldn't survive. What about the other people you mentioned?"

"Wilders," I growled. "Even lower than travelers. Cowards, criminals, perverts, eccentrics—anyone who can't accept the customs of society—flee into the Wild, living scarcely any better than truly wild adults. I would dislike being classed among them."

"So would we. Besides, our studies would be severely limited if we went into hiding."

"Are there any other options?" Ralphayers asked me.

"Two, as a matter of fact. First, we can try to settle in another town. Strongwood Thicket is closest. We have some *twilga* with its townsfolk and we can practice our professions there." I didn't elaborate on what I would have to do to become Strongwood Thicket's Weigher. I didn't think they would approve.

"That sounds more promising," Pamayers replied. "We could widen the range of our studies while still having a reasonable amount of security. But why do you say 'try to settle'?"

"Moving from one town to another is a pretty rare thing. We might be accepted, and we might not. The only way to find out is to go there."

"What if we aren't accepted?" Ralphayers asked.

"Then we try the other option. We go on to Mountainhole and seek Kraal's wisdom."

"Mountainhole?"

"The home of the shrines to the Ninety-Nine Gods. The High Priest of Kraal speaks for the wisest of the gods. His council doesn't come cheaply, but it's worth what you pay for it."

"You think a priest can help us?"

"Absolutely."

"Religious shrines!" Pamayers' eyes were shining. "Imagine what we could learn there, the data we could collect!"

"We're in agreement then," Ralphayers said to me. "On to Strongwood Thicket, and Mountainhole if necessary."

"So be it." I was pleased at how skillfully I had gotten them to see things my way. And having a definite plan of action made me feel a bit less lost.

We went on in silence. The humans' strange garments seemed to protect them from the bone-chilling wind, but they were swaying as they walked. Runt's tail was dragging in the snow. As for me, I was feeling more than uncomfortably cold and tired, though I made a point of not showing it.

Emerging from a stand of trees, we scrambled over the broken, treacherous ground at the foot of a sheer cliff. It vanished into the darkness above us.

Suddenly a monstrous, ground-shaking crash a pawful of strides behind us startled everybody. "What that?" Runt bleated.

"Nothing to worry about," I answered soothingly. No point in worrying, I added silently to myself, since there wasn't anything you could do about it. "Sometimes on cold nights the demon of the cliff throws huge boulders at evil creatures down here. Since you're a good *tagnami*, you have nothing to fear."

The explanation, which I had gotten from my priest, calmed Runt down. But he kept looking guiltily at the cliff.

Ralphayers came up beside me and spoke softly so that Runt couldn't hear him. "It could also be water freezing in cracks in the rock, breaking off chunks of the cliff face."

"Savants must lead drab, juiceless lives. I prefer my version."

Ralphayers twisted his face in a smile. "You know, so do I."

Following the cliff north a few hundred-strides, we came to a point where the ground rose at an almost unclimbable angle. I paused to sniff for anyone who might have claimed the sanctuary ahead of us. Kraal was with us for a change: nobody home.

"Do we have to climb up there?" Pamayers asked wearily.

"Yes. This is a place where travelers and mothers-to-be camp—I dropped all of my cubs here. It's as safe and comfortable as you're going to find in this part of the Wild. It's hard to reach, and there's no water, game or vegetation to attract unwelcome visitors. Come on."

Everybody, even the humans, used four legs to climb the ice-slicked, rubble-strewn slope. Fortunately, the knowledge that we were at the end of the night's journey lent our aching muscles strength. Panting and trembling, we reached the top.

In some ancient god-fight this part of the cliff had been pounded down into a shelf. About a square hundred-stride of former cliff top jutted out from the face. It was all bare graystone, swept clean of snow by the wind. A dimple in the face provided some shelter for helpless mothers and their cubs. The rock showed the scars of fires, but anything that might have attracted scavengers had been meticulously disposed of. Away from the face the sanctuary looked down on rustling treetops. The drop-off from the edges of the shelf was sheer; we had come up at the only climbable point.

The wind howled eerily. The sanctuary was a safe spot to camp, but nobody lingered when her business was done.

"You're certainly right about this place being out of the way," Ralphayers said. "But what do we do if a dangerous animal finds its way up here and attacks us?"

I grinned, baring my fangs. "The most dangerous animal you're ever going to meet is answering your foolish question."

"Point taken. And since we managed to forget our bows in all the excitement, I'm afraid we're also going to have to rely on your hunting skill for meat when our field rations run out."

"I had already assumed that. Is this campsite satisfactory? If not," I finished dryly, "we can go on—"

"It's fine!" the humans said together.

"Good." We gratefully shed our carrysacks. I got out my water jug and half-emptied it, then passed it to Runt. The humans drank more delicately from theirs.

"Runt and I will sleep there," I told the humans, pointing to the dimple in the cliff face. "Set up your half-egg downwind and as far from us as you can manage without falling over the edge." Even so, sleeping close enough to the humans to protect them wasn't going to be easy. I anticipated many fitful nights.

"Runt!" I said sharply to get his attention.

"Mommy want?" he yawned.

"I want you to go back down to the forest. Find running water and refill my jug. Be careful not to break it. Then sniff out some reasonably dry treefuzz and fetch enough for both of us to sleep on."

Runt stared at his hindpaws.

"You heard me! Get to it!"

"Runt no go! Runt cold, tired! Want sleep by fire!"

I should have realized how worn out he was and lightened his chores appropriately. But it was too late now. Disobedience couldn't be tolerated. I loomed over him and let him smell my anger. "Go! Do!"

"No!"

I batted him across the snout with a forepaw, claws retracted of course, but hard enough to knock him to the ground and make him yowl. "Go! Do!"

Runt just kept yowling.

I stepped forward to bat him again.

With a quickness I hadn't known the humans possessed, Pamayers put herself between us. She looked up at me and spoke in a strange voice. "Don't hit him again."

Shock at her incredible presumption fueled my anger. "This is none of your business!" I growled. "Get out of my way!"

"If you try to hit him again, you'll have to kill me first."

"Are you challenging me?"

"No, I won't fight you. But you won't lay a paw on him while I'm alive."

Runt was huddled behind Pamayers' hindlegs, peering fearfully around them at me. "Come here!" I demanded.

His little face disappeared behind her.

I bared my fangs at Pamayers and popped my foreclaws. She was trying to steal my *tagnami*! A red haze clouded my vision.

Waking from what was apparently stunned immobility, Ralphayers squawked something at Pamayers. She replied briefly but heatedly.

Ralphayers moved over beside his companion. "I'm

going to have to go along with Pam on this," he said
to me.

An evil demon whispered to me. The humans are
giving you ample cause to challenge them. Kill them
and you can go home. Your *tagnami*, your territory,
your life will again be the way they were before the
humans intruded. You can reclaim everything that was
yours.

Everything except honor.

I took a deep breath and struggled to master myself.
I must have been worn out, too. Otherwise I wouldn't
have been cutting such a poor figure as a parent and
a Weigher. But that was done. Now, somehow, I had
to extricate us from this mess.

"I don't want to punish Runt," I said stiffly to
Pamayers. "But he must obey me. If he doesn't obey,
he won't learn, and he won't become a dominant
adult. I love him too much to let that happen."

"I know you do." Pamayers seemed to be calming
down, too. "Let me try something."

She knelt so that she was eye-to-eye with Runt and
gently stroked his head. "It's all right now," she said
soothingly. "Slasher isn't going to hurt you."

The demonflier was still circling on that. But I was
curious as to what the human was up to, so I tried to
smell and look benign.

"You don't want to sleep on cold, hard rock, do
you?" Pamayers asked Runt.

"No."

"And you want to have some nice, tasty water to
drink when you wake up, don't you?"

"Yes."

"Then shouldn't you go do what your parent told
you to do?"

Pamayers kept stroking Runt while he thought
about it. Finally his usual grin returned. "Runt fetch
plenty treefuzz and water. You see."

Grabbing the water jug, he bounded into the darkness toward the descending trail.

Pamayers stood up and faced me. "I offer *twilga* in apology for my actions."

"I owe you for getting Runt to obey," I admitted stiffly. "The debts cancel. Good night."

I took my carrysack over to the dimple. Then I ran the bounds of our temporary territory and set my warnoffs. I decided it would be best to treat the humans like *tagnami* in this. Their strange spoor would be less likely to repel wild animals.

When I returned, the humans had their half-egg up. They were moving about inside, silhouettes in the lamplight which pierced the thin fabric. I was glad to have smelled the last of them for the night.

A pile of treefuzz appeared, walking on Runt's hindlegs.

"Well done," I told him. "Drop the fuzz over by the cliff face, out of the wind, and spread it into a nice, soft bed for us."

"Okay," he said tentatively and did as he was told.

I pulled the treeswinger-hair blanket out of my carrysack, and put the water jug and my beltpouch in. Then I took the blanket and carrysack over to our "bed," the latter to use as a makeshift pillow.

Runt was already curled up on the pallet of dark, fragrant treefuzz.

He stirred as I settled beside him and pulled the blanket over us. "Runt?" I whispered.

"Yes, Mommy."

"I'm not angry with you. When I punish you, it's because I love you. I want you to grow up to be a good adult. Do you understand?"

"Yes. Runt love Mommy."

I licked him behind the ear. "Good night, *shirwa*."

We cuddled together, partly to share warmth. The treefuzz was a poor substitute for a real mattress, but in my exhaustion it felt as soft as a cloud. The bitter cold, the moaning wind, my sore muscles and the too-close presence of the humans all faded away. Runt's little snores were a lullaby that I felt as well as heard.

I slept.

# CHAPTER TWELVE

I woke up just as the sun began to peek over the eastern horizon. My body felt like a bruised sack full of creaking bones and tight muscles. Runt was still snoring, and there were no signs of life coming from the humans' half-egg. Stifling a moan, I managed to stand up.

The sky was reddish-gold on the eastern horizon and pale blue everywhere else. Not even a wisp of a cloud in sight. The Wild spread out below my rocky roost: scarlet, maroon and purple foliage, dark trunks and branches, sparkling blue streams, all painted on a pure white canvas. The chill mountain breeze was invigorating and held no scent of danger. Things seemed a bit less disastrous than they had last night.

I decided to work out my kinks and rouse my little furball at the same time. Creeping up on Runt silently, I touched him with a forepaw and yelled, "Pounce!"

A heartbeat later I had what seemed like a pawful of Runts swarming all over me. I defended myself as best I could without hurting him. Our slashes were clawless, our fangs didn't break skin. Yowling enthusiastically, we lunged, writhed, wrestled and rolled. Treefuzz flew. Finally I managed to pin all of him. I

was panting and wore a couple of minor scrapes, but
the kinks were gone.

"Someday I win!" Runt bleated happily.

"Someday."

The humans emerged from their half-egg and came
over. "Morning, Slasher, Runt," they said pleasantly.

"Morning," I replied just as pleasantly and Runt
echoed me. By unspoken mutual consent, last night's
dispute was put behind us.

"We thought we heard some slaughter being done
out here," Ralphayers said, wiping sleep from his eyes.
"But I don't see any blood or carcasses."

"Runt and I were playing. We didn't wake you, did
we?" I asked innocently.

That deserved and got no answer. Instead Pamayers
looked out at the world. "What a glorious day to begin
our adventure."

"Adventure," I snorted. "I can think of several ways
to characterize our misfortune, but 'adventure' isn't
one of them."

"Party pooper."

That couldn't possibly mean what it meant. "The
best way to Strongwood Thicket is by boat. If we want
to get to the river in time to buy passage today, we'll
have to set a fast pace. Any objections?"

"None," Ralphayers replied. "Would you like some
of our . . . that is, like to buy some of our rations for
breakfast?"

I had tasted their food once. "No, thanks."

The humans returned to the half-egg to attend to
their morning routine and to break camp. Runt and I
groomed ourselves as best we could with a jugful of
water. Then I had Runt refill the jug and clean up
our campsite while I went down to hunt our breakfast.

Winter hunting in the Wild was about as challenging
as it got. I anticipated many hungry days ahead, but
this time I was lucky. I came across scrounger tracks
and followed them to their source. Soon I returned to

the sanctuary dragging a pair of the tasty furbags behind me.

The humans didn't show their usual interest as Runt and I ate. By the time we tossed the carcass over the edge and finished packing, the humans were ready to travel, too.

"We don't dare show our snouts near the territories," I told them, "so we'll follow this side of the mountains north. The Muddy River is about ten thousand-strides from here. It runs west through a gap in the mountains, then south past Coalgathering, but we'll be buying eastward passage. Boats usually leave Coalgathering around sunzenith, so we have that long to reach the river."

We half-walked, half-slid down the trail to the woods. I knew that the trail from Laketown in the south to the river passed nearby, but I didn't know exactly where. So I led my herd eastward into the snowbound Wild, figuring that we would have to come upon the trail eventually. And we did, after a few hundred-strides of plowing through drifts, scrambling over fallen trees, and jumping frigidly cold streams. Fortunately this wasn't a truly hard winter, like the one two years ago when even the river froze solid.

The trail was a breach in the vegetation wide enough to accommodate a wagon. There were wheel ruts, pawprints and scents of recent users, but none fresh enough to concern us. We had to contend with snow, ice and slush, but it was easier going than the woods. Taking the northern turn, I set the best pace I figured the humans could endure over a distance.

Shadows fought with shafts of golden light, losing as the sun rose. But it didn't bring much warmth; we were still following plumes of our own breath, and every sound was frozen to crystal sharpness. I liked the swaying trees, snow-crowned meadows and strange flavors in the air better than I had last night. But the root of my despair hadn't changed; I settled into a somber melancholy.

The others didn't share my mood. Runt was bounding here and there like a cub, enjoying his freedom from Bentback's log. The humans were almost as excited. They stopped frequently to collect samples and to use the box which supposedly showed what they were seeing to the skyboat. I had to keep after all of them like a mother waddler with her chicks.

Runt settled down and walked with Pamayers. She started telling him an improbable tale about a *tagnami* named Jack and a tall vine. I found his new attachment to her somewhat touching and smelled no reason to object so long as it didn't intrude on my parental authority.

I took advantage of the opportunity to have a private chat with Ralphayers. Dropping back beside him, I spoke in a voice that only he could hear. "Why did Pamayers interfere with my punishment of Runt last night?"

"You should ask her that."

"I would like to avoid renewing the dispute, if possible."

Ralphayers was quiet for a long time, then he said, "We humans disagree strongly on whether it's right to hit kids to discipline them. Some think it is, for the same reason you folks do—it's the quickest and easiest way. Others think it's bad for the kid and prefer non-violent persuasion. You can guess which side my wife takes."

Indeed. "I hope she understands that we do what tradition tells us is best for our *tagnami*."

"I'm sure she does," he replied. "But I'm also sure that if you try to beat Runt, you'll have to kill us first." There was iron in his voice.

It occurred to me that the humans' advanced knowledge might extend to child-rearing. Few people enjoyed punishing their *tagnami* and, if I could market a better method, I could rebuild my *twilga* balance in a hurry. Acquiring it from the humans for free would compensate me for their temerity. "I'll try your 'non-violent persuasion' as best I can."

"We'll help you," he replied, falling neatly into my snare.

Silence signaled the end of the topic, so I launched a new one. "A moment ago you used one of your alien words. I've heard it before, but I haven't been able to figure out what it means."

"Which one?"

"Wife."

Ralphayers paused. "That's going to take a bit of explaining, but here goes. Our kids take a lot longer to grow up than yours do—about eighteen years—and they need a lot of looking after. The usual setup is for a male and a female adult to live together, have kids and raise them. The relationship between the man and the woman is called marriage. Married men are husbands, married women are wives."

My jaw dropped. "Eighteen years! What use is a *tagnami* that needs so long to train?"

"We take the long-term approach. We can afford to since we live about twenty-five years longer than you."

"So you and Pamayers became husband and wife to drop a cub?"

Ralphayers laughed. "Pam and I have been married for six years. We haven't 'dropped any cubs' yet, but we hope to when things settle down."

"If I were you, I wouldn't count on that any time soon." Something about his explanation rang false. "How can you two have been married six years when you claim the skyboat grew you a couple of months ago?"

"Good point. I should have said the *original* Ralphayers and Pamayers, who still live on Earth and should be rather elderly by now. We were 'grown' from parts of them, like you grow plants from cuttings.

Since we have the same memories they did when the 'cuttings' were taken, we tend to forget we aren't them."

That should cure me of asking about human-things for awhile.

"Since we're on the topic of procreation," Ralphayers continued after a pause, "what's involved in dropping a cub? Rubbertail was a bit fuzzy on the details."

"Well, of course he would be. He's a male."

Ralphayers grinned.

"When a female knows her time is near," I explained, "she eats and drinks as much as she can. Then she goes into the Wild, to a sanctuary like the one where we camped last night. Between the birthing, recovering, and caring for the helpless newborn, she's laired up for three or four days."

"What's a cub like at birth?"

"Like Runt, only smaller and chubbier. About a half stride long, and ten to fifteen rock-weights. Short, fuzzy fur. Blind and not very active for the first couple of tenth-days. Four-legged. Slimy until licked clean." And absolutely the cutest, most lovable thing in the entire universe.

"What does it eat?"

"It lives off its fat until it's strong enough to hunt. Then it begins its life in the Wild, while the female goes home and celebrates with an old fashioned feeding frenzy."

"Amazing," Ralphayers said softly.

"Really? What do your newborns eat?"

He told me. I stared at Pamayers in amazement. Well, it did explain her top-heavy shape.

"How many cubs do you have at a time?" he asked me.

"One, almost always. The rare double-births are either sickly or stillborn."

We lapsed into a thoughtful silence. I imagine each of us was heartily glad not to be the other.

We plodded on, making occasional stops so that the humans could rest. The sun climbed toward sunzenith faster than I liked, but I figured we would reach the river first. The humans were holding up well and without complaint. Runt was doing more listening to Pamayers than frolicking, but he didn't smell dangerously tired. A still-sore back and wet hindleg fur were my worst complaints. Activity kept us from feeling the cold very much.

I was noticing a pattern to the differences between the Wild and my territory. Deprived of centuries of civilized tending, the web of being here was less ordered. Flora and fauna lived where they wished. Death, rot, overpopulation and other blights were everywhere. At first it seemed a tragic waste, then I began to sense the almost desperate energy born of this grimmer battle for survival. It made me feel younger, fiercer.

Emerging from a patch of underbrush, we found ourselves on the bank of the Muddy River. The brown water was running high and fast this time of year. The other bank was about fifty strides away. Round, maroon riverplant and chunks of ice were floating downriver. Flyfish jumped for airborne bugs, and lumpmeats scuttled among the rustling wandplants in the shallows. The rank smell would take some getting used to.

"River!" Runt bleated. "Where we go now?"

"Now we rest and hope a boat comes along," I replied.

"What if one doesn't?" Pamayers asked. "Could we hike to Strongwood Thicket?"

"Through the Boiling Swamp?" I laughed. "The only destinations on that trail are misery and death."

Looking around, I spotted a patch of ground under a fat tangletree which was free of snow and reasonably dry. I had Runt kick-brush it clean while the humans and I shed our carrysacks. The humans sat against the black trunk in a way that made my tail hurt just seeing it; Runt and I settled on our haunches. We all drank and the humans ate some of their rations. Then we relaxed. It would have been idyllic except for the brisk river breeze.

I was just getting comfortable, and thinking about emulating Runt's nap, when I heard the faint blowing of a thunderfish downriver. "Everybody up!" I said sharply. "Here comes our ride—I hope."

We grabbed our carrysacks and hurried down to the water's edge. As we reached it, the boat appeared around a bend in the river.

The boat looked old and decrepit. It was small for the river trade, fifteen strides long by five wide, and blockish. I knew it was flat-bottomed so it could operate in the shallows. The strongwood planks were poorly caulked and needed a new coat of waterproofing. The bow and stern cargo bins were covered with bigmeat hides and an awning of hide sheltered the cabin; all were much patched. The poles used for maneuvering were debarked branches, and poorly debarked at that.

The thunderfish puller was, on the other hand, a prime specimen. Over ten strides long, it was flat, wide, and tapered toward the tail. Its mottled hide was mud-brown. The widely spaced eyes in its flat head couldn't see very well, but its enormous whiskers enabled it to feel its way through the rushes where it liked to feed. Its fins were big and strong enough to pull a fully loaded boat upriver as fast as a person could walk. A rope harness ran back from its head to the bow of the boat, while reins attached to its whiskers kept going to the cabin.

The humans had their seeing-box aimed at the thunderfish. "I've been hoping to catch one of these in action," Ralphayers muttered.

"Look at that spout," Pamayers pointed. "It must

be an air-breather. How can something that size find enough to eat in a river ecology?"

"It's omnivorous, like you," I replied. "It prefers fish, but it can also graze on river plants."

As the boat came closer, I read the name *Splasher* painted up by the bow and got a look at the person in the cabin holding the reins. Old Wetsnout. I groaned.

"Is something wrong?" Ralphayers asked.

"Depends on what you mean by wrong. Wetsnout is a good sort, but he'll talk your ear down to a stump."

He laughed. "Your annoyance is our treasure trove of knowledge."

"It's possible to be too rich."

I boomed out my loudest hailing howl; Wetsnout's hearing wasn't all it used to be. He leaned out from under the awning and peered at us. "Young Slasher from Coalgathering, isn't it?"

Ignoring the giggles behind me, I yelled back, "Yes, it's me! Aren't you ever going to die?"

"Nope! Only thing I've never done, and I don't aim to!"

"My companions are my *tagnami*, Runt, and the distinguished savants from another world, Pamayers and Ralphayers."

His face split in a wide grin. "I've heard a binful about your business associates, most of it bad, but none of it boring! Since you vouch for them, I'll chance it!"

Wetsnout brought the boat as close to the bank as he dared. Then, while the thunderfish rested and sucked in riverplants, he poled the stern around so that it gently nuzzled the bottom mud an easy stride from the bank. Traveler though he was, he knew his trade.

"Come on, hop aboard!" he cackled. He looked as ancient and decrepit as his boat. His black-and-gray striped fur was falling out in patches and his fangs were worn down to nubbins. He stooped over midway between two and four legs. His strength and agility were failing but, even more than me, he had made up for the loss with expertise. His scent and expression revealed more joy than he had any reason to feel.

Runt was staring at the boat dubiously. "No go on boat! No go on water!"

I didn't have time to explain away his fear. Tucking him under one foreleg and my carrysack under the other, I jumped onto the stern. The humans followed with their gear.

The stern cargo bin was loaded unsurprisingly with coal. We quickly scrambled across the treacherous terrain and jumped down into the cabin. Runt yowled until I growled; then he shut up. I returned him to his hindlegs. He glared at me but didn't try to bolt.

The cabin didn't deserve the name. The deck and sides were bare planking and the paint was giving way to rot in places. The pilot's chair was the only furniture. An alcohol lamp hung from an awning support. Two big brass-bound trunks presumably held equipment, wares and personal belongings. To Wetsnout this was home; to me it was a wooden box.

Wetsnout slouched in the chair and took up the reins. He flicked them twice and the thunderfish began to pull the boat away from the bank. A flick of the right rein and the thunderfish turned upriver. The boat followed.

A plume of foul-smelling spray shot high and loud, drifting back to wet us. The deck moved disturbingly underpaw. We were on our way.

# CHAPTER THIRTEEN

"Now let's talk *twilga*, folks!" Wetsnout spoke without taking his eyes off the river.

"I'm representing all of us," I told him. "How much will four passages to Strongwood Thicket lighten our books?"

He named a ridiculous amount and the negotiation was on. He wasn't the hardest bargainer I had ever dealt with, but he was certainly the longest-winded. We went at it for several hundredth-days. Finally, we agreed on a price and entered it in our books.

Wetsnout kept the boat near the middle of the river. The thunderfish wiggled ahead on the surface, occasionally veering to suck in some riverplants or dive for a fish. The strongwood and firetrees lining the banks leaned over the river like canopies. Birdcalls could be heard over the sounds of wind and water.

Runt got over his aversion to river travel and set out to explore every hundredth-stride of the boat. Twice I grabbed him in time to keep him from falling in the water. Finally he settled on his haunches on the forward bin cover and watched the passing river, fascinated.

The humans were standing on either side of Wetsnout,

161

gripping the side of the boat for balance. (Sometimes four legs are a definite advantage.) They were talking with him, mostly listening.

Fetching a weighted line from one of the trunks, Wetsnout scrambled forward and took a sounding. When he was back in his seat, Pamayers asked, "Don't you know the river well?"

Wetsnout cackled. "I know it about as well as any mother's cub can! But it changes! Old channels silt up, the current digs new ones! Sandbars move! The river is like a fine mate—you have to court her every time! See that lighter water over yonder?" He pointed toward the left bank.

"Yes."

"It's a new shoal! Run up on it and I'd have to dump my cargo to get clear! The whole river is like that—one trap after another! But it hasn't caught me yet!"

I was discovering new reasons to dislike boat travel. The rocking deck was making my stomach complain and I was getting tired of thunderfish spray in my face. But the worst part was being penned with another adult in his "cabin," especially one who groomed himself as infrequently as Wetsnout.

As a distraction I joined the conversation. "What happened to Mudfur?" I asked Wetsnout.

"Mudfur?" Ralphayers whispered to me.

"His most recent *tagnami*."

"Not any more!" Wetsnout growled.

"Did he post a challenge against you?" I asked him.

"Worse! After all my hard work making a river trader of him, he decides to take up distilling in Crimson Dale!"

I was sorry I had asked. It wasn't the sort of shame any parent liked to tell. Or hear.

Ralphayers whispered to me, "Let me get this straight. He's unhappy because his *tagnami* didn't kill him?"

"Of course."

He looked puzzled which puzzled me.

Wetsnout resumed his monologue about life on the river. After the trouble in town, his reaction to the humans was a relief. Occasionally he asked them about the rivers and boats of Earth. But for the most part, they were no more to him than an interested, patient audience for his yarns. He didn't even object to them holding their speaking-box in front of his face.

We came upon a family of watersnorters wading in the shallows, feeding on wandplant and easing the weight on their legs. The long, mottled-gray mounds stared at us with their tiny eyes. There were a few tense moments as we passed within a pawful of strides of them, but they didn't charge. We left them behind.

The sun sank toward the treetops behind us as the afternoon wore on. Runt's vigil on the forward bin cover turned into a nap. I soon joined him, to keep an eye on him and to get some fresher air. The humans showed no sign of succumbing to Wetsnout's incessant verbal attack.

"White water coming up!" Wetsnout yelled to me. "Don't make no difference to me if you and your fur-ball have to swim for it, since you've already paid your way, but you might find the water a mite chilly this time of year!"

"By the time you get finished with a warning," I growled back, "the danger is past." I nudged Runt awake. "Into the cabin, *shirwa*."

"Why?" he yawned.

"We're about to go through some rough water. You don't want to fall in, do you?"

He scrambled back to the cabin and I followed.

The exposed rocks and frothy water ahead didn't look like a serious danger. But I knew from travelers' tales what to expect. "Runt, spread your paws. Ralphayers, Pamayers, hang onto the side."

"Are you sure there's a navigable channel through there?" Pamayers asked Wetsnout dubiously.

"Was last time I was in these parts! Of course, you never know what might have moved since then! But old Whiskers has a good nose for deep water, and so do I, come to it! Brace yourselves, drypaws—here we go!"

The boat veered toward a gap between two rocks. It didn't look big enough to let us pass and my pessimism increased as the boat rocked more wildly. The thunderfish was jumping and writhing against the fiercer current. The boat slowed, but that just made it less stable. The river noise grew until it blared like Kraal's own tuskhorn.

"No like bumpy water!" Runt bleated.

I was wishing for an enemy more vulnerable to fangs and claws, one I could at least die fighting. But I tried to comfort him. "Just be brave for a few more heartbeats, Runt. Then the water will calm down."

Something banged the bottom of the boat hard. Swearing enthusiastically, Wetsnout whipped his reins. The boat pitched so sharply that everybody staggered. I expected to see water gushing into the cabin, but it was dry. Runt had slid over by Pamayers. He was clinging to her hindlegs for physical and emotional support while she stroked his fur and whispered soothingly.

The boat seemed to be jumping then slamming down. Water shot over the bow and crashed where Runt had been sleeping—the spray was almost blinding. A fearsomely huge rock loomed in front of us, then magically whisked aside.

"Can the thunderfish survive this?" Pamayers yelled at Wetsnout.

"Can we?" Ralphayers echoed her.

"Yes and yes! This is nothing—just a rough patch! You should ride Hellchute or Fangstone Rapids sometime if you want some real fun!"

The white water seemed to go on for a very long time, but it actually took less than a hundredth-day. Finally the river settled down. The boat's gyrations subsided to what now seemed a gentle rocking, for which my stomach expressed its gratitude.

When we were well clear of the white water, Wetsnout let the thunderfish rest and feed. Everybody except the humans shook dry; they used cheats called towels. Having survived the experience, Runt was now eager to repeat it. We continued on upriver.

The sun was now below the treetops and the sky was beginning to darken. The breeze was stiffening. "There's a fair campsite up ahead!" Wetsnout announced. "Don't want to brave Boiling Swamp by night, that's for sure!"

I agreed heartily. Runt and the humans looked curious, but I didn't explain. No point in frightening them prematurely.

The boat headed for the southern bank where a rocky point sheltered a patch of calm water. Wetsnout poled the stern around, then backed the boat through sparse wandplant and grounded it. After dropping a pair of anchors from the bow, he coaxed the thunderfish alongside, fed it a handful of shriveled green berries, and took off the harness and reins. The thunderfish leaped and splashed toward deep water.

"What are we going to do for a thunderfish tomorrow?" Ralphayers asked Wetsnout.

"Don't you fret about that! Whiskers will fill his belly, get some fish-type sleep, and be back here at sunup ready to pull! I trained him myself! As long as I've got these," he waggled the bag of berries which he was putting back in its trunk, "he'll be good!"

"What are they?"

"Dried sourberries! I get them from a trader from down South—they don't grow in these parts! Thunderfish love them! Never have been able to figure out why—foul-tasting things! But they do, can't get enough of them!"

Pamayers was watching the monstrous fish swim away. "How do you go about training them?" she asked dubiously.

Wetsnout's laugh sounded like steam coming from a boiling kettle. "It ain't easy, I'll give you that! You catch a tad small enough to handle, use the berries to reward and a tree branch to punish, and teach him who's boss! Takes a pile of patience and stick-to-it-iveness! There are some tricks to it, but they'd cost you *twilga!*"

We jumped off the stern and scrambled up the bank with our camping gear. I saw why Wetsnout favored the place. A dense grove of firetrees lined the bank. The leafy canopy had kept the ground free of snow and reasonably dry; it also sheltered us from the wind. The trunks were thick with treefuzz and the dead wood on the ground would burn in a campfire. A quick sniff around assured both Wetsnout and myself that we had the place to ourselves.

Exploring the grove, we found a running stream with a well-used campfire clearing beside it. "Shall we make this commonland?" I suggested to Wetsnout.

"Okay by me!"

Wetsnout set his warnoffs around the landing. The boat was his territory; he would sleep aboard. I decided that the eastern end of the grove would be best for me and my herd. I ran the bounds and set my warnoffs, easily done since I hadn't set any that morning.

The humans had cleared some ground near the river and were setting up their half-egg. I found a protected spot nearby, but not too nearby.

"Runt!" I yelled.

He had been stretching his legs but came bounding back quickly. "Mommy!"

"Gather treefuzz and make us a bed, then refill the water jug."

"Okay!"

While Runt tended to his chores, I considered our dinner prospects. They didn't smell promising. I decided to try the river.

Wetsnout was already there. Being a river traveler, fish were what he mostly ate. He had attracted an audience; the humans and their seeing-box were watching him avidly.

He was knee-deep in the brown water, standing like a statue on three legs. The other forepaw was poised above a bulbbug that he had set floating on the water.

Suddenly, the forepaw slammed into the water and jerked out gripping a writhing orangefish. It was almost a stride long, definitely a full meal. Wetsnout emerged from the river, shook himself dry, then went aboard the boat to eat.

Having finished his chores, Runt joined me. "Fish taste good?" he asked.

"Better than nothing. I'll show you how to catch one. Watch closely and keep quiet."

I collected some bugs and waded out into the frigid river. My technique wasn't as polished as Wetsnout's, but I soon managed to catch another orangefish and a pair of smaller popeyes. I gave the popeyes to the humans.

"What about Runt?" Pamayers asked me.

"He'll have to catch his own."

"And if he doesn't?"

"He will. He's my *tagnami*, and hunger is a good teacher."

The humans returned to their camp to prepare their dinner. I watched Runt while I devoured my fish down to the bones. Runt was awkward and impatient at first, but he managed to catch another popeye before his legs froze.

By the time everybody was fed, dusk had given way

to night. Clouds were gathering, deepening the darkness and threatening poor travel weather for the next day. Wetsnout and I worked out a campfire agreement. Everybody brought their shares of dry firewood to the charred spot in the clearing; Ralphayers used his amazing fire-maker and we were soon crouched/seated around a warming blaze.

"Nothing like a campfire to warm a person's bones!" Wetsnout cackled, taking a swig from his jug. I was tempted to offer to buy some of his demonsweat, but I no longer had a single *twil* to squander.

"Yep!" he went on. "A good fire and good traveling companions! Can't ask more of Usu than that! Now's the time for traveler's tales—the muddier the better!"

"You wouldn't happen to have any recent news from Coalgathering?" I asked.

Wetsnout laughed. "Oh, I do indeed! You and your demons were the talk of the town when I put in there this morn! I imagine you'd be willing to pay well to hear what it was saying!"

"I would," I gritted.

"Alas, if I had something juicy to sell you, I would! But it's all no more than you'd guess! So I'll tell for the usual tale in return!"

Wetsnout paused. "The circle challengers say that you and your demons fled to escape! You've been branded a coward! The circle challengers have claimed your territory and put it up for sale!"

It was what I had expected. But that didn't make the reality any easier to bear. I wished bad fortune to whoever made my territory her own.

"What about our territory?" Ralphayers asked Wetsnout.

"The priests declared it cursed and the challengers gave up their claims! Bet it'll be a long time before anybody even goes near the place! For such puny creatures, you make a powerful impression on folks! I—!"

Wetsnout stopped talking and my back fur rose in the same heartbeat. A stranger was approaching.

Having come from downwind, by chance or design, she was very close. Everybody sprang to their paws as she stepped into the clearing.

She was the most miserable specimen of adulthood that I had seen in a long time. Her white-with-black-patches fur was off-white and ragged from poor grooming. A poorly healed scar ran from her chest to her left hindthigh. She was as tall as me, with the muscles of a miner. Her beltpouch and carrysack were well-worn and then some. She smelled dirty and dangerous.

"Wilder," I whispered to the humans. "Keep quiet." I pulled Runt behind me. The humans moved closer together.

"Nice boat," the wilder growled. "Who owns it?"

"I do," Wetsnout replied suspiciously.

"I challenge you for it."

So that was her ploy: a hijack. Well, that was Wetsnout's problem. I had my own.

I stepped forward. "Evening," I said to the wilder. "I'm Slasher of Coalgathering. My *tagnami*, these two savants whom I represent, and I have all paid for passage to Strongwood Thicket. If you win the boat, will you honor the bargain?" If not, I had my work cut out for me.

Pamayers started to say something. I silenced her with a sharp gesture.

The wilder looked us over, smelling surprised when she came to the humans, and cautious when she came to me. "I'll take you there," she growled. "My challenge is for the old male, so keep out of it."

"I would like to offer my services as a Weigher." Probably former Weigher by now, I reminded myself. "Maybe I can arrange a compromise between you—"

"By Usu, the river god, I don't need any Weigher to

speak for me!" Wetsnout shrieked. "Never have, never will! Respectable folks settle their own disputes!"

The wilder tossed her beltpouch and carrysack aside while Wetsnout did the same with his beltpouch. I was the only one who saw Wetsnout sneak something out of the beltpouch first. He stuck himself in the flank with the tiny needle-shape, then dropped it.

The opponents closed in on each other on four legs. The wilder was as silent as death, but Wetsnout wheezed as he moved. They circled each other warily, a couple of strides apart.

"You have to stop this!" Pamayers whispered urgently to me. "Wetsnout doesn't have a chance!"

"I don't have to stop this since it's not my business. And don't bury Wetsnout prematurely. You don't survive the dangers of the river as long as he has by luck alone." I was burning with curiosity to find out what the old dung-eater was up to. On the face of it I had to agree with Pamayers; it would be more slaughter than fight.

The wilder tensed to lunge. Suddenly Wetsnout let out the loudest, most ghastly wail I had ever heard. Then he fell over on his side. It was a horrible thing to smell or see. His body jerked in spasms that threatened to tear muscles and break bones. His face was twisted beyond any recognizable expression; his eyes were wide open, but glazed and unseeing. Frothing saliva shot from one end, piss and feces from the other. His yowling took all the pain in the world and turned it into sound. The stench of madness enveloped him. Runt and even the humans took an instinctive step back. I did, too, just in case my theory concerning the "fit" turned out to be wrong.

The wilder glared at Wetsnout suspiciously. Then, as she got a good whiff of the stench, her own scent turned fearful. She looked up with wild eyes and saw our retreat.

Letting out a frantic howl, she grabbed her gear

and fled into the darkness the way she had come. I put my ear to the ground until the sound of her all-out running faded. She wouldn't be back.

Pamayers started toward Wetsnout with the doctoring kit from her carrysack. When I figured out what she had in mind, I said, "I wouldn't do that, if I were you."

She stopped. "Why not?"

"Wetsnout wouldn't appreciate your interference. Besides, he should come out of it shortly on his own."

"He's suffering a major seizure! He could be seriously injured, or dying!"

"Look." I pointed at Wetsnout. The "fit" was fading fast.

"What happened to the wilder?" Ralphayers wanted to know. "Why did she run away instead of killing Wetsnout?"

"As everybody knows, except a few misguided savants, demons enter people and drive them mad. She smelled and saw that Wetsnout had been possessed and fled to escape his fate."

"His problem is medical, not theological!" Pamayers snapped.

"The wilder certainly believed otherwise."

Ralphayers was the first to catch on. "Self-induced!" he laughed boomingly. "Brilliant! But how?"

"Ask him," I growled. Wetsnout's eyes were focusing. He dragged himself to the stream and rolled in. The frigid water had a powerful restorative effect. He shook himself dry, then took a long pull from his jug. He looked himself again, though that wasn't saying all that much.

Runt came out from behind me, smelling bewildered. Pamayers looked mad at somebody.

"Never fails!" Wetsnout cackled as he fetched his beltpouch. "A bit of twitching and spitting and they take off like all Ninety-Nine Gods were after them!"

"How did you fake the seizure?" Ralphayers asked.

"Little thing called a crazythorn! Bought a bunch of them off a traveler from the Dead Lands, along with the trick! Leaves you with Usu's own sore muscles, and a headache you wouldn't believe, but it beats being dead!"

I couldn't hide my disgust any longer. "That was cowardly and totally immoral behavior!"

Wetsnout laughed. "That's mighty priestly talk! You taking up a new calling, Weigher?"

"No wonder you and the humans get along so well! You're woven from the same hair!"

"Anybody besides me ready to turn in for the night?" Pamayers asked cheerfully. Ralphayers nodded.

"Don't oversleep," Wetsnout warned us, "or you'll get left!"

Wetsnout and I managed to put out the fire without getting too close to each other. Then he headed for the boat and I took Runt back to our campsite.

"Why old male not dead?" Runt bleated.

"He is," I growled. "He just won't admit it."

Runt and I curled up in our makeshift bed and went to sleep. A light snow began to fall; our leafy roof protected us from it, if not the accompanying cold wind. Still, thanks to my active day, I slept reasonably well.

The snow was still drifting down when we woke at dawn. Wetsnout's abused muscles had tightened up; otherwise he seemed his old self, with the emphasis on old. We were both over our mads. Runt, Wetsnout and I breakfasted on fish while the humans ate some of their rations. We packed up, Wetsnout harnessed his thunderfish, and we started upriver again.

The snow fell over the river like a sheer, never-ending curtain through which we cleaved. The sky was a roiled gray plain. Wetsnout took soundings and swept snow off the deck and the awning; otherwise we all kept to the too-small cabin. I found myself dwelling on the thought that the boat was a tiny piece of civilization in the middle of the Wild.

Wetsnout was driving the thunderfish to its top speed. "What's the rush?" Ralphayers asked him.

"Got to get through Boiling Swamp before sunset! Nobody with brains between their ears runs the swamp by night or camps within scent of it!"

"Why?"

"Ask me again tonight, if you have to!"

The river entered a gap in a line of hills, part of the bowl which hemmed in the swamp. Immediately we noticed changes. The air became warmer and the falling flakes turned to a fine, clinging mist. The snow vanished from the banks and branches. The flora and fauna increased. Runt let out a low growl at the medley of strange, dangerous smells coming from upriver.

Leaving the hills behind, we entered the swamp. Wetsnout concentrated fiercely on his piloting, which included subduing the increasingly anxious thunderfish. The humans aimed their seeing-box, squawked at each other, and stared raptly. Runt seemed to be amputating Pamayers' hindleg in his quest for comfort. I kept my nose, eyes and ears open for trouble and tried to figure out what I could do about it if it came.

The river widened and small islands appeared until the boat was following one of a pawful of channels. "I hope you know where you're going," I growled.

"Reckon so!" he cackled. "But you never can tell!"

The water teemed with life. Riverplant, wandplant and gnarly knobtrees with exposed roots all but clogged the channels. The bugs were so thick that our tails and forepaws kept busy shooing them away. Big dark birds dove and came up with wiggling fish; some became prey instead of predator and didn't come up at all. Slitherers and water darters hunted in the rushes.

The hummocks were low, some even below the waterline. They wore thick pelts of strange plants: tall and narrow, with fronds instead of leaves, ranging from groundplant-size to giants taller than strongwood trees. Malodorous fungi and vines with delicate flowers clung to the stem-like trunks. Dabs of green clashed with the predominant red. Darters, direbeasts and their larger relatives moved through the vegetation, grazing, stalking, fighting and feeding. The air was filled with the savage din of their cries. Wetsnout made a point of avoiding them.

The god who had made this place slept uneasily. There were weirdly melted-looking outcrops of rock; some of them glowed with inner fire or leaked foul gases. In places the water boiled, sending huge plumes of steam into the sky. Elsewhere geysers erupted spectacularly. Even the ground shook from time to time.

"Fascinating," Pamayers exclaimed. "A tropical micro-climate created by tectonic activity."

Wetsnout scratched his head in puzzlement. "The boiling keeps it warm here, too! This is only a taste, of course—in the swamplands down South you can get a full meal! Don't reckon you'd want to, though—!"

"Look at that!" Ralphayers interrupted, pointing.

A long-necked, fat-bodied, long-tailed creature about twenty-five strides long lumbered into view on stumpy legs. Its hide looked like reddish-brown iron plating. It bit off and swallowed a frond-treetop.

"It can't be!" Pamayers gasped.

"Folks call them walkinghills!" Wetsnout explained. "I've seen bigger!"

The humans squawked at each other. The exchange turned vigorous, so I asked, "Something wrong?"

"We had monsters like that on Earth a long time ago," Ralphayers replied. "They disappeared—killed off by the weather changes caused by a huge meteorite strike. Your world didn't get struck, so your monsters survived. This proves the meteorite theory."

"Nonsense!" Pamayers snapped. "You're assuming

parallel evolution—I could postulate a dozen other theories to explain the data."

Shrugging, I let them continue their debate. Savants had gone to the challenge lawn over things nobody else understood.

The boat plowed on through the repellent, dangerous morass. Heartbeat by tense heartbeat, the day slowly passed.

The ground surrounding some of the hot springs writhed with worms over a stride long. The humans were delighted by the plants which used fumarole gas to send balloon-like seed sacs floating across the sky. Flocks of strange birds that flew by flapping their round, flat bodies attacked us several times, but we drove them off. Our worst moment came when an enormous, long-necked swimmer almost capsized the boat while trying to either eat or mate with it. The thunderfish worried the swimmer until it went away.

All in all, a pleasantly uneventful passage.

The sun was setting beyond the clouds as the boat emerged from the hills marking the Boiling Swamp's eastern border. The snow had stopped, but the chill in the air was even more bitter after the respite. I was heartily glad to have the swamp behind me.

We spent the night on an island. It meant eating fish again and drinking river water which tasted as muddy as it looked, but we camped undisturbed. The dawn brought a clear sky, almost windless and promising some warmth later on. We set out on the last leg of our journey; Wetsnout expected to reach Strongwood Thicket before sunzenith.

By midmorning we had settled into what was becoming our routine. Wetsnout was piloting and regaling the humans with his tall tales. The humans were listening and occasionally using their research boxes. Runt was napping on the forward bin cover, catching what sun there was. I was worrying about what kind of reception we would receive in Strongwood Thicket.

Suddenly the thunderfish, which had been swimming placidly, jumped high and dove into the water. What looked like the tail of a second thunderfish broke the surface for a heartbeat. The harness dragged the bow down, then went slack. The deck bounced under my hindpaws.

"What in Kraal's name is going on!" I yelled at Wetsnout.

"Fight!" He was jerking the reins savagely but futilely. "Best hang on tight unless you want to try your luck in the middle of it!"

The harness dragged the boat sharply to the right, then back. I dropped to four legs for balance. The humans were taking Wetsnout's advice. "Come here!" I yelled at Runt.

Runt was lying flat on the cover, reeking of fear. His eyes were wide and unseeing. I doubted that he even heard me.

Something very hard and very strong slammed into the bottom of the boat. Wetsnout was knocked from his chair. Runt was closer to the bow. Much more of this and he would be thunderfish bait.

I sprang to the forward deck and went to get him.

The uneven, spray-slicked bin cover was treacherous under the best of circumstances. With the boat gyrating unpredictably under me, I didn't have much hope. But I had to try.

The boat rocked violently. I danced frantically and managed to stay upright. A staggering step forward. Another. Another.

I was a stride from Runt when my luck ran out. The boat lurched just as one foreleg was taking over from the other. I stumbled. Pamayers screamed.

A club of anthracite coal bashed the side of my head. Paralyzed, lost in a swirl of colored light, I rolled over the side.

The river was cold, freezing, numbing. I couldn't see anything now. I tried to breath and choked on water. I fought the greatest fight of my life just to move my legs. And lost.

Consciousness was fading fast. My last thought was that I had found a pretty stupid way to die.

# CHAPTER FOURTEEN

I woke up smelling coal.

I was lying facedown on something hard, irregular, wet and cold. I tried to move, but I was as weak and blind as a newborn cub. Somebody was trying to pull my forelegs off by bending them behind me. I coughed up a couple lungfuls of river, then gasped for breath. The attacker released me. If I had been stronger, I would have rolled over and killed her.

The side of my head felt like Kraal had batted it. I was cold and sore from the bones out and my chest was waterlogged. Otherwise I felt pretty lousy. So far, conditions didn't match the priestly description of arrival in the Afterworld.

Strength was leaking back into me. I managed to open my eyes.

I was lying on the forward bin cover of Wetsnout's boat. Somehow I had survived. I would be properly grateful about that when I stopped feeling like grinner dung.

Ralphayers was getting up off my back; he looked as wet as I was. Pamayers had been hanging onto Runt. Now she let him go and he sprang over to hug me.

"Mommy okay?" he bleated. "Mommy not dead?"

I tried to speak and had a coughing fit instead. Finally I managed to croak, "I'll be fine in a few heartbeats. How about you? You don't feel like you fell in."

"Runt okay. Stay flat, not fall in. Runt okay now."

His warmth and love were driving the river-cold out of my body. I could have staggered to my paws; instead I wrapped my forelegs around him and held him close. Both of us had survived which raised several important questions.

Ralphayers had fetched the towel from his carrysack and was drying himself off. "You didn't do yourself any permanent harm that I could find," he told me. "Your lungs are clear. You banged your head on the side, but fortunately you have a thick skull."

"So I've been told on occasion."

Gently disengaging Runt, I managed to get to four legs without whimpering. Shaking myself dry gave me the parent of all headaches. Finally I stood upright. I was beginning to feel like a person again.

"Now I would like to know what happened to me," I said levelly. It didn't make sense that I could have gotten back aboard on my own and I was a poor choice for a miracle. But the only other explanation was even more fantastic.

"You slipped, banged your head, and fell in the water," Pamayers explained, smiling at me for some reason. "Our thunderfish drove off the other one, which is why you weren't eaten. Ralph dove in and rescued you." She put a foreleg around him.

Ralphayers had gone to considerable effort, and put his own life at risk, to save me! It didn't make sense. The humans were already rich; why would he crave my meager *twilga* balance?

"Meanwhile I persuaded Wetsnout to come about and pick you two up," Pamayers finished.

"How did you manage that?"

"I let Wetsnout name his own price."

I stifled a groan. There went the rest of my *twilga*. I would have been better off financially inside the thunderfish.

"Well, let's get to it," I growled.

"To what?" Ralphayers asked.

I opened my beltpouch, which had lived up to its maker's waterproof claim, and brought out my *twilga* book and writingstick. "I'm not a wealthy person, as you well know. But I value my life as highly as anyone of my advanced years would. Therefore, I'll pay a reasonable amount for your service. I won't even insist on a reduction for the way you manhandled me since it was in my interest."

The humans looked dumbfounded. Finally Ralphayers said, "Forget it. I'm not going to take payment for saving your life."

I was in no mood for alien foolishness. "You must! To do otherwise would shame me—you would be saying that my life is worthless! You would put me in your debt forever!"

"You don't owe me a damn thing."

I closed to pouncing range and bared my fangs. Then, getting precarious control of my rage, I froze. "Explain what you mean by that!" I growled.

Pamayers moved over beside her mate. Runt instinctively retreated toward the bow.

"You have a moral code which you live by," Ralphayers replied. He seemed determined rather than afraid. "So do we. We follow yours as much as we can since we're visitors here. But there are some things we simply won't do. Taking payment for saving the life of a friend is one of them."

"Why?" I demanded.

"In our morality some things are too valuable to be bought—they have to be earned by returning them in kind. Friendship is one of them. Now, if you still feel you have to, go ahead and kill me."

"Us." Pamayers corrected him.

A multitiered *twilga* system—what a fascinating concept! I started to calm down as I considered the implications. "If I understand you correctly, the only proper repayment for your service is my friendship?"

"Exactly," Ralphayers replied.

I still didn't like it, but the only alternative was to challenge them. So I would have to accept it. "My friendship is yours. Shall we enter the transaction in our books?"

The humans laughed, looking relieved. "This sort of transaction we inscribe in our hearts," Pamayers explained, "not on paper."

The matter was settled. Runt curled up on the bin cover to resume his nap; the humans and I returned to the shelter of the cabin.

Wetsnout was in his chair, tending the reins and whistling some tune as ancient as he was. Throughout my rescue and its aftermath he had properly minded his own business. "Damned foolish stunt you pulled there!" he cackled at me. "If it weren't for the strange ways of your demon friends, you'd be in Usu's gut about now!"

I was too glad to be alive to let his senile banter bother me. "We have a *twilga* debt to settle, I believe, for your part in rescuing me?"

"We do indeed! *I'm* not crazy!"

"Unless, of course," I turned to the humans, "the friendship you feel for me requires that you pay the *twilga*?"

Ralphayers grinned. "I think we can skip that gesture."

"How much were you promised?" I asked Wetsnout.

"Two hundred *twil*!"

It was an outrageous price for the service, but a cheap one for my life, so I didn't grumble much. It was a welcome return to propriety to enter the transaction in our books.

Shortly before sunzenith the mix of foliage along

the banks gave way to a strongwood forest. The ancient giants, for which Strongwood Thicket had been named, climbed straight and proud into the sky. In their deep shadow very little grew; the ground was a carpet of mouldering leaves and fungi. Here and there gaps in the leafy canopy let shafts of golden light nourish saplings and underbrush. Very little snow had reached the ground.

If the forest floor was unusually barren, the treetop terraces teemed with life. Even in winter they sheltered and nourished an amazing variety of creatures. Birds sang as they flew through the branches, hunting for bugs. Slitherers and tree darters climbed the vine-wrapped trunks. There were treeswingers ranging from small, noisy ones to adult-sized ones that were smart enough to be trained for simple tasks.

Most of this my nose and ears told me; my eyes saw only somber forest. The river wove solemnly through the gloom. Water slapped the bow rhythmically as the boat pushed against the current.

Wetsnout pointed to plumes of dark smoke rising into the sky up ahead. "Should be docking at Strongwood Thicket in another hundredth-day or so!"

"What's it like?" Ralphayers asked.

"Just another uppity drypaw watering hole! Never could understand why you folks take root, like diggerbushes, with a whole world to roam!"

"Somebody has to create the civilization which supports your parasitic lifestyle," I growled.

"Parasitic! You'd rot in your pretty towns if we travelers didn't tie them together! What kind of 'civilization' would you have without us?"

"A respectable one."

I couldn't smell any warnoffs when we reached the territories, but the land was noticeably tamed. Large areas of strongwood trees had been chopped down for lumber. In their place were carefully nurtured groves of replanted trees and new types of foliage to nourish imported game. Dirt roads came down to the riverbanks, where floating logs waited to be towed to town. We passed an adult and two *tagnami* at work in a waterwheel-powered sawmill.

One last bend in the river brought us to Strongwood Thicket.

The town was older and bigger than Coalgathering, with half again as many adults. Unlike Coalgathering it occupied both sides of the river; the rowboats in use and tied up at the docks linked the halves together. The town had spread beyond its original flatland site, climbing the surrounding low hills. Strongwood dominated its architecture and commerce. Even in the heart of winter there was plenty of activity.

Wetsnout docked on the south side of town, where I wanted to be. The dock's owner emerged from his tiny stall and Wetsnout settled the *twilga* with him. Meanwhile Runt, the humans and I disembarked.

"Thank you for a fascinating trip," Pamayers told Wetsnout.

"Been a positive pleasure having you two aboard!" he cackled, giving me a pointed look. "Don't meet up with many folks these days who appreciate good conversation! If you are demons, we could stand a few more demons in these parts!"

With that, Wetsnout headed for the town's Broker Street to sell his cargo.

"Now what?" Ralphayers asked me.

"I'm going to look into the possibility of our settling here. I assume you'll want to wander around and do some researching. I'll join you later."

"How will you find us?"

That was a silly question. "I'll sniff for flowers."

I was wondering what to do with Runt during the serious business ahead, when Pamayers seemed to read my mind. "Runt can come along with us, if you like."

"He's all yours. Try to stay out of trouble."

"You, too."

The humans, with Runt in tow, set out down the first street they came to. They attracted some attention from the townsfolk, particularly the *tagnami*, but not as much as I would have expected. I headed for the center of town.

Strongwood Thicket was richer than Coalgathering and flaunted it. The stalls were bigger; the pens were more crowded with game. Bright colors and elaborate carvings disguised the sameness of the strongwood construction. The streets were rows of planking, with bridges crossing the streams which ran down to the river. The townsfolk looked well-fed for this time of year.

As I strolled along Craft Street, admiring the furniture, musical instruments, books, burl sculptures and other town-made items, I gradually noticed a chill which came from the people around me rather than the air. It could have been the normal suspicion accorded strangers, but I had an ominous feeling.

The Weigher's stall, overlooking the snow-covered challenge lawn, was as fancy as the rest of the town. I noted several bits of remodeling I would do if I became its new owner. Sawpelt was busy with a weighing, so I stretched my legs circling the challenge lawn until he was free.

Sawpelt came to the doorway to welcome me. He was as I had imagined him from his letters, smooth enough to slip through a knothole. His solid black fur was perfectly groomed; even his fangs gleamed. His beltpouch was the latest fashion and he wore enough rings, bracelets and necklaces to keep several jewelers in business. A pawful of years younger than me, he had the long, lithe body of a fighter who relied on his quickness. But his professional reputation was that of a persuasive negotiator who rarely had to resort to the challenge lawn.

Stay sharp, I warned myself, or he'll snatch the prey right out of your jaws.

"Welcome, Slasher of Coalgathering," he said pleasantly. His scent didn't reveal a thing; I hoped mine didn't either. "After all our years of professional correspondence, it's good to finally catch scent of you. Come in out of the cold."

Showing that he knew who I was before I introduced myself was a dominance ploy, meant to put me off-balance, and it worked. "Thank you, Sawpelt. You honor me." I followed him inside. The stall's decor and furnishings were impressive, if a bit too modern for my taste. He had all the tools of our profession and then some. What was missing were the personal touches, the spoor of who he was. He had a careful style.

He gestured me to a chair by the warm hearthfire, then settled behind his desk.

"Well, Slasher, what brings you to our humble town? It must be important to fetch you from your territory at this time of year."

The casual tone in Sawpelt's voice was just a bit off, as if he already knew the answer to his question. I guessed the source of his information; several boats faster than Wetsnout's scow had passed us on the river. "The distinguished savants from another world, Ralphayers and Pamayers, are traveling to do research. I'm acting as their guide."

"The timing of their trip was fortunate. If they had lingered in Coalgathering another heartbeat, I hear, it might have been postponed permanently."

So he did know about the circle challenge. Point to him. "There was a minor disagreement concerning our departure, but that's all behind us now."

"And the whole world is before you. Adventure, exotic lands, mysteries to ponder—how I envy you. But, alas, I'm just a simple townsperson in a minor woodland village, rooted to his territory. It's good of you to honor us with a visit, however brief, before pressing on."

So that was how he was going to play it. Okay, that claw could cut both ways. "Familiarity has blinded you to the wonders of your town. Its fame has spread as far as travelers' tales, making it the Crossroads of the North. Its size and prosperity testify to the wisdom and industry of its townsfolk. I can think of no finer place for the humans to conduct their research indefinitely." I put a slight emphasis on the last word.

"Your dem—ur, savants—will indeed find much to interest them here." A sharpness was edging into Sawpelt's scent. "Our town is large, as you so astutely noted, and claims, among its own, many people who hold strongly to our hallowed traditions. They have noted with interest the results of your savants' innovations in Coalgathering. I'm sure your savants will enjoy an even more spirited exchange of ideas with them than they did with the fewer like-minded people in Coalgathering."

I smiled, showing my fangs. "I enjoy a spirited exchange of ideas myself from time to time."

"Then I imagine you would be included. In fact, your association with the savants would undoubtedly take up all of your time." The emphasis on the word "all" gave the sentence two meanings.

"I've always felt that we Weighers should practice our honored profession as long as we're able," I replied. "Don't you agree?"

"Of course. As long as we're able." Sawpelt glanced outside at the challenge lawn.

It would come to that if the humans and I settled here. A town only needed one Weigher. But Sawpelt and I were too experienced to let fight-lust drive us to it prematurely.

"The town would certainly welcome and benefit from your superior skill as a Weigher," Sawpelt went on. "My own poor efforts you can see for yourself."

He gestured to take in a broad arc of planked streets and well-maintained town wall. "Whereas your own long efforts, I hear, finally came to a dramatic conclusion."

The reference to my street-paving project, which had undoubtedly died under the claw of the circle challenge, hurt too much to hide. Shamefully I smelled Sawpelt's pleasure at his dominance victory.

"You flatter me," I said as sweetly as I could manage. "If we should put our skills to an objective test," it was my turn to glance at the challenge lawn, "I'm sure you would acquit yourself well. The gods admire and welcome bravery."

"I appreciate the invigorating drink from the deep well of your wisdom," Sawpelt replied. "So, if it comes to that, will the pawful of adults in their youthful prime who aspire to succeed me as Weigher. They foolishly believe that the only skill they require is their great fighting ability. I'm certain that from your many years of experience you will be able to teach them otherwise. The town will be well served by your lesson."

Well, I had the information I had come for. Now I needed some privacy to digest it. Rising, I said, "Thanks for a most enjoyable chat. I won't keep you from your business any longer."

"Alas, there's little business for you to keep me from. It's always a pleasure to have a straightforward conversation with a colleague and friend." Sawpelt walked me to the doorway. "I hope to catch scent of you again soon."

"Likewise, I'm sure."

I went out into the cold afternoon. The sky was darkening as another flock of clouds moved in; my weather-sense told me it would be snowing by sunset. I needed a relaxed place to think, and a hot mug of the usual to unwind from the word fight. The two needs merged conveniently. I set out for Tavern Street.

The street zigzagged up a low hill. I stopped in front of the Golden Leaf, a tavern clearly popular with tree-fellers. Its floor was a wooden deck supported by the trunks of trees in the slope below. A still-living strongwood rose through the middle of the deck; its lowest branches were part of the roof. The decor and furnishings could best be described as arboreal.

I howled for permission to enter. The owner, an overweight, harried-smelling male, came to the doorway and looked me over. "You Slasher from Coalgathering?" he grunted.

"Yes," I replied, thinking it a bad sign that my fame had preceded me.

His scent turned hostile. "Come in, if you must. But you won't find much hospitality here."

That made it a point of pride. I went in and found an empty table by the deck's railing with a panoramic view of the town.

There were only a pawful of folks in the place, but they made up in liveliness what they lacked in numbers. Two of them were playing a tree-feller game on the strongwood. They were clinging to its sides with their claws, the way they did when they climbed trees to top them, and one-by-one retracting their claws. The loser would be the one who fell first. The other regulars were noisily encouraging and betting on them—until the owner whispered something to them. Then their volume faded and their hostile attention turned my way. I pretended to ignore it.

The owner came over. "What will it be?" he asked sullenly.

"I'll have a mug of fermented direbeast milk, warmed, with a dash of darter blood."

"We don't serve cub-drinks here. You can drink it cold and straight, or drink it somewhere else."

I repressed an urge to carve off some of his fat. "Cold and straight it is, my good fellow."

Eventually he slammed the mug down in front of me. We settled the tab and he went away. Sipping my drink but not particularly enjoying it, I considered the situation.

Stripped of its excess verbiage, Sawpelt's message was clear. The humans-as-demons notion had arrived here ahead of us and there were plenty of fierce conservatives ready to defend tradition with a circle challenge. He wouldn't take any side in the dispute but his own. Even if I challenged him to a deathduel and became the Weigher, it wouldn't help our cause; the local aspirants to the position would cut my career very short.

I wasn't sure I could sniff out dishonesty from him, but he wasn't the sort to lie when cleverly delivered truth would serve. The reception that I was receiving from the townsfolk certainly supported his claim. The hope which had comforted me during the trip died; Strongwood Thicket wasn't going to be my new home. I was still landless and adrift. I emptied the mug in one gulp.

On to Mountainhole! I wasn't too proud—any-more—to admit that I needed help. It would take Kraal's own wisdom to unravel the knot into which the humans had tied my life.

The humans . . .

They were wandering around down there, as careless and ignorant as *tagnami*, among townsfolk who were hungry for an excuse to post a challenge. And Runt was with them. I realized that I had better round up my herd fast.

If it wasn't already too late.

Leaving the unfriendly atmosphere of the Golden Leaf, I hurried back down Tavern Street toward the docks. I soon caught a fresh scent of groundflowers plus hostility. Turning onto Woodwork Street, I tracked the scent to its source.

The humans were aiming their seeing-box at a paper-making stall. A *tagnami*-powered roller was squeezing a tray of wood pulp into a big sheet of paper, while the owner cut dried sheets down to size. The humans were oblivious to the hostile attention of the townsfolk around them, but Runt smelled and looked anxious.

"Mommy!" he bleated as I joined them. "No like here!"

"Me neither." I scratched behind his ears and he calmed down.

"Your small-scale industrialization is amazing," Ralphayers said to me. "Given the limitations of your culture, you work wonders."

"Slasher, some of the people here have been turning their backs to us when we ask them questions," Pamayers added. "What does that mean?"

"It means we aren't wanted here. If we don't get out of town fast, we'll be staring at another circle challenge. Come along!"

"Where?"

"Back to the dock. Hopefully Wetsnout hasn't left yet." Fleeing to save the humans was becoming a distasteful habit.

As usual, the humans wanted explanations when action was called for, so I had to drive them with threatening growls. Runt, bless him, followed my tail smartly and quietly.

Apparently the conservatives here were as willing to settle for driving us out as their brethren back home. The hostile attention followed us, but no challenges were posted.

Wetsnout's decrepit boat looked beautiful to me still tied up at the dock. The thunderfish was thrashing about, eager to be away. I knew how it felt. The cargo bins were open and empty, and Wetsnout was nowhere in sight.

"Now what?" Pamayers asked, glancing anxiously at the crowd of townsfolk poised behind us.

"Now we wait."

Which we did, tensely. Runt again sought the comfort of Pamayer's hindleg, while she spoke soothingly to him. Ralphayers showed a foolish contempt for survival by aiming the seeing-box at the crowd. I commended my soul to Kraal, just in case.

Finally Wetsnout arrived, followed by four runleg-pulled wagons loaded with the lumber and wood products which were his new cargo, plus some items for the boat and himself. The brokers from whom he had made his purchases unloaded them on the dock. Noticing us, Wetsnout came over. He was grinning smugly.

"Come to see me off!" he cackled. "Now that's what I call neighborly!"

I forced the embarrassing words out. "I wish to buy passage for the four of us to Mountainhole."

Wetsnout slapped his hindthigh and laughed so hard that it became a wracking cough. "Wore out your welcome already! And they say travelers comb your fur the wrong way!"

"How much will it cost?" I demanded.

"Well now, thanks to the generosity of the brokers here, my *twilga* book is pretty fat! No need to take on any bothersome passengers this trip!"

"But we really need to leave here now," Pamayers told him. "Our lives are in danger."

"I'd enjoy *your* company, truth to tell, and I suppose I could put up with your fancy friend! But you'll have to earn your passage!"

"How?" I demanded.

"By loading my cargo!" Wetsnout gestured to the mountains of goods.

"Me, a Weigher, load cargo like a *tagnami!*" I

erupted. "Absolutely not! I'll pay double your outrageous fee, but not that!"

Wetsnout turned toward his boat. "Have a nice run! Smells like the townsfolk here will get you off to a brisk start!"

The humans walked over to the cargo. "Show us where and how you want it," Ralphayers said to Wetsnout.

Wetsnout did, in detail, and the humans went to work. Runt soon bounded over to join in the strange new game. I watched and fumed.

Finally I gave up and grabbed a board. I was still duty-bound to the humans; I couldn't let them go on upriver without me.

"Look at it this way," Ralphayers said cheerfully as he lifted the other end. "The sooner the cargo is loaded, the sooner we're out of here."

The world had turned upside down and all the honor had spilled out. While I performed manual labor to the amusement of the gathered townsfolk, Wetsnout sprawled comfortably on the dock. He still managed to spot and vocally correct every mistake. I did the best job I could just to shut his mouth.

When the last item was stowed, Wetsnout bestirred himself. He inspected the bins, then buttoned the covers in place.

"Tolerable piece of work!" he cackled. "You've earned your passage! Hop aboard or get left!"

The humans and I went into the cabin while Runt scrambled forward and crouched on the bin cover. Wetsnout cast off the lines, then settled into his chair. Flicking the reins, he yelled, "Get along, Whiskers! We're pissing daylight!"

The thunderfish wiggled toward deep water and the boat pulled away from the dock. As Strongwood Thicket slipped picturesquely behind us, I prayed for a swarm of woodbugs to devour it.

# CHAPTER FIFTEEN

During the next five days, we left the part of the world I knew behind.

The mountains and wooded valleys gave way to soft hills, which in turn gave way to a seemingly endless plain. Wetsnout told us it was called the Endless Plain. The river's winding course straightened, heading southeast. Occasionally it spawned marshlands, but for the most part rolling prairie met the eye in all directions.

There wasn't any snow here, but twice we had to ride out demonic thunderstorms at anchor. The omnipresent groundplant was a type new to me: tall and reddish-gold, with a whorl of seed-bearing spokes on top. The serenely waving carpet hid an ongoing struggle for survival. Small animals that used speed, camouflage or burrows for defense were stalked by larger carnivores. In addition to the normal birds, there were long-legged ones which ran better than they flew, and monsters like the demonflier which could carry off a fully grown grinner.

For Wetsnout the trip had been one long monologue, interrupted occasionally by work and sleep breaks. For some bizarre reason, the humans found his senile babbling fascinating; they listened attentively when they weren't collecting specimens or using their research boxes. Runt had made the forward bin cover his "territory." That left me free to torture myself with unanswerable questions about my future.

On the morning of the sixth day we encountered a boat heading downriver.

The other thunderfish was blowing as the boat closed the gap between us. It was like the *Splasher* in design, but smaller, newer and probably faster. It boasted a more cabin-like cabin and wooden bin covers.

Then Wetsnout recognized the owner's scent. "Shore-singer!" he yelled, leaning out over the side. "Good to cross your wake again! Last time was, let's see, down Laketown way when you were getting that rowboat built!"

Shoresinger leaned out of his cabin. He was about my age, big and easy-going; his accent marked him as originally from some coastal town. "Well met, old friend! I have news to sell, if you're of a mind!"

"May be!"

The thunderfish tried to attack each other, but they were reined into submission. Wetsnout and Shore-singer maneuvered until their boats were side-by-side and almost touching. This was business so they ignored us.

"So you've a juicy bit to sell!" Wetsnout cackled. "Well, so do I! Suppose we swap and call it square?"

Shoresinger smelled disappointed. "My news will buy gold and jewels for your coffers!"

"Mine will buy you a longer life!"

They haggled some more for the sport of it, then agreed to swap.

"Seller first, old friend!" Shoresinger yelled. "The herdfolk are wintering in these parts! I traded with them at Northford yesterday and have full bins of tusks and furs to show for it! They should make South-ford by this afternoon!"

Wetsnout slapped his hindthigh. "Now that's news worth buying! Which clan?"

"The Swift! Now pay me fairly, old friend!"

"Eight days ago a marauder tried to take me just downriver from the Boiling Swamp! Big, mean bitch, but none too bright! Came to my campfire before bed-time! Might still be around!"

"I'll give her a wide berth! Best we both hoist anchor!" The thunderfish were becoming increasingly hard to control. "Fare well, old friend!"

"I'll still be on this river when you're in some fish's belly!" Wetsnout cackled.

The two boats resumed their courses and Shoresing-er's soon disappeared from sight. I had only a vague idea what his news meant, but Wetsnout smelled very pleased with it. After some visible thinking, he reached a decision.

"Up yonder the river forks!" he told us. "The north fork, the one Shoresinger came down, goes on to Mountainhole! But being a generous sort, I'm going to throw in a sidetrip on the south fork for no extra *twilga!*"

"To a place called Southford, perhaps?" Ralphayers asked dryly.

"Your birth-mother didn't drop no dumb demons!"

"Kraal curse it!" I growled at Wetsnout. "We bought passage straight to Mountainhole!"

"You bought passage to Mountainhole—weren't no straight or crooked about it! Don't get your fur up! We'll make Mountainhole just a couple of days later than you figured! From what the demons tell me, you aren't exactly pressed for time!"

Keep calm, I told myself. If you let his blood out, who would pilot the boat?

"What's this Swift Clan you're going to trade with?" Ralphayers asked Wetsnout.

"They're herdfolk! The bigmeat herds roam south to winter, then back north! The clans go with them! Each clan has its herd, or the other way round—depends on how you figure it!"

"A whole new culture to sample!" Pamayers exclaimed. "And a migratory one—with that kind of range, they should be a gold mine of data!"

I could hardly believe my ears. "The herdfolk are barbarians, ignorant savages!" I gave Wetsnout a dark glance. "No decent person has anything to do with them!"

"Nonsense," Ralphayers laughed. "Some of our best friends are barbarians."

That shut me up.

"Since we're looking for a new home," Pamayers went on, "we might even join the clan, if possible. At least for one migratory cycle. It would be an incredibly valuable experience." She looked at Ralphayers, who nodded in agreement.

"But . . . but they're shiftless!" I sputtered, horrified by the notion. "They never stay more than a pawful of days in the same place!"

"What's your point?" Wetsnout cackled.

"Bentback tell tale about wild herdfolk!" Runt bleated from the bow. "No school, no smelly town, no cabin chores—just hunt bigmeat! We go be herdfolk! Please!"

"It's not as if we have a town ready to welcome us with open arms," Ralphayers pointed out.

"We could at least explore the possibility," Pamayers added.

I was hot enough to fight, but you can't fight reason. Shrugging, I growled, "I'm not making any promises, but I'll look into the possibility."

Wetsnout laughed and slapped his hindthigh. "Slasher of the Swift Clan! The noble savage!"

"I hear they take the pelts of their enemies," I growled back. "Even mangy ones like yours."

We soon came to the fork in the river. Wetsnout flicked his right rein and the thunderfish pulled the boat into the southern branch. The sun climbed through the cloudless sky to sunzenith, then past it.

The land changed somewhat. The reddish-gold sea of groundplant became uneven: bulging in mounds, rising and falling like broad waves. Worn outcrops of softstone poked through. Bushes and even some small trees grew in sheltered spots. The river up ahead widened and turned a lighter shade of brown.

"An ancient mountain range almost completely eroded," Pamayers said to nobody in particular.

"That there's the ford!" Wetsnout pointed to the lighter water. "Only way past it'd be to empty old *Splasher*, and there ain't no point in that since there ain't nobody to trade with upriver!"

He steered for the right bank about a thousand-stride shy of the ford.

"Why not put in closer to the ford?" Ralphayers asked him.

"Cause I don't want a few thousand thirsty bigmeats coming aboard!"

Wetsnout grounded the boat's stern, dropped the bow anchors, and freed the thunderfish. Runt was the first one off the boat. The humans and I grabbed our gear and followed him.

The sky was a great blue bowl that came all the way down to the ground in every direction. The groundplant reached to my hindknees and spread out forever. A pawful of strides away from the bank, you couldn't see the river. The birdcalls and niknik chirps were swallowed by a vast, awesome silence.

I realized that the world was a pretty big place, and that I desperately wanted to go home.

Runt ran up to me. "Where wild herdfolk?" he bleated plaintively. "Where bigmeats?"

We certainly seemed to have the Endless Plain to

ourselves. "They will be along soon, I imagine."
Unfortunately.

Runt bounded off to chase a long-ear while the
humans stuck groundplant seeds into one of their
boxes. A nearby mound offered a good vantage point,
so I headed for it.

From the top of the mound, I smelled and saw a
lot more of the same. The only danger threatening me
was boredom. I dropped my carrysack and brought
out the water jug for a drink. Flattening some
groundplant into a pallet, I stretched out to rest my
middle-aged bones.

Wetsnout was acting peculiarly, even for him. Having set warnoffs around the landing, he was claw-
mowing a circle of groundplant about twenty-five
strides across. When he finished, he fetched items
from his trunks and bins aboard the boat. He set them
out individually around the circle.

The humans were interested, too. They hurried up
the mound for a better view.

"If that's a challenge lawn," I said to them, "he
has certainly come up with a strange way to commit
suicide."

"It's a trading circle," Pamayers explained, while
Ralphayers aimed the seeing-box. "Other parties put
what they are willing to trade for an item next to it.
If Wetsnout is satisfied with the best offer, he takes
the offer, and the offerer takes the item. A primitive
but effective method for trading through a language
barrier."

"For someone who has only been on our world for
a pawful of ten-days, you speak with great certainty."

Her face turned red. "It's my profession."

When all of his items were in place, Wetsnout
leaned against the boat's stern and sucked on his jug.
Runt tired of his game and curled up beside me for
a nap. The humans discussed savant matters. I waited.

"What's that?" Pamayers asked, pointing north. A line of what looked like smoke was rising into the sky.

"Looks like a range fire," Ralphayers suggested.

Putting my ear to the ground, I confirmed my suspicion. "It's the Swift Clan and their herd. Mostly herd."

The dust cloud swelled as it approached. The breeze acquired the tasty scent of bigmeat. Runt sprang to his paws and watched the cloud eagerly. The humans were peering at it, too, with their seeing-box ready.

A deep rumbling came from the dust cloud. Faint at first, it grew steadily louder. Soon it sounded like continuous thunder. The ground shook under us. Runt put his paws over his ears.

There was a dark brown patch under the dust cloud, like a shadow on the groundplant. The patch grew with the cloud, evolving into a herd of bigmeats. A Kraal damned huge herd of bigmeats! At least five thousand of them were stampeding for the river, flattening the groundplant in their wake.

Now they were close enough to make out details. Half again my length and five times my weight, they made incredible speed on their six massive legs. They were almost as bulky as watersnorters, but some of that was thick brown scales. Single, upwardly curving horns jutted from the middle of their flat, bony faces. Last year's cubs were almost fully grown; this year's were still in their mothers.

Individually they were fearsome creatures. Collectively they became a force of nature, seemingly irresistible.

But for all their power, they were still herd animals, so they could be herded. The members of the Swift Clan, roughly forty in number, surrounded the herd. Acting from plan or custom, some would charge in howling and nipping flanks to turn the herd or change its speed. It was a spectacular, almost unbelievable sight.

Behind the herd, more slowly, came a procession of the clan's wagons. They were simple by Coalgathering standards: wooden boxes with fur covers and big solid wheels. They were pulled by a strange species of dwarf runleg. *Tagnami* walked ahead of them, guiding them. The wagons held their parents' property, such as it was.

The herd slowed as it reached the ford. Soon the thousands of bigmeats were placidly drinking and grazing on both sides of the river. The clan members went back to their wagons, while some of the *tagnami* took over watching the herd.

The adults spread out around the herd to claim territories. Judging by the bounds they were running, the territories were like wheel spokes with the herd as the hub. They were tiny compared to civilized territories, since they didn't have to provide game. The best ones were, of course, claimed by the most dominant clan members. The herd ground and the riverbanks were commonland; so was a bowl-like area which they would probably use for some kind of gathering.

Pitching camp didn't take them much longer than it took us. The runlegs were hobbled, then unharnessed to drink and graze. Colorful multipeaked tents the size of cabins went up. They were of sheercloth—a very thin/strong/valuable fabric woven from spinnerbug webbing—and had decent ventilation, unlike the humans' half-egg. Soon a wide range of camp activities were under way: mending, crafting, teaching, drinking and socializing.

"A symbiotic relationship!" Pamayers exclaimed into her speaking-box. "The clan guides the herd to the best grazing and protects it from danger. In return the herd provides food and organic products. Note—find out if the clan has a custom about hunting the old, sick and injured bigmeats first."

Oblivious to the rest of us, she started down the mound toward the herdfolk.

I stopped her with a gesture. "Where do you think you're going?"

"To make close-range observations."

"That would be a remarkably bad idea," I told her.

"Why? I only want to do the sort of things we did in Coalgathering and Strongwood Thicket."

"Those were civilized towns, and you almost got killed in both. These herdfolk are barbarians who slash first and sniff you out later."

Pamayers' professional ardor subsided. "There must be some way to make contact with them?"

"Of course there is," I replied. "But it won't be as easy as dropping out of the sky. Everything is a ritual with them and we don't even speak their language."

Ralphayers grinned. "You forget the translator—the gadget I used on you at our first meeting."

I *had* forgotten it. Now the possibilities roused my *twilga* sense. We would need some local *twilga* if we wanted to do any business here; Coalgathering *twilga* could only be brokered through Wetsnout at a murderous discount.

"It might be useful," I admitted. "But if you try to use it on a clan member the way you used it on me, you'll most likely lose your translator—at the shoulder. Will you let me handle the introductions? I think I can eliminate the language barrier, earn some clan *twilga*, and impress the herdfolk all in one ploy." And get retribution from Wetsnout for the indignity of loading his cargo.

"Sounds good to us. When do you plan to work your magic?"

I peered at the territories. The clan members had spotted Wetsnout's boat when they arrived at the ford. Now that their camps were set up, the most dominant ones were bringing their barter goods to trade with him. "Now."

I started down toward Wetsnout's trading circle and the humans followed. But Runt lagged reluctantly behind.

"What's the matter?" I asked him. "I thought you were hot to catch scent of bigmeats and wild herdfolk?"

"No want now!" he bleated wanly. "Bigmeats too big! Herdfolk smell dangerous!"

That they did. But I said soothingly, "You'll be safe, *shirwa*. I won't let the bigmeats trample you or the herdfolk eat you. Come along."

"Okay, Mommy." Runt followed my tail warily.

Wetsnout was circling his wares like a preydiver, watching the approaching clan members. I stopped at the boundary of his territory.

"What do you want?" he demanded.

"First, permission to enter."

"No time to chat! Got me some tall palavering to do!"

"That's why I'm here—to enable you to increase your profit."

That got his attention. "Come on in! But make it quick!"

We maneuvered through the trade goods to join him. "Can you talk with these barbarians?" I asked.

"In their clan lingo? Nope! I know a tad of their interclan paw-talk—enough to say how-do! Why?"

"If you could speak their language perfectly, wouldn't that improve your trading?"

"Sure would—I'd be able to do a proper job of dickering! But I ain't got the time for no lessons!"

"The humans have a machine which teaches languages in a pawful of heartbeats. For a modest fee, they will teach you the Swift Clan language."

Interest and suspicion fought in Wetsnout's scent. "Sounds like demon-magic!" he cackled.

"It's just a machine," Ralphayers assured him. "Completely safe."

"I've used it myself," I continued. "It feels . . . odd, but doesn't do any harm."

Pamayers fetched the translator from her carrysack. "Ralph or I will have to operate it. You attach this electrode to your forehead and one of the clan members does the same with the other—that's all there is to it." She demonstrated.

The harmless appearance of the translator settled the fight in Wetsnout. "Just how modest would this fee of yours be?"

We haggled quickly because the herdfolk were almost here. I neglected to mention the extra benefit we would derive from the transaction. When we finished, the humans and I were well financed for what I hoped would be a brief stay.

Wetsnout eyed the approaching clan members. There were twelve of them, arrayed by dominance. Most had *tagnami* carrying their trade goods.

"Best you stay here while I introduce you!" Wetsnout told us. "These folks don't take to strangers right off!"

The clan members stopped at the edge of Wetsnout's territory. They were living examples of the primordial savagery from which civilization had miraculously risen. Averaging half a head taller than me, they were thickly layered with supple muscles. Their pelts tended toward combinations of orange and black. To the gods' work they had added some decorative touches of their own: heavy gold ear and nose rings, dyed claws and fangs, and strange symbols painted onto their pelts. From their bigmeat belts hung mementos of their most impressive kills. Their scent made my back fur rise.

They stared at us, mostly at the humans. Runt disappeared behind me and kept quiet. The humans wisely stayed still; this wasn't the time for research.

The biggest, strongest, most bejeweled and painted clan member stood in front of Wetsnout. In a barbarian culture he would also be the clan's Weigher. They began an involved exchange of forepaw gestures which would have been amusing under other circumstances. It went on for some time, but the expectation of blood—probably mine—kept me from being bored.

Finally Wetsnout turned to us. "This here is Mountain-fierce-runner! He has agreed to go along with your magic—I think! But in payment he wants to learn our language!"

"No problem," Ralphayers replied. "We can do that at the same time."

Pamayers started forward. Her face had taken on a greenish tinge and Ralphayers looked none too happy, either.

Catching Pamayers' eye, I whispered, "No matter what, show no fear! That would make you legitimate prey!"

She gave no sign of hearing me.

Holding the translator in front of her, she slowly approached Wetsnout and Mountain-fierce-runner. The frowning glares of the other clan members were fixed on her. Even Wetsnout smelled tense. Runt whimpered. I honestly assessed my chances against the barbarian behemoth and would have bet my *twilga* on him.

Pamayers stopped between Wetsnout and Mountain-fierce-runner. She gave one of the half-bulbs to Wetsnout, who stuck it to his forehead as she had showed him. Wisely she didn't try to give the other one to Mountain-fierce-runner. She just stood there.

Mountain-fierce-runner glared at the half-bulb. He picked it out of her paw and glared at it some more. Then he glanced back at his rivals, who would pounce on any scent of weakness. Finally he stuck it forcefully to his forehead.

Moving slowly and carefully, Pamayers touched parts of the box in her paw.

Wetsnout's and Mountain-fierce-runner's eyes went wide and unfocused. Both males stiffened like wood carvings. I remembered what they were experiencing and hoped they were enjoying it as much as I had.

A pawful of heartbeats later Wetsnout snapped out of it, smelling and looking thunderstruck. For once in his verbose life he was speechless.

Mountain-fierce-runner woke up a couple of heartbeats later. His reaction was different.

Rage-scent shot from him. His face twisted maniacally. Claws popping, his right forepaw rose. Then it blurred as it slashed across Pamayers' throat.

# CHAPTER SIXTEEN

The glistening claws passed within a hair-width of Pamayers' bare hide. Her face turned as white as a bigmeat horn, but she didn't flinch.

Mountain-fierce-runner regained control of himself as quickly as he had lost it. He yanked the half-bulb off his forehead and threw it to the ground. When Wetsnout removed his, Pamayers all but ran back to Ralphayers. Runt hugged her hindleg.

Wetsnout said something to Mountain-fierce-runner in a language that sounded like coughing. The clan member replied in the same tongue, then asked, "Can you understand what I am saying?"

"Sure enough!"

Mountain-fierce-runner made a lengthy speech in his own language to his fellow herdfolk. They stared at him in amazement, and at the humans with suspicion.

Then he came over to us. "I am Mountain-fierce-runner, the Weigher for the Swift Clan," he introduced himself formally.

"I'm Slasher, from the town of Coalgathering." No point in risking competitive hostility by mentioning my former profession. "This is my *tagnami*, Runt. I'm serving as a guide for these savants, Pamayers and Ralphayers."

Mountain-fierce-runner faced the humans. "The old one says you are wizards practicing white magic, but you look more like demons."

"We're neither," Ralphayers replied. "The stars in the night sky are suns, and worlds circle them. We come from one of those worlds. Our 'magic' is only machines you haven't learned how to build yet."

Mountain-fierce-runner spoke to his fellow clan members again, and this time some of them replied angrily. A brief argument followed which he seemed to win. To the humans he said, "Our priests insist that you are demons and must be destroyed."

"What do you think?" Pamayers replied.

"If you are not demons, why are you here?"

"We're savants. We came here to learn the wisdom of your ways."

Mountain-fierce-runner took several heartbeats to think it over, then said, "I do not know what you are. But your words are good and you have shown your power. I think it is best to call you friends."

My back fur laid down. It looked like I was going to have a future to worry about after all.

"Thank you," Pamayers told Mountain-fierce-runner. "May we visit your camp?"

"My people do not welcome strangers. But you taught me this language, so I will repay you by clearing your path."

Dropping to four legs, he touched his forehead to each of the humans. I almost challenged him before I figured out what he was doing. Then he stood up.

"I have put my scent-mark on you," he explained. "You will be treated with respect as long as you deserve it. Do not dishonor me."

"We won't," Ralphayers promised.

"Now I will trade with the old one." Mountain-fierce-runner gestured to his *tagnami*, who had wisely kept clear of the encounter. They strode to Wetsnout's trading circle.

The trading went much as Pamayers had predicted. Mountain-fierce-runner took the snowy icestalker pelts and ornate tusk carvings which his *tagnami* was carrying and put them down next to some of Wetsnout's items. Their new language skills added an exciting and potentially dangerous element to the trading. But Wetsnout knew when to stop pushing, while Mountain-fierce-runner seemed to have a special tolerance for senile ranting. While they haggled, the other clan members came in turn to put down their trade goods.

Pamayers still looked a bit shaken by her ordeal. "Are you okay?" I asked her.

"Nothing a change of underwear won't cure. But I don't understand Mountain-fierce-runner. First he tries to kill me, now he wants to be friends."

"If he wanted to kill you, you would be dead."

"I don't get it, either," Ralphayers said.

I thought I did. "The effect of the translator scared him. He didn't dare show his fear, so he turned it into rage. He *wanted* to kill you for a heartbeat, but he couldn't because you hadn't done him any harm he could admit to. So he played a barbarian's game with you. If you had flinched from his mock-attack, you would have become legitimate prey. And dead."

"Nice peaceful little world you have here," Ralphayers remarked dryly.

"We like it."

"When some of the other herdfolk finish trading," I added, "I'll get Wetsnout to arrange language exchanges, so we can learn theirs." But remembering their reaction to the translator, I wasn't sure if there would be any demand for the service.

"We don't need to go through all that," Ralphayers said, grinning. "Now that the languages are stored in the translator, it can teach them to us without a donor."

When I figured out what he had said, I was greatly relieved. "Well, what are you waiting for?"

One by one we all stuck the half-bulb to our foreheads and got the treatment. Even Runt learned the Swift Clan equivalent of his pawful of vocabulary. Suddenly finding that you know another language as well as your own is an amazing and unsettling experience.

While waiting for Mountain-fierce-runner to finish his trading, we tried out our clan language on each other. It was a very simple language; expressing complex ideas would be a challenge. And it was hard on the throat.

Finally Mountain-fierce-runner loaded up his *tagnami* with some of Wetsnout's goods and they started back toward the camp. I gestured to my herd to follow as I carefully approached him.

"What do you want?" he growled in my language.

"I want to buy wisdom from the Swift Clan Weigher," I replied in his.

He smelled surprised but made no mention of my language skill. The word "buy" had caught his attention.

"We will go to my tent to do business," he replied, returning to his own language.

We followed the trail of trampled groundplant toward the camp. As we went, we passed other clan members on their way to trade. Reeking of amazement, they stared at the humans. But Mountain-fierce-runner's scent-mark muted their instinctive hostility. I gestured that it was safe and the humans joined me beside Mountain-fierce-runner. Runt kept warily behind us.

"Your adults have many *tagnami*, do they not?" Pamayers asked Mountain-fierce-runner, struggling to fit her meaning into the primitive vocabulary.

"I have four *tagnami*. At times it is too many—at other times it is too few. There is much work to do and the older teach the younger. But they are a great deal of trouble."

"You can not live with them," I quoted the old saying, "and you can not live without them."

"It is true."

Glancing back at Runt, Mountain-fierce-runner laughed boomingly. "Come walk with us, little one. I will not eat you."

Runt bounded up and Mountain-fierce-runner patted his head. Runt smelled awed but no longer afraid.

The huge clan member might be my kind of barbarian after all.

At the edge of the camp Ralphayers said to me, "We'll leave sounding out Mountain-fierce-runner to you while we explore the camp. Okay?"

I gestured agreement. "Remember to stay on commonland unless you get permission to enter a territory. I'll rejoin you after my talk with Mountain-fierce-runner."

The humans set out to circle the camp, aiming their seeing-box at everything they passed. They quickly collected a curious crowd, mostly *tagnami*. Runt stayed with me. Or, more accurately, with Mountain-fierce-runner.

We walked between two territories, around the herd, and across the ford to reach his territory. On the way I saw enough herdfolk ways to change my disgust to disgust mingled with grudging admiration.

Bigmeat milk was being fermented and grain alcohol distilled for drinking as well as other uses. Worn-out items of precious iron, copper and tin were being melted and recast. The inedible parts of the bigmeat carcasses weren't wasted; the horns, scales, hide, tendons and bones were being made into a wide range of things. Clan members used their numerous *tagnami* to provide more of their own needs than civilized people had to. At the same time, each one seemed to specialize in something and there was brisk, if informal, trading among them.

I saw clan members coloring sheercloth in pits full of river water mixed with what looked like groundplant roots. Others were supervising *tagnami* who were repairing precious tent-poles and rigging. Next to several of the tents were pole-and-rope frames pegged into the ground on which clan members and *tagnami* were weaving colorful rugs. One proud-looking elderly clan member was carving large flutes from bigmeat horns. Everything I saw was being crafted with real artistry. I hadn't expected this from barbarians. No wonder Wetsnout and Shoresinger had been so eager to trade goods with the herdfolk.

We arrived at Mountain-fierce-runner's tent. It was a brilliant patchwork of crimson, berry blue and golden sheercloth. His other three *tagnami* were busy with chores over by the wagon.

Mountain-fierce-runner growled some quick orders. The *tagnami* carrying his new property took it over to stow in the wagon. Meanwhile the oldest *tagnami*, a strapping female just shy of adulthood, hurried over with her own heavy burden. She unrolled an intricately woven rug in front of the tent, then set a jug and two cups in the middle. I assumed that in bad weather a pole-supported canopy would have gone up over the rug.

"Business is for adults," Mountain-fierce-runner said, looking pointedly at Runt. "Send your little one to play."

I turned to Runt. "Have fun, but don't leave this territory, and try to stay out of trouble."

"I stay out of trouble, Mommy!"

Runt bounded away. Mountain-fierce-runner's *tagnami* went with him, talking to him. That caused me a moment of worry; *tagnami* games could get rough even among civilized people. But the herdfolk *tagnami* smelled curious rather than playful.

Mountain-fierce-runner and I crouched on the rug. Skipping the polite conversation which bogged down most civilized transactions, we got straight to business. I told him what I wanted and, with a minimum of negotiation, we settled on his fee.

"You drink my fermented bigmeat milk?" Mountain-fierce-runner asked. "It charges like a mad lead bull."

I didn't expect much given the primitive brewing technology, but a bad jug was better than no jug at all. "I drink."

He filled our mugs, then emptied his noisily. I took a more moderate gulp.

He hadn't been exaggerating; the milk must have been spiked with alcohol and fresh blood. I managed to stifle a whimper. "It is good," I said hoarsely.

Laughing, he refilled his mug.

The first matter of business was acquiring some spendable *twilga*. Instead of books, the herdfolk used an awkward system of bone disks bearing a *twilga* amount and the debtor's mark. I turned the *twilga* the humans and I had acquired from Wetsnout into a pouch-bulging pawful of Mountain-fierce-runner's disks. I could have gotten a better price from a clan member who had yet to trade with Wetsnout, but this was more convenient.

Then I came to my main business. "We want to join your clan. Can this be done?"

"No townsfolk have ever joined the Swift Clan," Mountain-fierce-runner replied thoughtfully. "Certainly no demons have ever joined the Swift Clan."

"Ralphayers and Pamayers are not demons. They are savants from another world."

"Our priests will say they are demons, and many will believe it."

I was getting tired of hearing that. "Whether they are savants or demons, they have great power. They can do much good or much harm. It is wise to be friends with ones who are so powerful. You said this."

"So I believe and my belief will convince others. Even so, there is a Testing for those from other clans who would run with our herd. All of you must pass it."

None of the legends I knew mentioned a Testing. It must have been a new custom. It was definitely a curious one; why would anybody tolerate such an intrusion on free will? It sounded almost . . . human.

I also had a bad feeling that whatever the Testing was, the humans would have trouble passing it. Controlling my indignation I said, "This Testing might turn the friendship the Powerful Ones feel for your clan to anger. That would be bad."

Concern and determination mingled in Mountain-fierce-runner's scent. "Custom is custom. We will bear what comes."

"What is the Testing?"

"Come to the clan-meet tonight. Ask to join the clan and your question will be answered." He looked at me in a way that made my fangs ache. "It is bad luck to talk about the Testing. I have spoken."

That was his quaint way of telling me I had used up my consultation *twilga*. Finishing my drink, I stood up. "I have heard that bigmeats provide good sport and good food. May I hunt your herd? I offer *twilga* in payment."

"Only the Swift Clan may hunt its herd. We do not sell the privilege and we circle challenge outsiders who trespass. Now go!"

Curiouser and curiouser. With such a plentiful natural resource in their paws, why wouldn't they want to turn some of it into hard *twilga*? Mountain-fierce-runner's sudden anger suggested that I had struck a sore spot. But what?

Retrieving Runt, I set out across the camp to track down the humans. "Did you have fun?" I asked Runt.

"Yes! Creek-fish-jumping and I play question game. She tell about wild herdfolk—I tell about home. She nice."

Unlike her parent, I growled to myself. But to be honest I had to admit that the herdfolk Weigher wasn't quite the muscle-brained barbarian I had expected. He was quite capable and even, inside his range, sophisticated.

The humans were easy to find; I just sniffed for the crowd of curious spectators. I noticed that Creek-fish-jumping was in front. She got around and quickly, too.

The humans were seated on another rug in front of another tent, similar to but less impressive than Mountain-fierce-runner's. They were chatting with a withered old male who looked like a fur-wrapped skeleton. I howled for permission to enter and received it.

"This is Black-demonflier-stalks," Pamayers said to me, too excited to make a proper introduction. "He's the clan's loremaster—he provides what we call higher education to those who want it." She was putting their speaking-box away.

"For a price, of course," Ralphayers added. "We've been listening to clan legends and we've run up quite a tab."

The old bag of bones was sucking on a jug. He seemed asleep, but he woke up to collect some of Mountain-fierce-runner's *twilga* disks. Then he nodded off again, so we left.

"Can we join the clan?" Pamayers asked eagerly. "There's so much to learn here—a totally new set of environment-driven social interactions."

I gave them the gist of my consultation with Mountain-fierce-runner. "So we should go to this clan-meet tonight," I finished.

"Sounds good to us," Ralphayers replied. "What do we do until then? We're pretty hungry and we could use some rest."

"We'll pitch camp on that mound by Wetsnout's

landing. It's the best unoccupied land hereabouts—near water and with a good vantage. And it's near our transportation, in case the clan doesn't accept us."

I paused. The sun was setting and the camp's daytime activities were being concluded. A chill breeze thick with bigmeat-scent had sprung up. "But before we go, there's something I want to see. Come along. You might find it . . . interesting."

I led Runt and the humans to the edge of the herd ground. The bigmeats were still grazing and drinking, a roiling dark brown mass. At close range they looked even more dangerous than they smelled. Their long, claw-sharp horns could gut a person from snout to tail. They could also kill by butting, kicking and trampling.

"Do you still want to hunt bigmeat, *shirwa*?" I teased Runt. He retreated behind Pamayers' hindleg.

Thanks to the size of their meals, herdfolk only had to feed every three days. A third of the clan members were closing in on the herd, each flanked by his or her *tagnami*. The same event would be played out everywhere, so I concentrated on the clan member closest to us: a lithe male with bold orange stripes.

Conditioned by centuries of domination, the bigmeats watched the approaching clan member warily, but didn't react. They even moved aside as he entered the herd. He seemed to be hunting for a particular bigmeat. Finally he found it: an old one judging by its huge horn and ragged scales, but still powerful and deadly. Orange Stripes' scent became a challenge. His *tagnami* hung back, while the nearby bigmeats moved away. The chosen one lowered its head so that its horn was aimed at Orange Stripes. Steam came from its nostrils.

It charged.

It moved slowly, ponderously at first. But it accelerated quickly, until it was running as fast as a person. Its thunderous roars were deafening. Its driving hooves shook the ground.

Orange Stripes stood his ground. He was crouched, as if preparing to impale himself on the swiftly closing horn. His tense scent was all but engulfed by that of the enraged bigmeat. He looked like a cub in the path of an avalanche.

Only when the horntip was less than a stride from Orange Stripes did he act. In a blur of motion, he sprang aside. The bigmeat lumbered past him.

It took a few heartbeats to swing around and charge again. By then, Orange Stripes was crouched and ready.

But this time he was a split-heartbeat too slow with his sideways leap. The horn ripped a long gash in his left flank.

Pamayers gasped and Runt growled in excitement. But I could tell by the amount of blood staining Orange Stripes' fur that it was a shallow wound. Not seriously injured, he howled more from rage than pain.

Both opponents accepted that this fight was to the death. The bigmeat charged again and again. Each time Orange Stripes barely avoided it. Once he slipped on his own blood and was almost trampled; otherwise he came through unscathed.

Orange Stripes' *tagnami* and the nearby bigmeats were watching the fight, as if it were an everyday occurrence. Which it was. Other, similar fights were going on throughout the herd.

"What is this?" Ralphayers asked me. "Some kind of ritual?"

"It's either pre-meal sport or wearing out the prey. Or both."

"If I were a betting man, I'd bet on the bigmeat."

The bigmeat charged again and Orange Stripes jumped aside. But this time he landed like a coiled spring. Uncoiling, he pounced onto the bigmeat's back.

Orange Stripes planted his claws and hung on. The

bigmeat went berserk. Roaring even louder, it reared and bucked and spun. But it couldn't dislodge him.

His fangs bit deep behind the mighty head and tore out a mouthful of bloody meat.

The maddened bigmeat dropped and rolled over in an effort to crush its attacker. But Orange Stripes scrambled away just in time.

The bigmeat staggered up. Then it lunged forward to gore him.

Ducking under the horntip, Orange Stripes hurtled between the bigmeat's forelegs. There was barely enough space for him between its belly and the ground, but he squeezed through. A brilliant ploy— one I would remember.

The bigmeat turned and charged again. It tried to pound Orange Stripes into the plain with its hooves, but he rolled aside and leaped to his paws. I could smell his fight-lust.

The opponents closed for what both knew would be the last time. The bigmeat, staining the groundplant crimson behind it, was visibly slowed. But it thrust its horn at Orange Stripes' flank.

Diving past it, Orange Stripes sank his fangs into the bigmeat's massive right foreleg. Cracking bone came sharply through the din of the fight.

The bigmeat went down on its side. The ground shook as it landed.

Orange Stripes pounced on top of it, savaging it with claws and fangs. Blood puddled around them. The bigmeat struggled to rise, but vainly. Its horn swung back and forth as it tried to delay its death. But Orange Stripes kept out of its range. The bigmeat's mournful roars weakened.

Finally Orange Stripes chewed through the bigmeat's sinewy throat. Blood gushed. The bigmeat spasmed violently, then lay still.

Rising from the carcass, Orange Stripes howled

triumphantly. He licked his wound clean, then began to feed on his kill.

Other howls came from around the herd. But the herdfolk didn't have it all their own way. I saw one family of *tagnami* treating their seriously wounded parent, while a former eldest *tagnami* finished off his dead parent's kill. Now I understood why the herdfolk needed so many *tagnami*.

When the clan members were finished, the *tagnami* would eat. Then they would drag the carcasses back to their territories.

Excited and ravenously hungry, I had to keep myself from running out and challenging one of the magnificent beasts. "Wasn't that wonderful?" I asked the humans.

They didn't answer. Turning, I saw that their faces had that greenish hue again.

Omnivores.

# CHAPTER SEVENTEEN

We started back to the mound near Wetsnout's landing. The novelty of the humans was beginning to wear off; fewer stares, comments and *tagnami* followed us as we passed through the camp.

Evening twilight had swallowed the world. A low mist was spreading from the river, hiding the horizon. A chill, damp breeze made the groundplant ripple. The mournful howls of a wild adult were muted by distance. The golden fire that was the Endless Plain by daylight had turned into dull gray ashes.

I explained some of the finer points of bigmeat hunting to Runt, who found the topic exciting again now that it wasn't imminent. The humans showed an uncharacteristic lack of interest.

Approaching the mound, I sniffed it out to make sure it was unoccupied and otherwise free of danger. It was. I led my herd up to the wide crown.

"Runt and I will camp here," I told the humans as I gratefully dropped my carrysack where we had awaited the clan's arrival. Then I pointed downwind. "I recommend you lay your half-egg over there."

Ralphayers looked and nodded. "Works for us."

"We have about a tenth-day until the clan-meet

starts," I guessed. "Do what you like until then. The riverbank hereabouts is commonland, except what Wetsnout marked, if you need water."

The humans went over to their campsite and set to work. I sent Runt to fill the water jug, gather groundplant into a pallet, and fetch three big pieces of dry wood from along the bank. While he tended to his chores, I ran the bounds of my temporary territory and set my warnoffs. Then I went hunting for dinner.

I could smell Wetsnout stalking fish in the river, but the bigmeat hunt was too fresh in my memory for me to settle for a cold-blooded kill. Game would avoid the herd, so I ranged south. Catching a strange but tasty scent, I managed with great effort to run the creature down. It was gangly and long-legged: barely enough to feed the two of us. But I didn't have time to hunt a second course.

I ate my fill while it was warm, then dragged the carcass back to camp. Runt had finished his chores. While he ate, I drank from the jug, took a comb to my matted fur, then stretched out for a bit of rest.

The foggy night was almost pitch black. Even with my darksight, I couldn't see very far or well, so I relied more on my nose and ears.

The humans rejoined us. Wetsnout howled for permission to enter and I granted it grudgingly.

"What do you want?" I growled as Wetsnout came puffing up the slope.

"Evening to you, too, young Slasher!" he cackled. "Came by to tell you I'll be hoisting anchor tomorrow about sunzenith! If you're of a mind to go on to Mountainhole, don't dawdle or you'll get left!"

"And if we decide to stay, I'll be there to get some of our *twilga* back."

"How did your trading go?" Pamayers asked Wetsnout.

"Best ever! Knowing the lingo didn't hurt none at all!"

"Are you going to the clan-meet tonight?"

Wetsnout gestured an emphatic negative. "And leave my boat lying about for any marauder to snatch? Don't be cub-witted! I've got full bins of treasure to guard—mighty tusks from the shagfurs of the far North, sheercloth in shades to dazzle the eye, glossy icestalker and chewer pelts, bone jewelry carved with exquisite craftsmanship—"

"A simple no would suffice," I growled.

"Have fun at the tail-chase!" Wetsnout said to the humans. Ignoring me, he headed back to his boat.

I picked up one of the three pieces of wood Runt had fetched and told the humans, "One for each of you."

"What are we going to do with them?" Pamayers asked as she and Ralphayers each picked one up.

"Throw them on the clan's fire. If we don't contribute, we can't attend."

We set out for the commonland hollow in the clan camp which I had spotted earlier. In the distance I could make out a tiny-seeming flicker of flame; the clan-meet was beginning. Nothing important would happen for a while yet, so I kept to an easy pace. The humans were using their lamp-rods to compensate for their inferior darksight. Runt was playing a game of pouncing on the circles of light as they moved.

The territories were deserted except for the very young *tagnami* sleeping in their parents' tents; a pawful of older *tagnami* were tending the placidly grazing bigmeats and runlegs. Everybody else was at the clan-meet. Occasional roars and whinnies pierced the night's stillness. The fog made the tents and wagons seem vague, dream-like.

The hollow, on the other paw, was alive with activity. A big fire was blazing merrily in the middle. The ground was bare by the fire, while the surrounding groundplant had been scythed low. A crude challenge lawn had been laid out beside the fire. The clan members were conversing, guzzling from jugs, and betting on dice games. *Tagnami* weren't permitted to attend clan-meets, so they skulked around the edge of the hollow, watching. The breeze was rich with festive smells and sounds.

The preliminary socializing was well under way. Soon the clan members would turn their attention to clan business. Their migratory, herd-sharing existence required more group customs than townsfolk had. I doubted they found consensus any easier to achieve and I began to feel some respect for their Weigher's skill.

At the edge of the hollow I stopped Runt. "I'm sorry, *shirwa*, but you can't come in. You can watch from out here, or play."

"I go play with my friend, Mommy."

"You do that. Be good."

"I will." Runt bounded into the darkness.

"Do what I do," I told the humans. They made their head gesture of agreement.

I stepped into the hollow and they followed. The socializing paused as everybody turned to stare at the humans. The clan members looked even more savage than usual in the flickering yellow light of the fire. The dominant scent was hostility.

If any of the local conservatives were going to challenge our presence, now would be the time. Bracing myself, I strode briskly to the fire and threw my piece of wood on it. The humans did the same. Then I led them to a spot far from the fire, where the least dominant clan members were. We crouched/sat on the cold, damp lawn.

Nobody challenged us. The hostility began to fade and the clan members resumed their socializing. But we were conspicuously ignored.

"When do we ask about joining the clan?" Pamayers whispered to me.

"After all the other business. We aren't even *in* their dominance ranking."

Finally the clan members had enough fermented bigmeat milk inside them to get down to business. Mountain-fierce-runner rose and stood by the fire, where everybody could see him. The conversations stopped.

"I am the Weigher of the Swift Clan," he said formally. "Who challenges this?"

Nobody spoke.

"I am the Weigher of the Swift Clan," he repeated. "Custom brings us here to settle disputes. Who challenges custom?"

Nobody spoke. The humans were surreptitiously using their seeing-box and speaking-box.

"I am the Weigher of the Swift Clan. If you want me to settle a dispute, I am here. If you want to settle a dispute by fang and claw, the challenge lawn is there."

The first pair of clan members decided to hire Mountain-fierce-runner to settle their boundary dispute. The cases that followed were, despite the cultural differences, familiar enough to make me ache for my lost profession. Instead of weighing books, he relied on an impressive collection of remembered legends. His negotiating style was crude but, backed by his fearsome fighting skills, very effective. None of the cases went to the challenge lawn, much to the disappointment of the clan members. Deathduels were apparently part of the festivities.

The fire was burning low when the last case was settled. Mountain-fierce-runner's last call went unanswered, so I decided it was my turn. I started to get to my paws.

Four strange herdfolk strode out of the darkness.

They were big, powerful adults, but their gaunt physiques and matted fur suggested that they had been living in the Wild for some time. The symbols painted on their fur had been crudely cut off. Their scent told of determination overcoming shame.

They held themselves proudly as they walked to the fire and threw their pieces of wood on it. Everybody was staring at them; the sudden silence was ominous. The hostility that had welcomed us returned almost as strongly.

"What's going on?" Ralphayers whispered to me.

"I don't know. But I don't think they're members of the Swift Clan."

The biggest newcomer approached Mountain-fierce-runner. "I am Blue-sky-dawn," she growled.

"I am Mountain-fierce-runner, the Weigher of the Swift Clan. Why do you not name your clan?"

"My companions and I were of the Brave Clan, but the Brave Clan is dead. Our herd is no more."

That was big news to the Swift Clan members judging from the volume of the excited conversations it spawned. The hostility didn't lessen, but an undercurrent of fear joined it.

Mountain-fierce-runner's growl cut through the babble. "Why do you come here?"

"We come to join the Swift Clan."

The conversations stopped abruptly. You could have slashed the tension with a claw.

"To become Swift Clan, you must survive the Testing."

"We know this—it was the same in the Brave Clan. I will go first." Blue-sky-dawn dropped her beltpouch and went over to the challenge lawn.

Mountain-fierce-runner turned to the other clan members. "Only the strong may be Swift Clan. I will defend the clan from weakness. Who challenges this?"

Nobody spoke. Fight-lust swept the clan members, as Mountain-fierce-runner joined the newcomer on the challenge lawn.

"This is crazy," I whispered to the humans. "Mountain-

fierce-runner is accepting a challenge for . . . for what?
For nothing!"

"I don't think so," Pamayers replied. She smelled
sick. "I'm afraid he has a very good reason."

There were no preliminaries. Mountain-fierce-
runner and Blue-sky-dawn dropped to four legs and
circled warily. Low growls and killing scents came
from them. The spectators from both clans moved to
get better views.

Suddenly Blue-sky-dawn thought she saw an opening. She became an unbelievably quick blur as she
dove at Mountain-fierce-runner's foreleg.

But he was even quicker. He sprang aside and her
jaws snapped shut on air.

They squared off again. Blue-sky-dawn slashed at
Mountain-fierce-runner's snout with a forepaw. He
reared up, then raked his opponent's foreleg with his
own claws. Blood sprayed across the challenge lawn.

Blue-sky-dawn backed up to lick her wound. The
spectators were excitedly discussing the finer points of
the fight and making bets. Mountain-fierce-runner was
heavily favored.

He charged Blue-sky-dawn like a furry bigmeat. She
stood her ground. They came together in a crash that
shook the ground and made me wince.

Both fighters staggered, but neither went down.
Blue-sky-dawn tried to slash Mountain-fierce-runner's
eyes, but he caught her foreleg in his jaws and worried
it.

Howling, she jerked it back minus some fur and
hide.

She charged Mountain-fierce-runner. He held his
ground; apparently it was a point of honor to do so in
a herdfolk fight. She slammed into him thunderously.

Mountain-fierce-runner was knocked over on his
back. The tufts of groundplant in which his claws had
been planted were uprooted. He threw them at Blue-
sky-dawn, momentarily distracting her.

Before she could pounce on him, he wrapped his tail around her neck and squeezed. Her eyes bulged. She twisted to catch the tail in her jaws, but he whipped it away barely in time.

Mountain-fierce-runner squirmed around and sprang on her. He bore her over on her back and came down on top of her. Howling fiercely, they sank their claws into each other's chests and bellies in a death-grip.

They rolled across the challenge lawn, writhing and lunging. Blood stained the groundplant dark in their wake. Mighty leg muscles strained against each other, while slavering jaws sought throats. The flickering firelight amplified the savagery of the struggle. Disdaining the ploys of civilized fighting, it was strength against strength, quickness against quickness.

Slowly, but inexorably, Mountain-fierce-runner was winning the contest. Blue-sky-dawn's back creaked as it bent backward. Her attacks weakened as her position worsened and her throat was less protected. Imminent death filled her scent and eyes.

Finally Mountain-fierce-runner's fangs sank into her throat. Biting deep, he tore out a mouthful of meat. Blood gushed in his face. Blue-sky-dawn went limp.

Rising, Mountain-fierce-runner growled, "This one fails the Testing." He gestured for his *tagnami* to drag her from the camp and to retrieve her beltpouch. Then he went back to his pallet, to the disappointment of the clan's medicine-witch who had her spell-bag in paw.

Another Swift Clan member went to the challenge lawn. He was the mean-smelling brute who had stood closest to Mountain-fierce-runner at Wetsnout's trading circle: apparently Number Two in the dominance ranking. He fought the next former Brave Clan member, and won. Numbers Three and Four fought the remaining newcomers in turn. Number Four won too, but Number Three's opponent became a Swift Clan member (and a wealthy one, at that) over her dead body.

While the post-fight conversations raged around us, I turned to the humans. "Are you ready to take the Testing next?" I asked dryly.

Pamayers swallowed. "Isn't there . . . some other way? *Any* other way?"

"No. I asked Mountain-fierce-runner."

"Suddenly going on to Mountainhole looks very good to me," Ralphayers said. Pamayers nodded her agreement reluctantly.

Mountain-fierce-runner returned to his place by the fire. "Who else comes here to join the Swift Clan?" he asked, looking at me.

I gestured no. The clan members had a good laugh at what they considered our lack of courage, then resumed their socializing.

The fire was glowing embers and the clan members were nodding when a low-ranking youngster staggered to his hindpaws. He smelled like a hothead, and a jugful of the local demonsweat had drowned his judgment without improving his mood.

"Why do you squawk at each other like treeswingers?" he slurred at the humans, who were conversing in their own language.

Startled, they looked up at him. "We talk about . . . your customs," Pamayers replied quickly.

She was such a poor liar that even the herdfolk hothead caught her at it. "You speak falsely! You insult me!"

He was working himself up to a challenge and he didn't have far to go. I futilely wracked my tired brain for a way to defuse the situation before it got out of paw. I wasn't eager to fight; intoxication just made herdfolk harder to hurt. Quiet set in around the fire as the clan members enjoyed the unique dispute.

"I mean no insult," Pamayers assured him. "We talk . . . savant-talk. You would not understand."

"You say I am stupid! You say you are better than Black-demonflier-cub!"

"No!"

He was within pouncing range. If he lost control and struck without a proper challenge, I wouldn't be able to save Pamayers. But I would avenge the harm to my honor.

"You pretend to be demons or wizards! Wise! Powerful!" Black-demonflier-cub ranted. "I smell only puny, clawless pets!"

If the humans had had any honor, the fight would have begun then. Ralphayers' flat face had reddened and his stringy muscles were tensed. But Pamayers replied as calmly as she could manage. "If I answer your question truthfully, it will be a bad thing. You will be hurt."

Black-demonflier-cub growled fiercely. "Words only hurt cubs! Now you say I am cub-witted! Tell me what you hide from me! I do not ask again!" He loomed over her ominously.

"I will tell you," Ralphayers replied. I didn't need a scent to tell that he was furious. "I will tell all of you!"

Ignoring Pamayers' quick alien words and brushing aside her restraining forepaw, he strode like a dominant person to the fire. Horrified, I braced myself to go down fighting. But, with the exception of Black-demonflier-cub, the clan members were amused and curious rather than offended. Mountain-fierce-runner even yielded to the human, returning to his pallet to listen.

"My companion and I are savants." Ralphayers spoke loudly enough for everybody to hear him. "We come among you to learn your ways. Our eyes and ears tell us how you live now and your legends tell us how you lived before."

"*Gurroth!*" Black-demonflier-cub growled. "You say nothing!"

Ralphayers ignored him. "Long ago the bigmeat herds roamed the Endless Plain. The herds were much bigger then, and there were more of them. The first herdfolk came to hunt them. The clans ate well."

The familiar tale was boring his audience. All except Pamayers, who was frowning.

"The clans grew," Ralphayers went on. "More big-meats were killed for food, but more calves were not born. The herds began to shrink. The wise among your ancestors saw this. Clan customs changed to save the herds. You ate more from your kills, but less often. The clans became smaller and the Testing kept them so. You stopped letting outsiders hunt your herds."

"Be quiet!" Black-demonflier-cub growled drunkenly. "Your foolishness fouls the air!" But the herdfolk enjoyed good stories, true or false; other listeners shouted him down.

"But the changes came too late. You still killed too many bigmeats—the herds kept shrinking. The smaller herds are gone. Their herdfolk," Ralphayers glanced at the new clan member, "are dead or elsewhere."

His anger had passed; now he seemed sad. "In another hundred years, the herds and herdfolk will all be gone. Swift Clan will be gone. You do not believe me because you do not want it to be so. But it is. Nothing you can do will stop it." He paused. "That is what my companion and I were talking about."

With that he returned to his seat beside Pamayers. Most of the audience showed their amusement by howling and slapping the ground with their tails. But a few, including Mountain-fierce-runner and the ancient loremaster, smelled troubled.

Black-demonflier-cub smelled violent. He lurched toward Ralphayers. "You dare threaten me! I will—!"

"You were not threatened," Mountain-fierce-runner cut in. "If you could smell, you would know these savants carry my mark."

Black-demonflier-cub sobered up dramatically and headed for his territory.

The clan-meet was over. Mountain-fierce-runner conducted a brief closing ritual, then the clan members started drifting back to their territories.

"Time to collect Runt and return to our camp," I told the humans. "You two have tested your luck enough for one night."

"Absolutely," Ralphayers agreed.

We properly let the clan members leave the hollow ahead of us. Everybody, even Mountain-fierce-runner, pointedly ignored us. Whether that was because we were outsiders or because Ralphayers had slashed a nerve, I didn't know. But it now seemed an even better idea to leave with Wetsnout tomorrow.

I found Runt's spoor amid that of the many *tagnami* who had been watching the clan-meet and tracked it through the almost pitch-blackness. Instead of coming to me like a good *tagnami*, he seemed to be playing hide-and-seek. If so, he was in big trouble; I was too tired for games.

I found him in a secluded area between the hollow and the herd. He wasn't alone. Creek-fish-jumping stood stolidly behind him.

"Come along, Runt," I growled grumpily. "We're going back to our camp."

"Fish-friend say we wait here," Runt bleated. "She want talk to humans."

"What's going on?" Pamayers asked.

I explained to the humans. "But of course you can't speak to Creek-fish-jumping. Runt should know better."

"Why can't we?"

"It isn't proper to talk to another person's *tagnami*, except on that person's business."

"Why?"

I twitched from exasperation. "Because she has no *twilga*. And because Mountain-fierce-runner would resent the intrusion on his parental authority."

"Creek-fish-jumping knows that," Ralphayers replied, "but she's here. Let's find out why."

Using their lamp-rods to illuminate the immediate area, the humans went over to Creek-fish-jumping. "I am Pamayers and this is Ralphayers," Pamayers said.

"I am Creek-fish-jumping," the *tagnami* replied formally. She held herself like an adult. I suspected that she would soon be challenging Mountain-fierce-runner and I wasn't sure who would have the edge.

"I heard you speak at the clan-meet," Creek-fish-jumping said to Ralphayers. "You are wiser than we. Did you speak the truth? Is the Swift Clan dying?"

"I spoke the truth. I am sorry."

"How can we save ourselves?"

Ralphayers paused. "To do so, you would have to make your herd bigger or your clan smaller. But you cannot make cows drop more calves, and the clan is as small as it can be to do what it must do. I see no hope."

Creek-fish-jumping's concern for the future of her clan marked her as excellent Weigher material. I was impressed by her reaction to Ralphayer's words; her thoughtfulness and determination didn't waver.

"When the last bigmeat is eaten," she said at last, "we will have to range far to live off the Wild. The clan will end. We will become uncivilized animals again. Is there no other trail for us?"

Pamayers said something to Ralphayers in their own language. They squawked at each other for a few thousandth-days. Then Pamayers turned to Creek-fish-jumping.

"You can save your clan," she said. "But it will be hard. You will have to adopt new ways. You—"

"A moment, please," I interrupted. I couldn't let this go on. "The wisdom of the humans is valuable. Do you offer *twilga* for it?"

"We can't stand by while a whole culture starves to

death," Pamayers said firmly to me. "I'm going to tell her my notion."

Creek-fish-jumping drew herself up. "I will pay for what I receive."

"But you have no *twilga*," Pamayers replied.

"I do have honor. For your knowledge I will pay you half the light of my world." Lifting a forepaw to her right eye, Creek-fish-jumping popped its longest claw.

"No!" Pamayers gasped. She looked at me frantically.

"It's their custom," I explained.

"There must be another way! You're a Weigher— help me!"

The reminder of my loss stung me. Was I still a Weigher? I considered the problem and came up with a possible solution. It was based on the humans' bizarre reason for being here. "Can you write?" I asked Creek-fish-jumping.

"I can," she replied proudly.

I turned to the humans. "You can't have learned everything about the Swift Clan in one day. Would a journal of day-to-day life be valuable to you?"

"It sure would," Ralphayers replied.

To Creek-fish-jumping I said, "For their wisdom the humans require this—you will keep a Book of Days of the Clan for the next year. Is this acceptable to you?"

"It is." Creek-fish-jumping's forepaw dropped from her eye.

"Your clan must give up wandering," Pamayers told her. "Settle in a place with good weather and water. Split up the herd among your clan members. Claim territories big enough for the bigmeats to graze during the warm season, and for growing groundplant to feed them during the cold season."

"The cold and snow kill the groundplant. How can the bigmeats feed?"

"You gather it and store it. The western towns have

much wisdom about this—they will sell the knowledge to you. Wisdom and hard work will make your herds grow and your clan will grow, too."

Creek-fish-jumping was silent for a pawful of heartbeats. "I think I understand," she said finally. "It can be done. I must become the Weigher. Then I must persuade the clan and take those who will not be persuaded to the challenge lawn. If Orglo wills it, I will succeed."

"Good luck," Pamayers said.

You'll need it, I thought. Creek-fish-jumping was too young to recognize impossibility when she challenged it. Still, I would be an eager listener to herdfolk news in future years, to learn what (if anything) came of tonight's chat.

"Thank you," Creek-fish-jumping said. "I will begin your Book of Days tomorrow. Now I must return to my parent's tent, before he misses me." She turned to leave.

"Bye, Fish-friend," Runt yawned.

"Good-bye, little one. I enjoyed our question-games."

Creek-fish-jumping disappeared into the darkness.

"If you're done saving the herdfolk," I said dryly to the humans, "we'll return to camp now."

# CHAPTER EIGHTEEN

Wetsnout set out downriver shortly after sunzenith and we went with him.

Resuming the routine of river travel was almost comforting. Wetsnout told his tales to anybody who would listen and to himself the rest of the time. The humans bought permission to study the goods he had received in trade from the Swift Clan. Runt napped on the bow and wore Pamayers' ears down with his growing vocabulary. I prayed to Kraal for deliverance from my unhappy fate.

The only good news was that I didn't have to become a barbarian.

The thunderfish had easy work at first as the boat rode with the current. Coming to the fork in the river, we took the branch which wended its way northeast through the rolling grasslands. Six days later we entered a region of wooded foothills which reminded me painfully of home. The river became narrower and faster and rose through fearsome rapids. The lofty white peaks of the Great Mountains loomed ahead of us.

Winter was waning, but it still had a sharp bite here. Snow blanketed the high meadows; icicle lace hung from gaunt branches. Blizzards and bitter cold made traveling miserable and camping even worse. Huddling with Runt between my inadequate blanket and the frozen ground, I desperately missed my snowy-feather bed.

The woods thinned as we climbed and the bare bones of the mountain range began to appear. On the eleventh day after leaving the Swift Clan camp, we arrived at Mountainhole.

Snow was drifting down in flurries and the afternoon sun was hidden by a sullen gray overcast. The thunderfish was struggling to pull the boat against the vigorous current. Emerging from a sheer-walled gorge, we found ourselves in a wide mountain valley. Townsmoke rose from the far end.

"Ever been here before?" Ralphayers asked me.

"No. I've meant to make a pilgrimage, but . . . well . . . it's hard for a Weigher to get away . . ."

"You seem to know quite a bit about it," Pamayers said.

"Well, of course. It's famous."

Wetsnout was busy keeping out of the way of other boats. They were oddly wrought craft pulled by odd fish, bearing pilgrims and goods from far lands.

The valley floor was roughly five thousand-strides across. The river rushed rapidly down the middle, fed by numerous streams. The various types of conetrees still wore their crimson needles, while the puffseed and goldenfruit trees were bare. Snow-draped bushes looked like fat clouds. The vegetation grew sparser as the slopes steepened and became forbidding softstone ridges.

The valley teemed with a surprising amount of fauna. Shaggy, magnificent tuskers and fleet sticklegs grazed on the winter foliage. Nutcheeks, darters, bulbbodies and several unfamiliar species of smaller creatures scurried about. Birds and slitherers filled the treetops. The medley of delicious aromas made me ache to go ashore and hunt.

I couldn't, though. The breeze also told me that every square stride of good land had been claimed for territories. Not surprisingly, considering that it was such a limited resource.

"You folks certainly picked an out-of-the-way place for your holy of holies," Ralphayers commented.

I was inclined to agree with him. "According to legend, the Ninety-Nine Gods fought here at the beginning of time to determine their dominance ranking. The blows blasted great holes in the mountains, which became the Sacred Underworld."

"A cave system?" Pamayers asked. "With limestone strata and running water, it could be quite elaborate."

"That's how the savants explain it."

Mountainhole had grown up on a rocky point of land on the left bank, which nobody would have wanted for a territory. There was no wall, making the town unnaturally visible. It was even bigger than Strongwood Thicket, both in size and in the number of stalls. And it was much richer. Fanciful structures trimmed with gold, silver and brass teased the eye. The docks were busy, as were the roads zigzagging down the northern and southern ridges. The town was aboil with activity. I could smell the reek from here.

"How can this valley possibly support such a large town?" Pamayers asked me.

"It doesn't—the gods do," I explained. "Most of the population is pilgrims. They leave a lot of *twilga* here—priestly instruction, guest territories, souvenirs and so on. Religion is very profitable."

"Well, what do you know," Ralphayers said. "There are universal laws of nature."

Wetsnout joined the conversation. "Mountainhole has gotten to be quite a crossroads! All that *twilga* draws traders like wingbugs to a carcass! Reckon I'll find some Eastern runleg-packers about to dicker

with, maybe sell a passage or two, and be on my way
back downriver before dark!"

"Then this is where we part company," Pamayers
said to him. "We've enjoyed traveling with you. We'll
miss you."

"You've said that before!" Wetsnout cackled. "Try
not to wear out your welcome so quick this time!"

"Our travel-luck has to improve eventually," I
growled at him.

"And calm water to you, too, young Slasher!"

Finding a vacant berth, Wetsnout maneuvered the
boat in and tied up. He went off to settle the *twilga*
with the dock owner while I disembarked my herd.

"What we do now, Mommy?" Runt bleated.

"That's a good question," Ralphayers echoed him.

"It's too late to make a pilgrimage today." It might
not have been, but now that I was here I found myself
strangely reluctant to try my last hope. "Tomorrow
morning will do. Our first order of business is to hire
a guest territory."

"Will you need us with you to do that?" Pamayers
asked. She was staring raptly at Mountainhole.

"I think we should stay together for the time being.
This is a very devout town, needless to say, and I fear
the reaction to you two might be even less friendly
than usual."

"That bad," Ralphayers muttered. "Together it is."

Shouldering our carrysacks, we left the dock. Runt
followed my tail closely and the humans followed his.

The lightly falling snow was like a veil through
which everything seemed softly blurred. It lay like a
pelt on stone roofs or turned to mud in the well-
trodden dirt streets. Up close the stalls were even
more impressive and the crowds were even thicker.
The town-reek and town-din attacked my senses. I
didn't know where the local Broker Street was and I
didn't care to buy the information, so I set out to find
it.

The nearest people smelled/saw the humans. They stopped and stared and I braced myself for a hostile reaction to the "demons."

It didn't come. There were some excited conversations, mystic sign-making and amulet-kissing, and a pawful of *tagnami* came as close as they dared. But then everybody went back to whatever they had been doing, ignoring the humans as if they were a common scent here. I couldn't believe it. But as we mudwaded toward the center of town and kept meeting the same reaction, I finally had to.

"No mob with torches and pitchforks," Ralphayers commented. "We must be losing our touch."

I thought I had it figured out. "We've found the one place where you don't stand out," I replied, feeling relieved. "This is a religious town—people *expect* to find demons here, or won't admit it if they don't. I wouldn't say you were welcome, and trouble could still come. But only after considerable theological debate, by which time we should be long gone."

"If you say so," Ralphayers said dubiously.

The humans were trying to aim their seeing-box at everything and everybody. Runt's eyes were as big as moons. Relaxing a bit, I let myself do some gawking too. Mountainhole was famous for its spectacle as well as its holiness.

The shrines and other stalls strove to outdo one another in garish splendor. A ziggurat of gold-veined white blocks climbed majestically toward the clouds. A great jeweled Eye beckoned us to enter, while a blackglass statue of Vigah, the god of winged creatures, surmounted a street-spanning arch. A tavern built in the likeness of a bigmeat glared at one emulating a longfang. The bower of a centuries-old redcone tree held the shrine of some forest god. Most of the stalls had their upper-wall flaps in place; music, chanting, pungent odors and weirdly colored smokes came from open doorways.

The unpaved streets were eddying currents of people and wagons pulled by runlegs or other beasts. Vendors hawked plaster busts of the gods, snack bugs and maps at the tops of their voices. A wandering prophet recited his scripture, hoping to attract disciples to his new sect. There were jewel-bedecked priests, shaved and painted priests, and priests wearing the hides of their totems. Religious arguments abounded and well-attended fights were under way on three challenge lawns. Most of the townsfolk as well as the pilgrims seemed to come from somewhere else: shaggy Northerners, foul-smelling swampfolk, desert dwellers with their kinky fur, off-white and other odd Eastern colorings, salt-bleached seafarers, hulking barbarians from the plains, and even some dwarfs from Kraal-knew-where.

"The shrines are magnificent!" Pamayers sighed. "Simply magnificent! Which is the one where you worship Kraal?"

I had to laugh. "These are the shrines of the lesser gods. More impressive than preaching in the street, I grant, but not to be compared with the sacred places of Kraal and the other Great Ones."

"What makes one god more important than another?" Ralphayers asked.

"The number and dominance of their worshippers. All this—" I gestured broadly to take in the town, "—reflects the ongoing divine competition. New sects arise and grow and old ones fade. The shrines tell the tale."

Runt slipped in a puddle of slushy mud and bounced up yowling and licking. "This being such a wealthy town," Ralphayers said to me, "you'd think the townsfolk would pave the streets like in Strongwood Thicket."

"The streets aren't paved for the same reason there are three challenge lawns and no town wall. Mountainhole doesn't have a Weigher."

"That's perfect!" Pamayers exclaimed. "We could settle here. You could be the Weigher and we could carry on our research. So much of your world comes here—the pilgrims, traders and other travelers would be a marvelous source of data."

"That would be an incredibly bad idea," I replied.

"Why?"

"For you two, because the question here isn't whether you're demons, but only what kind. When it's settled, you can expect plenty of challenges. For me, because Mountainhole isn't an attractive career opportunity. A Weigher would be anathema here—too much uncompromising religious certitude."

"Everywhere we go it's the same!" Pamayers muttered angrily. "Why are your people so intolerant and hostile?"

"Would I be more welcome if I visited your world?"

She didn't reply. The topic was dropped by unspoken mutual consent.

I finally found Broker Street. There were several stalls dealing in guest territories; I picked one which was between customers.

The broker smelled us coming and met us at the doorway. He was from some Southern oasis town, sleek and well-groomed from his black-with-white-tufts fur to his heavy, gold tail rings. His scent made me want to keep a close eye on my *twilga* book.

"Welcome, welcome to my humble establishment!" he enthused in my language; to do business in Mountainhole you had to be a linguist and a judge of origins. He peered at the humans for a heartbeat, then went on with his pitch. "Your presence testifies to your exceptional judgment—my guest territories are the finest to be had, accommodating the needs of the spirit as well as the body."

"They sound expensive," I replied cautiously.

He dismissed the notion with a gesture. "A pittance

only, I assure you. Come in out of the cold, please, and share my modest comforts."

We followed him inside. His stall was a dome with a tall silver spire on top. The furnishings were fine imported sandwood and elegant brass lamps made up for the lack of sunlight. Best of all, there was a blazing hearthfire.

"Please be seated, good pilgrims." The broker gestured to comfortable chairs around the hearth. After the humans and I shed our carrysacks and sat down, with Runt crouched obediently beside me, the broker perched across from us like a hungry grinner.

"I'm Drywind from the Blue Oasis," he introduced himself, "a humble dealer in territories."

"Pleased to meet you," I replied. "I'm Slasher from Coalgathering, and these are the distinguished savants from another world, Pamayers and Ralphayers."

Drywind peered at the humans again. "A customer by any other name would be as welcome, so they say. How many territories will you be requiring?"

"Just one."

"I see . . . do you have any special requirements?"

"I'm making a pilgrimage to the shrine of Kraal, so I would like to be close to it."

"Of course, I have just the territory for you." Going to an elaborate wall map of the valley, he pointed to a square of land near the northern ridge. "A secluded retreat for the truly devout and practically on the doorstep of the great Kraal's shrine."

I compared the map to what I had seen of the valley. "It's a rocky slope with no vegetation and less game," I said dryly.

"You don't seem the sort to stalk nutcheeks and darters when there is better sport to be had."

I licked my lips. "The webwings still swarm?"

"They blot out the stars."

"How much do you want?"

"One hundred and eighty *twil* per night."

It would do for a brief stay. And I was prepared to forgive a lot for good webwing hunting. I managed to haggle the price downward, but not much.

Settling the *twilga* was easy. Mountainhole being what it was, *twilga* from practically everywhere was good here. I got rid of the last of our herdfolk disks and used our own books to cover the balance. Drywind showed me on the map where the boundary cairns were. Then he politely hurried us out so he could tend to his next customer.

Above the clouds the sun was dropping toward the western horizon. The snow had stopped, but the cold wind was stiffening. "Where to now?" Ralphayers asked. "Our territory?"

"One quick stop first," I replied.

I had spotted Goods Street during my search, so I had no trouble finding the stall I was looking for. It was a round structure with two levels. A bedlam of raucous cries came from the ground level where the owner apparently stored his excess stock.

"What does this stall sell?" Pamayers asked curiously.

"You'll see. Wait here—I'll be back in a heartbeat."

I hurried up the circling steps to the upper level, not wanting to leave the two trouble-magnets on their own any longer than necessary. When I returned, I was the proud owner of a first-class webwing hunting outfit.

Pamayers peered into the cage at the pair of fat, noisy birds. "They're darling! I don't recognize them— do you know what they're called?"

"Mountain greenwings, I believe—you only find them around here. I wouldn't get too fond of these two if I were you."

Pamayers noticed Runt eyeing the cage hungrily and frowned. "You aren't going to eat them, are you?"

I was enjoying my little dominance game. "I promise you I won't eat them. Come on. I don't want to have to hunt cairns in the dark." Or miss the swarming.

The town was starting to empty out. The trails were crowded with runners and wagons, and hired boats were carrying a steady stream of people to the far bank. Finding a trail which went in the right direction, I led my herd toward the northern ridge at a brisk pace.

The trail wound through thriving stands of trees, across streams and white meadows. Branches swayed in the moaning wind. Nutcheeks scurried up trees, birds fluffed their feathers against the cold, and a tusker bellowed mournfully in the distance. The web of being was slowing as the day ended. Fresh woodland scents cleared the town-reek from my nostrils and invigorated me. Still, I wished that I had come here in high summer instead of winter; the wildflowers of the Sacred Valley were praised in many legends.

The humans were collecting bits of plants and sticking them in one of their research boxes. Runt was bounding here and there, even happier than I to be away from the town. That left me free to concentrate on finding our territory and keeping us at a polite distance from the other pilgrims and townsfolk on the trail.

The land became tumbled and started to rise. The trees thinned. Rock outcrops and patches of claw-bushes appeared; the tasty game-scents which had been so strong near the river faded. The quality of the territories we passed diminished, as did the number of our fellow travelers. We soon found ourselves alone on the trail.

Sunset was dimming the snow-mantled beauty of the valley. It was also making my hunt for the boundary cairn increasingly difficult. But Kraal's own luck was with me. I found the pile of rocks beside an old tree stump.

"Here we are," I announced, gesturing to the

shadowed terrain upslope. "If I know my maps, the territory runs all the way to that spur of the ridge."

"It doesn't seem big enough for a territory," Pamayers said dubiously, "especially with so little vegetation. Is there enough game here for the guests?"

"The owner undoubtedly keeps it stocked from the breeders' pens and, of course, there are the webwings. We won't go hungry. But I can't say I enjoy being packed so close to other folks, like firebricks in a wall." The scents of our neighbors as well as the recent occupants of this territory made my fangs ache.

"Look at that!" Pamayers exclaimed, pointing back to the river.

We had climbed well up the paw of the ridge and had a panoramic view of the valley. The darkness was now almost complete. Hundreds of tiny, flickering yellow lights—campfires and hearthfires—spread below us. As we watched, more lights appeared.

"Isn't it beautiful?" she asked me.

Herd animals. "If you say so. Runt and I will camp in those redcone trees by the stream. Feel free to lay your half-egg anywhere downwind."

Pitching camp had become a routine. The humans found a hollow sheltered from the wind and went about their mysterious rituals. Meanwhile, Runt and I scrambled up the rough slope to the small stand of trees. The ground under the snow-bowed branches was clear, soft and reasonably dry. While Runt collected treefuzz for a pallet and filled my jug from the stream, I ran the bounds of the miserable excuse for a territory. It didn't take long.

Evening had given way to night by the time I finished. The humans were waiting with Runt when I returned to my meager camp. "What's for dinner?" Ralphayers asked.

"Webwing, if I can get the knack of sky fishing. I've never done it, but I've heard enough bragging on the subject. They should start swarming soon." I took off my beltpouch and picked up the birdcage. "Runt, come along. You're in for a treat."

"Webwing good to eat?" Runt asked.

"Very good, I'm told. Let's find out."

The humans held a brief conversation in their own language. "Pam is going to collect specimens," Ralphayers said to me. "But I'd like to watch, if you don't mind."

"Just keep quiet and out of my way."

I loped and slid down the treacherous slope to a level, open space suitable for sky fishing. Runt bounded around my hindlegs excitedly and Ralphayers followed with the seeing-box.

Suddenly the woodland tensed. The birds in the nearby trees stopped singing; the nikniks stopped chirping. Nutcheeks and darters scurried for cover. Runt's tail went rigid. Even Ralphayers noticed it. "What's going on?" he whispered.

"The webwings are swarming. They sleep by day in the Sacred Underworld. Each night they range far and wide to hunt. Get back by that bush, both of you."

While Ralphayers and Runt retreated, I put the cage down. There was a coil of line inside made from the same stuff as sheercloth: thin, light, strong and expensive. Twenty-five strides of it joined the leather thong at one end to the barbed hook at the other. Opening the cage, I brought out the line and one of the birds. The bird seemed used to handling and didn't struggle as I clipped the hook to its wire neck ring. Slipping the thong around my right forepaw, I held the coiled line in that paw and the bird in my left.

"Enjoy your last flight, little one," I said softly to the bird as I walked to the middle of the clearing. I heard the seeing-box humming. "Fulfill your role in the web of being."

Kicking snow aside, I managed to plant my hindclaws in the frozen ground. My darksight had kicked in and it would stay sharp as long as I kept my back to Ralphayers' lamp-rod. My muscles tingled with extra-energy. Anticipation and the wind rippled my fur. I was ready.

A black cloud rose from the bare slopes beyond Mountainhole. It spread in all directions, broke up, and became thousands of black specks. The ones heading my way grew quickly.

I let the bird go. Flapping hard to compensate for the extra weight of the line, it climbed into the dark sky. When the line went taut, it started to circle as it had been trained to do.

One of the specks swelled until it became a huge . . . thing. According to Rubbertail, webwings weren't birds, but rather distantly related to us. This one's body was as long as mine, but bigger around the middle. Daylight would have shown me that its short-cropped fur was brown. Its wings were enormous leathery pinions, like a demonflier's. The almost-snoutless head was dominated by moveable, cup-like ears; webwings were guided by sound rather than sight because they lived in darkness. Its two claw-tipped legs were folded under it.

The webwing spotted the circling bird and dove at it. The bird tried frantically to escape, but it couldn't.

The webwing caught the bird in its claws. The bird's terrified cawing was stilled as the webwing swallowed it.

Now! Yanking the line hard, I set the hook in the webwing's jawbone.

I thought I was well braced. But the next thing I knew, I was being dragged across the ground.

My forelegs felt like they were being yanked off. The snow piled up in my face, blinding and choking me. Rocky ground tried to peel the hide from my belly and flank. I imagined I was leaving a wide trail of blood and fur.

This was embarrassing, not to mention painful and

possibly fatal. A brief glimpse past the snow showed a rock outcrop ahead. Its broken, ice-encrusted edges glistened like knife blades.

I curled, lunged, and managed to come to my hind-legs. The webwing was still towing me toward the rocks. It flew in eerie silence except for the hollow flapping of its wings. It might have been trying to escape, but webwings were supposed to be clever; maybe it thought of me as prey, too, and planned to shred me for easier eating.

I sprang to the outcrop to get some slack on the line. Planting my hindpaws away from the sharp edges, I anchored myself firmly.

The line snapped taut. My bones creaked and my muscles screamed with pain. The line hummed. Then it went slack, as the webwing came around in a tight half-circle.

And dove at me.

I dashed back toward the middle of the clearing to get some maneuvering room. An enveloping shadow and a fetid scent gave me a split-heartbeat of warning. I flattened and claws parted the fur along my spine.

The webwing climbed, then flipped over and dove at me again, claws first. I stood my ground until I could almost see the individual hairs on its weird, eye-less face. Then I sprang sideways. As it passed behind me, I slashed it with my hindclaws. Black blood sprayed across the snow.

Three more times the webwing attacked me with the same results. Finally it gave up. Realizing that I was too big a bite for it to swallow, it decided to seek easier prey elsewhere. It started to flap away.

I still had hold of the line. When it went taut, I dashed a few strides to the left, planted three paws, and yanked hard on the line.

The trick to playing a webwing was to get the line at as big an angle to its course as you could manage. You had to be firm to turn it, but not so firm that you broke the line or tore out the hook. I got it right the first time. The webwing veered to ease its agony.

I ran sideways to the webwing's new course, planted, and yanked again. It tried another direction with no better luck.

Now all it wanted to do was escape. It tried every aerial stunt it knew: climbing, zigzagging, feinting, circling and gliding. I barely managed to keep a stride ahead. My muscles ached, my wounds burned and bled, and I was gasping for breath. My extra-energy was fading fast.

But the webwing's strength was fading, too. It realized that escape was impossible. It would have to fight for its life, while it still could.

It dove at me, a spreading blackness that blotted out the sky. I reared up to give it a warm welcome.

It crashed into me. I was knocked over backwards and it came down on top of me. Stunned, sickened by its foul reek, I struggled to fend off its jaws and claws.

We rolled across the clearing, slashing and tearing at each other. The webwing's pinions were folded into its back. My raking foreclaws made sure they would never carry it aloft again.

The webwing's teeth were designed for smaller prey than me, but they were worrying my left shoulder and doing some damage. My fangs were busy gnawing through a sinewy leg. Fortunately I happened to be on top at the moment. I reared up, bringing the webwing's head with me. Then I hammered it into the frozen ground.

Its grip on my shoulder weakened momentarily. I tore free, stifling a whimper of pain. There was its furry neck, right in front of me. I let go of the leg and sank my fangs deep into the juicy meat. Bit. Ripped out.

Hot, black blood splashed in my face. The webwing spasmed, then lay still.

Rising on four shaky legs, I sent my victory howl booming across the valley. Other howls signifying other kills echoed mine. I made sure that my wounds weren't serious, then licked them clean.

Ralphayers and Runt were hurrying toward me, but I growled them back. The former's questions and the latter's appetite would have to wait. The kill was mine.

I hadn't had such good sport since Boulder's party. My blood was up and I was ravenous. Webwings were supposed to be delicious, despite the unappetizing scent. Time to find out.

They were.

# CHAPTER NINETEEN

The morning that confronted me upon waking was gray and foreboding. No snow was falling, but a strong wind roiled the clouds and whipped the treetops. Eerie whistling came from the ragged ridge. Of last night's victorious exhilaration, all that remained was soreness and a trace of the fetid scent of webwing.

Runt sprang from our miserable excuse for a bed, disgustingly cheerful. "We go see Kraal place today, Mommy?"

"Yes, *shirwa*," I replied as I struggled to my paws. "We're going to make a pilgrimage to the shrine of Great Kraal."

"Why?"

"The High Priest of Kraal is very wise. If he can't help us find a new home, nobody can." I didn't like the way that last part came out.

"Why we need home? I like smelling new places."

My blood ran cold. If I didn't get Runt back to a civilized life soon, he might end up a traveler.

We went about our morning routine with well-practiced speed. I watched proudly as Runt stalked and caught his own darter for breakfast. My exile had at least done this much good: he was filling out splendidly, making up for his lack of size with thick yet lithe muscles. He was on the trail to becoming a powerful fighter.

I caught a pair of grinners scavenging the webwing carcass. After making one of them my breakfast, I took the other to the humans, who were starting to stir in their camp. They cut some of the meat into chunks, put it in a pot with some water, roots and leaves, and boiled the mixture. They called it stew; it looked like something that had already been eaten.

"Ralph told me about your air fishing," Pamayers said to me while they ate. "There's one thing I don't understand."

"Only one?"

"If the sport is so popular, why isn't Mountainhole facing the same dilemma with webwings that the herd-folk are with their bigmeats?"

"One, webwings are only part of the town's food supply. Two, they breed like rotbugs—the hunting just keeps their population under control. Three, they win about half the fights."

"Oh."

Caching our carrysacks against possible theft by a trespassing marauder, we set out for Mountainhole. Runt carried the cage with the line and the remaining greenwing; the humans had some of their research boxes hanging from their belts.

The sun was barely up beyond the sullen cloud cover, but Mountainhole was already bustling, noisy and smelly. Our first stop was at Drywind's stall where I bought us another night in his guest territory. Then I returned the cage and its contents in exchange for a partial refund of my payment. At my age I had to pace myself when it came to such sport. From another Goods Street stall I bought a pitch-soaked torch. Finally I found a street vendor who smelled reasonably trust-worthy and bought a map to the shrine of Kraal.

"Now what?" Ralphayers asked me.

"Now I'm going to worship and buy some divine guidance at the shrine of Kraal. Runt will come with me, to learn. You've said you want to come along, too. Do you still or would you rather explore the town?"

"The town will be here tomorrow. We want to go with you to the shrine."

I felt nervous enough about the pilgrimage without the humans following my tail. "It'll cost you a lot of *twilga*, even if you don't seek instruction."

"We can afford it."

They could. "But you aren't worshippers of Kraal."

"We're prepared to be open-minded," Pamayers replied.

"There are dangers."

"With you to protect us, we feel perfectly safe."

I gave up. "Come on then. The sooner we get there, the less likely we'll have to wait."

Falling in with the flow of other pilgrims, I led my herd to the eastern edge of town and onto a well-worn road. At first the road followed the riverbank, but it soon veered north toward the ridge. In addition to the paw traffic, there were wagons hauling swirlstone blocks from the nearby quarries.

The shape of the land changed. The woods gave way to rising tables of softstone, barren except for snow plus occasional bushes and stunted trees. Tall, flat-topped columns were banded in shades of gray and white. There were no sharp edges; the terrain had a melted-down look. The wind carried the putrid scent of sulphur.

"This is where the gods fought their challenges," I whispered. Thousands of thousands of years had passed, but the land was still scarred. Walking in the shadow of the gods, I felt awed and humble. "Now that you see their power, what do you think?"

Ralphayers paused from aiming the seeing-box. "Very impressive. Of course, erosion and geothermal activity could have the same effect."

Savants.

Pilgrims were leaving the trail, disappearing into the trackless wilderness on the way to their shrines. I got out my map. Orienting myself from landmarks, I figured out our route. Soon we were scrambling up slopes and through gorges toward the ominously looming ridge.

It was definitely four-leg terrain and the humans weren't equipped for it. They were soon lagging behind. "May we rest a bit?" Pamayers gasped.

"Keep up or go back," I snarled.

We went on. In a pawful of thousandth-days, I would come to the end of my long quest. Could even Kraal lift me out of the pit trap I had dug for myself? I was as devout as the next person, but I had the same doubts, too. What if Rubbertail and the other savants were right; what if the High Priest only had faith, not answers? My taste of the wandering life had confirmed my belief that I couldn't live this way.

I pushed the weakening, blasphemous thoughts from my mind. Kraal was all-wise and all-powerful. He wouldn't fail me.

We passed a shaggy Northerner going the other way. By her thoughtful expression, I figured she was returning from her pilgrimage. She didn't respond to my friendly greeting. She didn't even notice the humans. I wondered why she had come and what the High Priest had told her.

We came to a steep slope, with the black mouth of a cave a pawful of strides up it. The mouth was a wide, almost level crack. At its tallest point an adult could just walk into it upright without stooping. A ramp of rocky rubble led up to it.

"This is the entrance to the shrine of Kraal," I announced proudly for Runt's benefit.

"After the shrines in town," Ralphayers said, "I was expecting something more elaborate."

I subdued my shock by reminding myself that he

didn't know any better. "This is the territory of the gods. To try to embellish their work would be presumptuous. Besides, don't judge the lumpmeat by its shell."

"What does that mean?"

"You'll see."

I lit the torch. It burned with a flickering yellow flame and gave off dark smoke. The humans turned on their lamp-rods. "Follow my tail closely," I warned Runt, "and don't make a sound."

"Okay, Mommy!"

Overcoming a final attack of doubt, I led my herd into the cave.

The floor had been worn smooth by countless priests and pilgrims, but it descended sharply and slanted to the left, making walking difficult. The roof was soot-darkened softstone. Warm, fetid air flew toward the mouth, bending the torch's flame. Runt was right behind me, smelling nervous, while the humans brought up the rear side-by-side.

"Excellent ventilation," Pamayers whispered. "The cave system must be extensive, with many openings."

"I was right about the geothermal activity," Ralphayers replied.

The cave soon widened into a chamber so big that its sides and roof were beyond even my darksight. The unusually level floor was covered with hundreds of boulder-shapes, most of them about my size, the rest smaller. A sound like a vast bellows echoed hollowly. The fetid smell was overwhelming.

Pamayers started over to one of the boulder-shapes. Stopping her with a gesture, I whispered, "What are you doing?"

"Getting a closer look. Those boulders could indicate ancient water flow."

"Those 'boulders' are sleeping webwings."

Squeaking like a scuttler, Pamayers sprang back

beside Ralphayers. "Just how nocturnal are they?" she asked me very softly.

"We should be safe enough if we don't disturb them by getting too close. Or talking."

The rest of our trip through the chamber was made in silence. I took a meandering route which kept us as clear of the webwings as possible. Occasionally one of the furry mounds moved and my tail went rigid. But it was just sleep-shifting. We reached the far end of the chamber without incident.

When we were safe, Pamayers whispered, "That floor didn't feel like rock."

"Even *your* nose should be able to smell the answer to that riddle. It's webwing guano."

After checking the map again, I followed the clammy softstone wall until I found a round hole barely big enough for me to squirm into. I led my herd through to the next chamber. Scrambling to our paws, we played our torch and lamp-rods around.

And stared in wonder.

Fangs of living rock jutted down from the roof and up from the floor, some smaller than me, others rivalling a full-grown strongwood. In places roof-fangs and floor-fangs had merged into majestic columns. Also before us were multipeaked mountains in miniature, rippling cascades like frozen waterfalls, and formations which defied description. All were elaborately wrought, with the look of melted candle wax. Tints of pink, gold and lavender vied in splendor with gleaming moon-white. Hollow echoes of dripping water filled the chamber.

"This is the Sacred Underworld," I announced, when I could speak. My doubts were banished.

"It's . . . magnificent!" Pamayers gasped.

"And what do you think of your savant's explanation now?"

"I think . . . your data is very persuasive. Let's go on," she finished eagerly.

The chamber was actually the beginning of a great cave, descending gently with many turns and branching passages deeper into the gut of the world. I led the way down the worn pilgrim trail. The rock formations were damp to the touch and the path was slippery. The dripping water collected in dark pools, then became a small stream flowing beside the trail. The fetid smell faded, while the reek of sulphur grew. Runt was trying to look everywhere at once. The humans were busy with their research boxes. Such behavior must not have been offensive to Kraal because he didn't do anything about it.

The air grew warmer, and wisps of steam thickened ahead of us. The cave floor became cracked; it was from the cracks that the steam rose. Pools of scarlet and green mud bubbled like the Snake's warming pots. I would have appreciated the beauty of Kraal's work more if I hadn't been coughing from the foul smell.

Coming to the end of the cavern none too soon, we emerged into the biggest chamber yet.

Natural pillars of rock supported the domed roof. The far end of the chamber was lost in the darkness, but, based on what I could see, it was roughly circular and at least five hundred strides across. The floor dipped somewhat toward the middle. There were a pawful of cave mouths in the walls; streams frothed noisily from some of them. The water flowed down to a small lake set in the middle of the chamber like a black jewel.

But awesome as the chamber was, it only held a fraction of my attention. Mostly I was gaping at the dense forest between the lake and the walls.

A forest, but unlike any I had ever seen before. The "trees" were thick stalks split at the top into many drooping, bulb-tipped branches. There were several types of them, varying in size. The "underbrush" consisted of misshapen lumps of stuff like nightmarish treefuzz. Smaller "plants" clung parasitically to bigger ones. Shades of gray and white dominated, with much mottling. The sick-sweet smell of rot attacked my nose. Bugs abounded, including a gossamer-winged one the size of a small bird, and there were several unfamiliar species of darter.

"A complex subterranean ecosystem!" Pamayers breathed, her eyes alight. "Guano for nutrients . . . geothermal warmth . . . mineral-rich water . . . fungal growths evolved to fill ecological niches . . . !"

"You say there are more of these . . . shrines?" Ralphayers asked me in an amazed tone.

"A pawful. Some greater, some lesser, but all part of the Sacred Underworld. This chamber is the territory of the High Priest—the trail leads to his Place of Instruction."

"He *lives* in here?"

"Of course. He has a cabin somewhere, probably well away from where he does business. The weather is ideal year round and High Priests can afford all the lamps and alcohol they need. As for game, there are webwings, darters and fish from the lake."

"This place would get on my nerves fast," Ralphayers muttered.

I was tempted to agree, but not within Kraal's hearing. "It must appeal to the religious soul."

I howled for permission to enter. If the High Priest was occupied with personal matters or another pilgrim, we would have to wait. But the permission howl came back promptly from the direction of the lake.

We set out down the trail. It wound through the weird forest, avoiding bubbling pools and rock outcrops. The flying bugs didn't show the usual interest in my torch or the humans' lamp-rods. That didn't surprise me. Like the webwings, the other creatures of this eternal darkness were probably eyeless.

The humans knew better than to collect samples in somebody else's territory; they settled for aiming their seeing-box at everything. Runt stayed very close to me.

The unnatural foliage seemed to close in around me and breathing became harder. Just a pawful of heartbeats now. The High Priest of Kraal was reputed to be the wisest person alive, able to call upon divine knowledge; he would be much more formidable than the town priests I had known. My hindpaws dragged. It was almost like being a *tagnami* again. I wasn't afraid, of course. Just ... tense.

The wind was coming from behind me so I didn't have any warning. The trail came to a sudden end and we all came to an equally sudden halt. We were standing at the edge of the Place of Instruction.

It was a circle of bare softstone roughly fifteen strides across, polished to gleaming perfection by uncounted paws. In the middle, the blue-gray rock reared up to three times my height. By divine or artistic craft, the formation had the aspect of a great fighter crouched to spring at an enemy. Twin lamp-eyes cast their illuminating gaze on the near half of the circle and purple smoke rose from braziers set on the forepaws. Niches around the base held the Writings of Kraal and the other tools of the High Priest trade. Sheercloth pillows were scattered across the ground between the forepaws.

The High Priest of Kraal stood four-legged atop the mighty stone head, watching us. His gray fur sported tufts of white on the face and belly. The twang in his permission howl had told me that he was from one of the lake towns south of Coalgathering. He was a pawful of years older than me but in fighting trim from his gleaming fangs to his firm belly to his lithe muscles. His scent and eyes marked him as the most dangerous sort of fighter: a very smart one.

"Who comes to the Shrine of Great Kraal, Sharpener of Fangs and Claws, Kindler of Bravery and

Ferocity, Arbiter of Victory?" he chanted. His words rang out boldly.

"Slasher of Coalgathering," I replied in awe.

"What brings you here?"

"I seek Kraal's enlightenment."

The High Priest ran down the stone shoulder and foreleg to the ground in front of me. His pelt bore many scars, including some which were only half-healed. I suspected that he had recently acquired or defended his position.

"I am Fastswimmer, the High Priest of Kraal," he said to me. "Are you of the True Faith?"

Stepping close to him, I whispered the secret name of our god. I had learned it long ago from Fireeyes, the Coalgathering priest of Kraal.

The High Priest smiled. "Welcome, pilgrim." Properly ignoring Runt, he turned to the humans. "I smell three where only one should be."

I didn't say anything. Let the humans explain their presence themselves, if they could.

Ralphayers stepped forward. "My name is Ralphayers and my companion is Pamayers. Contrary to popular opinion, we aren't demons—we're savants from another world."

"I know something of demonology," the High Priest replied, "and sky-science too, since the savants originally learned it from priests. Judging by your scent and appearance, I deem the latter explanation more likely. Is Great Kraal worshipped in your world?"

"Not by that name," Pamayers said. "We've come here to learn about the Shrine of Kraal and because Slasher's pilgrimage involves us. We offer *twilga* in payment."

The High Priest was silent for a pawful of heartbeats, then he gestured agreement. "If the True Faith were to become known in your far world, Kraal would be pleased. Welcome, savants."

The High Priest went over to a niche and returned

with his *twilga* book and writingstick. I negotiated for myself and the humans, too. The High Priest asked a high price for instruction, but that boded well for its quality, so I put up only a token effort. We reached a quick agreement and entered it in our books.

The High Priest gestured to the pillows. "Make yourselves comfortable," he told us. "Free yourselves from physical distractions so that we may ascend to the spiritual territory."

He settled himself under the giant head. The humans sat and I crouched on pillows facing him, while Runt settled on the softstone behind me.

"Slasher," the High Priest said, "I smell that you're troubled. What do you seek?"

"A new home for the humans and myself. We were . . . driven out of Coalgathering."

The High Priest stared at me in a too-seeing way that made my back fur rise. "Your mind and your heart are not as one in this matter, but I'll help you despite yourself. Tell me your tale."

Not daring to be offended, I set out to explain how my life had been ruined since the arrival of the humans. The High Priest was a very good listener. He guided me and drew me out with cogent questions so that I found myself going into great detail. I soon forgot the cavern, the humans, even Runt: everything except pouring my tragic story into the High Priest's receptive ears. It was long, throat-drying work. When I finished, I was surprised (and embarrassed) at how deeply I had bared my soul.

Silence returned to the Place of Instruction, except for dripping water and the sighing of the wind. The humans were looking at me oddly.

"Now I must commune with Great Kraal," the High Priest said at last. "Wait here."

The High Priest went over to one of the niches. Pouring a careful measure of a thick green liquid from a jug into a small cup, he gulped it down. Then he ran to the top of the stone head and crouched there. His eyes unfocused. He seemed to be half-asleep.

"A natural narcotic or hallucinogenic," Pamayers whispered.

"Probably from one of these cave fungi," Ralphayers agreed.

Ignoring their blasphemous remarks, I cleared my mind of everything except my devotion to Kraal. I begged forgiveness for my lapses from honor and pledged to buy instruction more frequently from my town priest (as soon as I reacquired one). Above all, I prayed for Kraal's divine guidance.

A couple of hundredth-days passed. Finally, the High Priest awoke from his holy trance. Rising, he shook himself vigorously as if drying off. Then he ran down to rejoin us. As he settled onto his pillow, I noticed that his scent and eyes were . . . strange. Disturbingly so.

"Great Kraal deigned to speak to me of your need, Slasher of Coalgathering," the High Priest said. His voice sounded strange, too.

My tail went so rigid you could have used it as a prybar.

"I am to say this to you. You will find no rest until you complete the circle."

The High Priest's scent and eyes returned to normal.

"Ur, what's the rest of the divine instruction?" I asked tentatively.

"There isn't any more."

"Complete the circle? What does that mean? Am I supposed to go back and face the circle challenge?"

"That is a literal interpretation—there are others. One or more of them might apply."

"Are you saying there's no hope? Then my whole journey was for nothing—I should have stayed and fought and died?"

"I say what I say. Every part of a circle is needed for it to be."

My confusion and disappointment were turning to anger. "I paid my hard-earned *twilga* for guidance, not riddles."

"Divine wisdom is a seed which will only grow in fertile soil. For it to be of use to you, you must be wise enough to use it."

"I demand what I paid for!" I sprang to four legs, eager to drown my loss in blood.

The High Priest matched my move in an effortless blur. "You have received it," he growled. "You might give it thought, in which case you might profit from it. But if you challenge the High Priest of Kraal, you will lose much more than your life."

Horror came over me as I realized what I had almost done. I quickly regained control of myself. "I accept your instruction. I just wish I knew what it meant."

"You will. Now my part is done and other pilgrims seek Great Kraal's wisdom. It's time for the three of you to go."

So we left.

# CHAPTER TWENTY

We stayed in Mountainhole four more days.

The humans spent as much time as they could in town. I suppose they were doing research although I didn't ask and didn't let them tell me. They were indecently pleased with themselves, studying the things they bought by day late into the night. Sometimes I had to go with them to negotiate purchases and settle disputes. Fortunately they were better at civilized behavior; they only offended a pawful of people and I managed to get those to accept *twilga* rather than blood in compensation.

Runt spent his free time with the humans. That was convenient because I wanted to be alone with my thoughts. But it bothered me. The humans seemed determined to leave me with nothing, not even the love of my *tagnami*.

I attended to my obligations automatically, my mind elsewhere. Then I would climb the valley's northern ridge, above all the scents of civilization, to a windswept crag poised between the sky and the world. There I would crouch for tenth-days, my mood in harmony with the snow and howling cold, trying to figure out the meaning of Kraal's instruction.

Complete the circle. I wracked my memory for usages of the phrase, possibly particular to some trade or profession, but I couldn't come up with anything except the obvious one. I knew that priests loved metaphors, but if it was a metaphor, what was it supposed to be telling me? The end of a circle was its beginning. But I couldn't go back in time to when the humans arrived and handle everything differently, even if I knew what I should have done, which I didn't. I could go back to *where* they arrived, Coalgathering, but what would I do when I got there? Accept the circle challenge and die?

Complete the circle. Was Kraal telling me that he would imbue me with his divine strength so that I could beat Shrubfur and the others? There were legends of great fighters who had completed circle challenges against tremendous odds. But I knew in my middle-aged bones that I wasn't one of them. I would die.

Was that the answer then? Was accepting the circle challenge my only honorable course of action, and eternal sleep the only home I would ever find? The notion had a kind of sick, seductive appeal. But my fighting instinct and my sense of honor both rejected it.

The humans had offered their services in trying to figure out Kraal's message, but I had growled them away. This riddle wasn't one which their alien wisdom could solve. Nor would I have had them do so even if they could. It was my responsibility, my test to pass or fail.

Around and around my thoughts flew, over and over again, fruitlessly. My mind had no trouble completing circles. But the various interpretations did have one thing in common. I finally decided to run Kraal's trail as far as I could follow it; hopefully the rest would then be revealed to me.

And if it wasn't? I didn't let myself think about that possibility. I was down to some pretty dismal options.

That evening after dinner, I left Runt to his chores and went down to the humans' camp. They were sitting around a fire outside their half-egg, burning the tusker haunch I had cut for them from my kill. I tried to ignore the foul scent. The day's collection of purchased books, tools and so on were piled beside the half-egg; tomorrow they would be resold to used-goods brokers.

"Good evening, Slasher," Ralphayers said cheerfully. Pamayers echoed him.

"Evening," I growled back. "How is your research coming along?"

"Very well," Pamayers replied. "Mountainhole is an amazing resource—it has an extensive fund of knowledge about this part of your world. Today we collected artifacts and anecdotal data."

"In other words," Ralphayers said dryly, "Pam went shopping while I traded drinks for travelers' tales in taverns." He paused, then added, "By the way, I think Pam started a new religion."

I had to ask. "How did she manage that?"

Pamayers' face turned pink. "One of the street priests came up to me and offered to be my . . . ah . . . disciple. I tried to explain that I wasn't a demon or prophet or whatever he thought I was. But he insisted on paying me for my instruction and hurried off to write the Holy Scripture of Earth, the god of the stars."

Under other circumstances I would have found that amusing, but I wasn't in a laughing mood. "I came here to tell you that Runt and I will be leaving Mountainhole tomorrow afternoon. If you still intend to travel with me, be prepared to leave then."

The humans squawked at each other in their own language. Then Pamayers said to me, "We would like to continue our research here for a few more days.

We offer *twilga* to compensate you for the inconvenience of delaying your departure."

"Refused," I growled. "I plan to leave as soon as I can buy passage. Stay or come as you choose."

"There's no choice to make. We'll go with you, of course—we still wouldn't survive long without your guidance and protection. May we ask where we're going in such a hurry?"

"Back to the Wild near Coalgathering. I'm going to establish a territory there. With spring coming, there should be adequate game and I can build some kind of cabin."

The humans did some more squawking. Then Pamayers spoke to me. "We have knowledge which can help us survive, even in the Wild. But the life of a wilder doesn't seem like much for any of us to look forward to."

"Why there?" Ralphayers asked. "Have you figured out Kraal's message?"

"Not completely," I admitted. "But the solution to my problem somehow involves Coalgathering—of that much I'm sure. So I'm returning as close as I dare until I figure out the rest." Something inside me was saying that the homeward journey would be taking me in the right direction.

The humans were quiet for a pawful of heartbeats. Then Pamayers said softly to me, "We realize that your divine instruction is a very personal matter, and we respect your privacy. But the answer you're looking for might be found through reason rather than religion. We might be able to help you, if you will let us."

"Your 'help' has already cost me everything but my life!" I growled. "And it may cost me that too!"

"We know—"

"You know too much and too little! Don't speak to me about this again!" Showing them my tail, I strode stiffly back to my camp.

The morning brought a gray sky, a freezing wind, and snow. Even so, the weather was more pleasant than my mood. Chatter was kept to a necessary minimum as we attended to our morning routines. Then we packed up our meager belongings including a sack of the humans' purchases which Runt carried. We set out for town at the best pace Runt could manage.

Mountainhole was buried under a thickening pelt of snow. Any sensible town would have been half-deserted, its folk laired up until the foul weather passed, but Mountainhole was just as crowded and busy as on any other day. The shrines and stalls were flapped and *tagnami* scurried about removing snow from doorways and roofs. Thick columns of smoke rose from chimneys like pillars supporting the sullen overcast. The pilgrims plowing through waist-high drifts in the streets reeked of religious fervor; the miserable conditions were enabling them to do penance and/or prove the strength of their faith.

I helped the humans resell their purchases to used-goods brokers with a minimum of negotiation and even less concern for getting a good deal. The humans could afford the loss. My thoughts were dominated by an overwhelming hunger to be on my way. I had had my fill of shrines and priests and instruction that didn't instruct. I bought some things that Runt and I would need in the Wild, then led my herd to the docks.

I had my choice of boats. A pawful of owners were quickly stowing their cargoes, eager to escape from the dangerous weather. I looked for a boat without any other passengers since I was in no mood for company. I settled on one like Wetsnout's, but better kept, bound for the coast. Its thunderfish seemed to be somewhat undersized, but that wouldn't matter traveling downriver. The owner was a young female with salt-bleached gray fur and a refreshing no-nonsense manner. She showed only a brief, cursory interest in the humans. We settled the *twilga* for four passages, then I led my herd aboard. Shortly after sunzenith the boat left Mountainhole in its snow-veiled wake.

The homeward trip was much like the one to Mountainhole and we soon settled into the familiar routine. The boat owner was a taciturn sort, tending to her boat and teaching her young *tagnami*. Runt found the forward bin cover as comfortable a perch as Wetsnout's had been. The humans spent much of their time discussing/arguing about things they had learned during the journey. I continued my mental efforts to figure out what Kraal wanted me to do.

Traveling with the river current, the trip went more quickly than it had the other way. The snowbound mountain slopes gliding past the boat's sides gave way to wooded hills. Tall groundplant rippled in the wind whistling across the Endless Plain. Trees and commerce continued to thrive in Strongwood Thicket. A shower of volcanic rock and ash almost sank us during the passage of the Boiling Swamp. The weather was gentler, although we hadn't left winter entirely behind us.

All the while I futilely pondered Kraal's instruction. As the thousand-strides flowed by, my frustration grew, and with it my anger. I could tell that my scent was worrying the boat owner. Runt took to spending his free time with Pamayers. Even the humans sensed my mood and kept their distance.

My control had been clawed and battered almost to the breaking point. Camping for the night near where the marauder had attacked Wetsnout, it snapped.

I had found a sheltering ring of fuzzyfruit trees for Runt and me to camp in. The humans had set up their half-egg in a small clearing beyond the stream we were sharing, while the boat owner kept to her "territory" well out of scent/sight/hearing. Loper was rising in the cloudless night sky. Nikniks chirped and a brisk wind bent the bare branches.

It was time to turn in so I went over to the humans'

camp to retrieve Runt. I was going to have to have a stern talk with him. *Tagnami* owed their parents proper respect and Runt wouldn't forget that while I still had fangs and claws and breath in my body. Wading across the frigid stream sharpened my resolve.

The fire in front of the half-egg had burned down almost to embers. Ralphayers was doing something inside the half-egg. Pamayers and Runt were sitting/ crouching close to the fire, making strange noises. At first I couldn't figure out what they were doing. Then memories from my days in Bentback's school cleared up the mystery. Pamayers was teaching Runt her language!

My back fur rose and my tail went rigid. Smelling my anger, Runt scrambled into a fearful, subservient crouch beside Pamayers.

Pamayers looked up and smiled at me, oblivious to my mood. "Good evening, Slasher," she said.

"Who's idea was this?" I growled.

"I want to learn funny talking," Runt bleated. "Pammy use teaching-box. But words hard to say, so Pammy show me."

"And how are you going to pay for your language lesson?"

Runt hung his head in shame.

"I don't expect any payment," Pamayers told me. "It's a worthwhile scientific experiment."

"Runt, return to our camp!" I growled. "Now!"

"Yes, Mommy!" Runt dashed into the darkness like a startled stickleg.

Pamayers came to her hindpaws, looking confused. I closed the gap between us and glared down at her. "You've been trying to steal Runt from me ever since we fled into the Wild! Now you're corrupting him to your alien ways! Those are challenge offenses, *kiroma!*"

"I'm doing nothing of the kind," Pamayers replied softly. "He's curious and enjoys my company, but you're the only one who can destroy his love for you."

"What do you mean?" I growled.

"You've become increasingly depressed and hostile ever since we left Coalgathering. At first Ralph and I thought it was simply displacement shock, but now I realize it's something more serious."

The notion of the humans discussing me like one of their research subjects burned white-hot. "What I think and feel is none of your affair!"

"It is, Slasher, because we care about you. You've . . . shown us your tail, and that hurts."

"Then pain repays pain! You seduced me with your talk of cooperation, turned my town against me, and got me exiled! You're evil burdens that I can't escape!"

Pamayers shook her head. "We aren't your enemies. Neither is Runt or even Kraal. You're fighting yourself. And because you're so strong and stubborn, you'll keep on until you kill yourself."

"Your words don't make any sense!" I growled.

"You're suffering from some kind of internal conflict. I wish I could be more specific but I don't know enough about your psychology. If you were willing to talk openly about it, maybe I could help—"

My forepaw rose and the claws popped out. I slashed at her bare white throat.

Her surprised backward lunge was much too slow. But something turned my forepaw so that the clawtips only grazed her. Four thin lines of blood as red as a person's traced her jawbone.

She didn't whimper and she didn't run. Staring up at me steadily, she asked, "Did that make you feel better?"

Sudden coldness extinguished my rage. I was ashamed of my lapse of control. I had let a weak, puny human lay a heavy dominance paw on me. "You were very close to death, human. You still are."

"Killing me won't resolve your conflict."

"Don't teach Runt any more of your alien ways.

And don't speak to me about this again." Turning, I strode back toward my camp.

Runt was nervously waiting for me. I was too tired to instruct him on proper behavior so I just told him to stop spending his free time with the humans. Then we went to bed.

The next morning we set out on the last leg of the river journey. Runt was attentive to his chores; otherwise, he was unusually quiet and he kept to himself. The humans spent their time talking to each other. The claw marks on Pamayers' throat were covered with a hide-colored concoction. The boat owner may have noticed the conversational chill, but she tended to her piloting and ignored us. Freed from distractions, I tried to plan my next step toward "completing the circle."

White cloudscapes hurried across the pale blue sky, riding a brisk north wind. In the early afternoon the boat owner put us ashore in the same spot where Wetsnout had picked us up less than four ten-days ago. (It seemed like a lot longer.)

I led my herd to the southbound trail and we reversed our other hike in the shadow of the Low Mountains. Once I worked the kinks out, it felt good to be traveling on my own paws again. I set an easy pace so the humans could keep up and so I could think.

We reached the sanctuary where we had spent our first night of exile shortly after sunset. So close to home, yet still so far. Fortunately the sanctuary wasn't already occupied.

"We'll camp here for tonight," I told the others. "In the morning I'll scout around to find the best land for territories. I don't know how long it'll take me to figure out the meaning of Kraal's message, so we should prepare for a lengthy stay—just in case."

"Why can't we settle here?" Ralphayers asked.

"Sanctuaries are commonland," I reminded him. "If

we tried to claim this one, the whole town would come out here to circle challenge us."

The night passed quietly and without incident. After the morning chores, I left Runt to guard our camp and the humans to continue their research, and set out on my territory hunt. Unencumbered, I ran like a ray of sunlight through the woods and across the white meadows. I rejoiced at my temporary freedom. If only I could remain free, return to Coalgathering and my life.

But honor was all I had left. A few thousand-strides south of the sanctuary I found a vale of the Low Mountains with a stream running through it. The flora and fauna left much to be desired, but they were as good as I would find in this part of the Wild, and barely good enough. I ran the bounds of my new territory and set my warnoffs. Then I fetched my herd.

I showed the humans the scruffy woodland east of my territory—close enough for me to protect them, but not too close. "Will this land suit your needs?"

"It's a bit out of the way," Ralphayers replied. "But there's water plus plenty of edible fruits, nuts and plants. It'll do."

"Claim as much of it as you want and are prepared to hold."

The humans went off to carve their new home out of the Wild. I used the last of the daylight to search for the best available site on which to build my new cabin. Straddling the stream was beyond my skill, so I settled for a low knoll beside the stream. I had Runt set up our camp in its lee while I hunted something for dinner.

My prey-luck was poor, even for the Wild and the time of year. Evening had become night by the time I finally pounced on a crawler. Stripping out its stinger and poison sac, I ate my fill of the cold, tough meat. Then I took the rest back to Runt and the humans.

The latter had set up their half-egg in a sheltered clearing near the stream.

Following an uncomfortable but uneventful night, the morning began cold and overcast. The humans came to visit me after breakfast. They forgot to request entry permission, so I fiercely reminded them that we weren't sharing a territory now and that living in the Wild didn't mean we had to act like uncivilized wilders.

That settled, Ralphayers asked me, "Any closer to completing the circle?"

"No."

"So now what?"

"So now I'm going to start building my cabin. I suggest you two do the same."

"Our half-egg will hold up a while longer," Ralphayers replied. "If we're still here in the spring, we'll build something then. It'll be a lot easier in warm, dry weather."

"We have extensive information on a wide range of building techniques," Pamayers said. "It could make your task go quicker and better. Would you care to buy some?"

My back fur rose. "We've managed to build cabins for thousands of years without your alien knowledge. I'm sure I'll be able to manage on my own. But I will be busy for a pawful of days, so you'll have to tend to your own affairs as much as possible."

"We've got plenty to keep us busy," Ralphayers replied. "Chopping firewood, digging a dung/piss hole, doing our washing and so on. In our spare time we'll study this region and analyze our data."

The humans left. I fetched from my carrysack the tools I had bought in Strongwood Thicket: a saw, a trowel, a hammer and a couple rock-weights of nails. Not much with which to build a cabin. But combined with hard work, time, and my educated layperson's knowledge of building, they would suffice.

While scouting the vale, I had noted the building materials available. There were some strongwood trees, but not enough for a log cabin like my former one. Graystone chunks of all sizes were piled at the bottom of a cliff, while the stream bed held deposits of a fair grade of clay. Many a sturdy cabin had been built with less.

My course of action was refreshingly straightforward. Clear and mark the ground. Cut strongwood trunks into pillars, dig post-holes, and set the pillars in place. Build lower-walls and a hearth out of stone chunks mortared with clay. Cut and nail strongwood branches into a roof framework and add bark shingles. Then set wooden tile blocks snugly for a floor. One basic cabin, ready for occupancy.

Come spring, I would be able to cure hides for upper-wall flaps and harvest redberries to brew a weatherproofing concoction. Then I could turn my attention to furniture, lamps and other amenities.

"Come along," I told Runt. "Time to start building our new cabin."

"Okay."

We went to the top of the knoll. The field of snow with its scattered bush-bumps was a long way from being a cozy home. But I had all the time in the world. Just take one stride at a time, I reminded myself, and eventually you will be done.

We set out to clear the knee-deep snow from the cabin site plus some extra ground for a work area. After trying the dignified but slow trowel, I gave up and copied Runt's technique of using his forelegs to send snow flying behind him. We had to pause frequently to warm our paws, but we finally excavated a patch of dirt and flattened groundplant.

Pacing off a rectangle representing the floorspace of my old cabin, I marked it by scraping lines in the ground with my hindclaws. Then I marked the places where the doorway, the hearth and the nine post-holes would go. In his eagerness to help Runt scuffed through some of my marks, so I growled him back.

I started to dig the first post-hole and ran into a stone wall. Almost literally. The ground was frozen rock-hard, too hard for my trowel. Clawing and growling at it didn't help. I managed to find enough dry wood to build a fire and used water boiled in my camping pot to thaw the ground. Digging was still slow, messy work, but by noon I had all of the holes done. I didn't know how deep they were supposed to be, but a stride had to be more than enough.

After a bit of rest, I sent Runt to collect some rocks and clay. Meanwhile I went to the nearest strongwood stand. Picking out nine trees with trunks about two paws across, I started sawing. That turned out to be harder than I thought it would be, too. The saw blade kept binding. I ended up having to make wedge-cuts, widen and deepen them, then put my shoulder into it. When all the trees were felled, I shortened them to the right length, sawed off the branches, and stripped the bark. As each log was finished, I had Runt drag it back to the cabin site.

The sun was setting, I was aching from snout to tail, and my fur was a mud-matted mess. Nevertheless I was determined to see the first pillar of my new home in place before I quit for the day. I turned a small rock and a cord from my carrysack into a crude plumb line. Then I wrestled one of the logs into a post-hole, and used the plumb line to get it standing straight. I filled in the hole with rocks and clay and plenty of hindpaw pounding, until the pillar was firmly anchored.

Stepping back and looking at it in the last of the daylight, I tried to muster some enthusiasm. But I was cold, tired and sore, and it was still a long way from being a cozy home.

Runt and I cleaned up at the stream, then we returned to our camp. Runt was tired and difficult; I had trouble getting him to do his chores. All I could hunt up for dinner were some bugs. The humans settled for boiled roots. They asked me how the cabin was coming so I told them briefly, but I didn't ask them about their day. A bitter wind was coming up. Having had enough of this day, I rounded up Runt and went to bed.

I woke up cold, stiff and sore. When memory poured back between my ears, I managed to feel even worse. Poking my head out from under the insufficient blanket, I watched the stars fade as the sun came to brighten the sky. It looked like I was going to have another clear day for cabin-building. The scents in the wind were unfamiliar but not dangerous. The woodland noises were muted, befitting a winter dawn in the Wild. Runt twitched nervously in his sleep beside me.

I felt unnaturally lethargic and hopeless. There was work that needed doing, I knew, but I couldn't stir up any motivation to move. I finally made myself get up. There were no signs of activity coming from the humans' camp. I growled at Runt and he woke up yawning. We silently drank and groomed ourselves at the stream; I was in no mood for his chatter. Then I set out to run the bounds and hunt up breakfast. I took Runt along to teach him how to do the former and to start him doing the latter for himself.

But first I ran up to the top of the knoll. I wanted to see how the cabin site had weathered the night, particularly the pillar. Coming to the patch of bare ground, I froze in my tracks.

The pillar was tipped over about thirty degrees.

Useless! All that hard, dirty, miserable work, and it couldn't even hold itself up, let alone a roof! Kraal curse it! Everything I did was worthless!

My howl of pain stilled the woodland noises. Runt cringed, then fled toward the humans' camp. I kicked the pillar and it fell the rest of the way to the ground.

I raked it ferociously with my foreclaws, sending strongwood chips flying. But it just lay there and mocked me.

Moving stiffly, half-dazed, I ran down the far side of the knoll and into the woods. Not to set my warn-offs or to hunt or even to retrieve Runt. I just ran. I wasn't going very fast, but I stumbled several times. Low branches I could have avoided whipped my chest and face. I heard myself whimper.

The pain lashed me back to rationality. Regaining control, I stopped my headlong, goalless plunge through the forest. I gasped for breath and let the bitter realization come.

This wasn't going to work. There was no point in pretending otherwise anymore. My town, my world, even my god had turned their tails to me. Now my last-ditch effort to cling to a scrap of civilization had collapsed. The only trail left for me led down into darkness. I could survive in the Wild indefinitely, of course, but mere survival wasn't enough.

As much as we people pride ourselves on our individualism, scratch us and you will find underneath creatures as socially interdependent as any hiving bug. I had been torn from my secure place in Coalgathering's social structure. In one swipe of the claw I had been disgraced, had lost my position and territory, and had been driven into exile. I was actually beginning to feel *lonely*. The humans were interesting and all too friendly, but they weren't people. We had too little in common.

Kraal curse the day that they had dropped into my life to destroy it!

No, I had hidden behind that excuse long enough. They weren't the ones who were to blame. They had provided the opportunity, but I had seized it to trample tradition and hurt people. Yes, hurt! Only now was I beginning to see, through their eyes, how wrongly I had dealt with Shrubfur and the others. In the

arrogance of my convictions I had forgotten that they
had a right to their own. For that there had to be
*twilga*, and I would pay it the rest of my life.

I sagged against the slick black bark of a forest giant
and for the first time since the day I killed my parent
I cried.

How long I cried I don't know. What stopped me
was a scent on the chill morning wind. A half-familiar
scent. A hostile, dangerous scent. Even in my present
state of mind, it snapped me back to animal awareness.

A wild male was coming this way. Not a wilder who
had turned his tail to civilization, but a cub who had
never been caught and raised as a *tagnami*. As an
adult he would be a very successful predator, unedu-
cated but cunning, a winner in the hard fight for survival in the Wild.

Worse yet, I could tell that he was in rut. He wasn't
looking to kill me for trespassing on his supposed territory. Not this time.

My back fur should have risen in outrage. I should
have rushed to challenge and gut the animal for his
effrontery. As a *tagnami* I had heard the dark tales of
travelers or wilders coupling with wild adults, but I
hadn't really believed them. Some things were just too
disgusting to be conceivable.

But I didn't move.

The wild male crept warily on four legs from a
patch of iceberry bushes. He was panting and his eyes
were aflame as he came toward me. At such close
range he had to know that I didn't share his lust, but
being an animal he wouldn't care. He would take what
he wanted.

He was an impressive physical specimen. About
Irongut's age, but even bigger and more thickly mus-
cled. His mottled gray-and-black pelt was so scarred
that it looked like a badly made quilt. His fangs had
seen hard use; they were worn down and chipped. He
stank from a lack of civilized grooming habits.

Still I didn't move.

This would end it. The body and the brain would go on, fulfilling an unwanted obligation. But the soul would be extinguished. No more pain, no more loss, no more loneliness. All I had to do was yield.

I made myself give off an acquiescent scent. Then I turned away, crouched low, tucked my tail to the side to protect it from his brutal passion, and spread my hindlegs for him.

# CHAPTER TWENTY-ONE

The sun was well past zenith when I loped back to the boundary of the humans' territory. I kept going without howling for permission; propriety didn't matter to me anymore. The woods fell silent where I passed. A freezing wind moaned through the gaunt branches, but I didn't care.

Coming to the camp clearing, I slowed to a walk and rose on my hindlegs. The half-egg looked like a giant redberry dropped in the pristine snow. Ralphayers was stacking firewood on a crude stone platform while Pamayers was perched on a log talking to her speaking-box. I wasn't surprised to find that Runt was with Pamayers. Since my *tagnami* preferred the human for a parent, so be it. Obligations no longer yoked me.

Runt smelled me and scurried behind Pamayers in terror. A few heartbeats later the humans noticed me. Dropping a log and putting the speaking-box away, they ran to meet me. Runt followed warily.

"Where have you been?" Pamayers demanded. "Runt showed up here terribly upset and told us about the cabin pillar! We tried to find you at your territory and in the Wild. You've been gone most of the day!"

I thought I was beginning to recognize some of the

287

humans' odd facial expressions. She seemed to be worried as well as afraid for me. But their feelings meant nothing to me now.

The perverted mating was a secret that I would take to Kraal, but they needed to know what had come afterward. "I've been doing what I should have done a long time ago—thinking clearly instead of just reacting to events." I paused. "I've come to my senses. I can't live like this."

"What do you mean?"

"Just this—I'm returning to Coalgathering. Now."

Ralphayers spoke before Pamayers could. "Have you come down with frostbite of the brain, Slasher? You've made quite a point of the fact that we can't go back! You said the circle challengers would be waiting to perform surgery on us without anesthesia!"

I nodded.

"Have you figured out what the High Priest meant by completing the circle? Or some other way for us to get around the challenge?"

The will to do something—anything—to regain control of my destiny brought back some of my old vigor. My memories of the wild male still burned like demonfire, but I would again be true to my name. "I'm going to accept the challenge for you. I'll complete that circle, if my skill and luck last."

"You can't possibly hope to win seven fights in a row!" Pamayers blurted. "What's wrong with you? Are you trying to commit suicide?"

That fang bit too close to the heart. "Why I do it is my own business." I growled.

"Really? What about Runt? What happens to him if you get yourself killed?"

"I'm sure you'll adopt him—you've already stolen his love from me. Still, we do have a business agreement. If you come with me, I'll do my best to keep you safe."

"How are you going to manage that after the circle challengers kill you?"

"If you want to find out the answer to that, you'll have to come along with me to town. But you aren't obligated to do so. We can terminate our arrangement here and now. With your alien knowledge and machines, you might make a life for yourselves as wilders."

"Without your help we won't survive the winter," Ralphayers disagreed. "Starvation, exposure, attack—take your choice."

"Besides," Pamayers added, "we can't learn much about your world hiding out here in the Wild. And we can't study your culture safely without your guidance—our travels made that clear. We need you."

The humans were trapped, but so was I, and I had no sympathy for any of us. "I'm leaving now," I told them. "If you're determined to hold me to our agreement, pack up your gear and meet me at the stream."

Turning, I headed for my own territory and camp. Runt, torn between duty and fear, followed at a wary distance. Behind us I heard the humans taking down their half-egg and squawking at each other.

Arriving at my meager campsite, I told Runt to clean up the area. He obeyed sullenly and silently. I doubted that he understood what was happening, but then neither did I, so I could hardly explain it to him. I stuffed my pawful of belongings into my carrysack—everything except the cabin-building tools which I threw away. Slinging the carrysack on my back, I led Runt to the stream.

The humans arrived just after we did, which was a good thing for them, because I wouldn't have waited. They looked as grim as I felt.

Turning my tail to the Wild, I set out for home. I tromped through the woods toward the trail which climbed west over the Sunrise Pass. Without a word the humans fell in behind me. Runt walked beside Pamayers, paw in paw.

The silence suited me. I didn't want to have to explain further. When you have lost everything you have to lose, right down to your self-respect, you reach at last a kind of peaceful equilibrium, the firmness of rock bottom. I wanted to enjoy it while I could.

I set an easy pace up to and through the pass, conserving my strength for what was to come. Even so, the humans were hard put to keep up. They squawked softly to each other from time to time. Runt trudged along warily, reverting to his animal instincts.

At the summit I paused to catch my breath. The wide river valley spread below me like a white pelt with a brown line wandering down the middle; Coalgathering was hidden under a cloud of dark hearth-smoke. Everything smelled and looked the same as before I was driven out. I took a long, deep breath. Then I started down, taking the most direct commonland trail to town.

I wanted to arrive before my former fellow townspeople closed up for the day and headed for their territories. The sun hung low over the treetops beyond the river when I came to the South Gate. Rising onto my hindlegs, I walked proudly through the stone archway. Runt and the humans followed closely, but not too closely.

I expected our arrival to cause quite a stir and I was right. Enough time had passed for the whole town to learn about the circle challenge, but not enough for the juicy gossip to fade from memories. As we walked along Savant Street toward the challenge lawn, most of the adults and *tagnami* stopped whatever they were doing, stared at us, and started talking eagerly among themselves. I knew what they were looking forward to; I didn't intend to disappoint them.

No one spoke to me. I didn't catch scent of Rubbertail, but there were others whom I had once counted as friends who made no more effort than the rest to hide their disgust. A growing crowd followed us at a safe distance. Others spread the news from street to street, like the ripples created by a rock tossed in the river.

The challenge lawn was deserted when we arrived, either by coincidence or advance warning. It had been cleared of snow by recent fights; the dormant ground-plant was crushed flat and reddish-brown instead of its usual crimson. I shrugged off my carrysack at the edge of the lawn, then walked out to the middle. Runt and the humans followed me nervously.

The challenge lawn was soon surrounded by hundreds of people—most of the town's population. The late afternoon was golden with shafts of light filtering through the treetops. Excitement and blood-lust saturated the air which was still but breath-misting cold. A beautiful day for fighting.

And dying.

"Don't say or do anything unless I tell you to," I growled at the humans. Then I turned to Runt. "Stay with Pamayers."

"Why?" Runt bleated.

"I don't have time to explain. Just do as I say."

Pamayers opened her mouth to speak, then thought better of it. She reached out with her forepaw and touched my shoulder. I should have been offended by her presumption; instead I found it oddly reassuring.

The spectators were staring at me and conversing noisily among themselves, but still nobody spoke to me. I was branded with a coward's shame. Then the hundreds of voices suddenly became silent. From seven points in the ring of spectators, persons stepped forward onto the lawn. Shrubfur, Greeneyes, Gulper, Longfang, Mudplayer and a couple of priests I didn't know by name. I recognized their scents from the dark night at Coldcrag. The circle challengers. The enemies who had done me so much harm. Controlling my rage,

I glared at them one by one. Finally I confronted Shrubfur.

"I'm glad to see that your courage has returned at last," Shrubfur growled. "One thing I never thought of you was that you were a coward. At least you will die with honor."

"The grievances between us have become complicated," I replied in a calm voice. "The humans and I are eager to settle them. I suggest that we get a judgment from the Weigher. You do have a new Weigher by now, don't you?"

I had been steadfastly refusing to look at my stall . . . my former stall. Now I glanced over at it and felt a stab of loss. It looked wonderful; the new owner hadn't changed a thing.

Shrubfur laughed boomingly, thoroughly enjoying some private joke. "That we do, Slasher. One more to my taste than his predecessor, despite his lack of years. I wonder if you will approve. Ah, here he is now."

Irongut stepped through the ring of spectators onto the challenge lawn.

My first reaction was outraged astonishment. He was a mere cub! But an unusually mature and thoughtful one, a fierce fighter with a serious interest in Weighing and powerful new friends among the hidebound traditionalists. In the absence of a high-ranked candidate, those qualities had apparently sufficed to win him the position. He wasn't the Weigher I would have picked. Knowing how he felt about the humans, I couldn't expect any help from him. Love wouldn't stop him from doing his duty any more than it would me. He would be fair, but fair according to his own beliefs.

He came over and stood between Shrubfur and myself. His expression when he looked at me was professionally pleasant, but I thought I smelled a faint trace of concern. Maybe he still felt something for me despite our differences.

"Afternoon, Slasher, Shrubfur," he said. To me he added, "I'm Coalgathering's Weigher now. Are my services needed here?"

It suddenly occurred to me that if my scheme went wrong, I would have to fight Irongut. I felt old. Too old.

Shrubfur growled, "Greeneyes, Gulper, Treeback, Longfang, Ashpelt, Mudplayer and I issued a circle challenge to the creatures called Ralphayers and Pamayers. Slasher intervened on their behalf. The three of them fled from us and abandoned their territories. Now that they have returned, we are reposting our challenge." The other six gestured their agreement.

"Will you accept a *twilga* settlement negotiated by me to resolve your grievances?" Irongut asked.

Before I could reply Shrubfur growled, "We will not! This is a blood dispute!" One by one the other circle challengers echoed her.

Irongut turned to the humans. "Then you must fight. Which of you will accept first?"

"No!" I shouted. Everybody had to hear this. "I claim that this challenge is unjust! I want the Weigher to judge if it's proper!"

The spectators had quieted to eavesdrop on us; now their excited chatter erupted again. Questioning the validity of a challenge was far from common. But for one this unusual, particularly a circle challenge, it was a legitimate request.

"You know I don't like to waste my *twilga*," Shrubfur said to me. "But my share from the sale of your territory was substantial, so I'm willing to pay to prove what I already know."

The other circle challengers smugly agreed to the weighing. We all got out our books and settled the *twilga*.

"Shall we go to my stall?" Irongut suggested.

I gestured no; the spectators were important to my plan. Shrubfur said, "We'll end this here and now." The other circle challengers agreed.

"Very well," Irongut replied. "Slasher, why do you claim that this challenge is unjust?"

"Because Shrubfur, Greeneyes, Gulper, Treeback, Longfang, Ashpelt and Mudplayer have no legitimate grievance against the humans."

"No grievance!" Shrubfur growled. "They have spread their evil knowledge from Outside which damages our businesses. Worse, they have seduced you so that you think like them and deal dishonorably with your own kind. The whole town knows about the perverted trick you used to get Greeneyes, Gulper, Longfang and me to agree to your street paving foolishness."

I took a deep breath. "Yes, I dealt with you dishonorably! I don't deny it! But Pamayers and Ralphayers have done none of you any harm. The knowledge they sell has greatly improved our trades and professions. Many here have bought from them and profited from the transaction. If you refused the chance to improve your businesses while your competitors didn't, whose fault is that? It's nothing less than cowardice to try to put the blame on others for your own mistakes. Knowledge isn't evil, but it can be used for evil. When it is, blame the user. Surely you aren't claiming that mere words can turn a good person bad? If you are, you're accusing everyone here of being so weak-minded that we can't control ourselves."

I was prepared to go on in the same vein but it wasn't necessary. My carefully crafted speech had already had the desired effect. Hostile scents and growls were coming from all around the ring of spectators and they were directed at Shrubfur. Many of the townspeople had done business with the humans and hoped to do more. Moreover, accusations of cowardice and stupidity always cut to the bone.

Irongut turned to the circle challengers. "Do you have anything to say against Slasher's claim?"

They smelled and looked like they wanted to bite something. But apparently none of them could think of a way to counter my argument. They didn't reply.

Irongut took a long time to consider the matter. Then he spoke loudly enough for everybody to hear him. "Slasher has made a valid point. I can't see that you have a legitimate grievance against the two creatures."

Tremendous relief surged through me. I wouldn't have to fight Irongut. I even found myself admiring his professional skill; he had made the proper judgement despite his own personal feelings on the subject.

Shrubfur and the other circle challengers were clearly unhappy with the weighing. But they also realized how bad they would look if they tried to pursue the matter further. Nor did any of them, even Shrubfur, seem inclined to fight Irongut over his judgment.

"Do you accept my weighing?" Irongut asked formally.

"I accept it," I replied, matching his youthful seriousness. The circle challengers agreed grudgingly.

Irongut acknowledged the presence of the humans for the first time by frowning at them. "I regret that you've returned to plague us again. If you keep to your evil ways, the next grievance will be legitimate. But for now you're not under challenge. Your territory and property are restored to you. Since they are considered evil and taboo, they haven't been sold and you should find them unmolested."

The humans stood straight and Ralphayers made the gesture of acknowledgment. Neither of them said anything stupid. I was almost proud of them; they just might manage to survive without me.

Irongut turned back to me, and his scent became even grimmer. "You've been very clever in your defense of the creatures. But you've as much as admitted that the challengers have a legitimate grievance against you. If they choose to press it."

Shrubfur smiled fiercely. "I do." The other circle challengers echoed her.

"Then," Irongut said levelly to me, "you'll have to complete the circle, if you can."

It had been a good life, until recently. Now I was ready to leave it in style. "I accept the challenge," I growled.

"We decided our order of challenge before we went to Coldcrag," Shrubfur announced. "I fight first, and there won't be a second."

Pre-fight excitement spread through the ring of spectators. Tactics were debated, advice/encouragement/insults were shouted at us, and the wagering was brisk. Fight-lust inundated us, not that we needed it. Irongut and the circle challengers stepped off the lawn.

I led Runt and the humans over to where I had dropped my carrysack. Taking off my beltpouch, I let it fall to the crushed groundplant. Runt was staring up at me, his eyes wet, reeking of fear and confusion.

"You don't have to do this for us," Pamayers whispered urgently.

"I'm not," I growled back.

"Good luck," Ralphayers said to me. "You're going to need it."

I turned away from the humans and dropped to four legs, cutting off any further comments from them. They didn't matter anymore. Nothing mattered except tasting Shrubfur's blood. I moved to the middle of the lawn.

Shrubfur was ready to fight, too. She slinked toward me slowly, also on four legs. Her pelt glistened like water in moonslight and her belly didn't droop a bit. She was still wearing her fierce smile.

"I hope you aren't going to run away again," she growled.

I returned her smile. "No. I owe you a debt of blood and I intend to repay it in full."

The preliminaries out of the way, Shrubfur and I closed in on each other. The chatter from the spectators faded as their excitement became rapt attention. A smallwing chirped in a nearby tree.

I wanted Shrubfur's life. She had chosen to make herself the symbol of my ruination. Whether I then fell to the second, third or fourth challenger didn't matter. But beating her wouldn't be easy; she was a paw taller than I and a mass of muscles from her trade. In age and quickness we were evenly matched. Well, maybe I had the edge in cunning. Maybe.

We circled warily, sniffing out each other's mood. Shrubfur was hot with anger, but she held it under rigid control: a good fighting attitude. I had no warning when she sprang at me.

She leaped over me, a flashy but effective move. Her foreclaws raked at my back. But I wasn't there; I had dropped to my belly, rolled and crouched. I tried to hook one of her hindlegs with my tail, but missed.

I scrambled around in time to meet Shrubfur's second attack. She feinted right, then lunged for my left flank. The feint was good enough to put me off-balance momentarily. Before I could recover, her fangs bit deep and tore out a mouthful of fur and flesh.

I jumped back several strides. The wound was bleeding freely and it burned like demonfire. But it would take more than a cub's nip to drop me.

I made my counterattack before Shrubfur expected me to. Springing at her left foreleg, I clawed it to the bone with a sideways forepaw swipe. Her eyes glazed for a heartbeat or two.

Pursuing my momentary advantage, I jumped high

and came down on top of her. Her legs buckled. She
slammed into the frozen ground and the breath
exploded out of her. I planted my claws in her flanks.
Then I set out to gnaw through the thick muscles in
the back of her neck, to sever her spine.

Shrubfur rolled frantically across the challenge
lawn, trying to dislodge me. My head hammered the
frozen ground again and again. The world blurred. I
hung on as long as I could, then scrambled away.

I almost made it. But Shrubfur's tail curled around
my hindleg, tripping me. By the time I yanked free,
her claws were raking my hindquarters. More demonfire
poured through me. I swallowed a howl of agony;
Kraal curse it if I was going to shame myself in front
of most of the town. I kicked backwards to discourage
Shrubfur.

She did stop carving my backside. Instead she caught
my right hindleg in her jaws and started gnawing.

We wrestled across the challenge lawn while
Shrubfur did her best to take my leg off above the
ankle. We slipped and slid in puddles of our mingled
blood. The pain was worse than I had ever known,
almost more than I could bear.

I had only a pawful of heartbeats left to save my
leg. Arching until I could feel my spine creak, I swung
a forepaw back and down, and caught the tip of her
snout with my claws. Red blood spurted. Taking
advantage of her momentary distraction, I jerked my
leg free.

By unspoken mutual consent we disengaged to
catch our breath. Panting, trembling, we glared warily
at each other across a pawful of strides and licked our
wounds. Shrubfur was a mess: her snout split, the back
of her neck chewed up, her flanks scored, limping on
her slashed foreleg, her pelt matted with blood. I figured I looked just as bad, if not worse. But we both
had plenty of fight left in us.

We started circling again, closing in. Neither of us

spotted an opening so we sped up. Soon we were running flat out, chasing each other's tails in a dangerously tight circle. We probably looked foolish playing the *tagnami* game, but this wasn't a game. Whichever of us tired or slipped first would almost certainly lose everything she had to lose.

Everything except Shrubfur's back became a vague blur. I was gasping for breath and my heart was pounding against my ribs. Even with claws extended I couldn't get good traction on the blood-slicked, frozen ground. My extra-energy was all but gone.

A nip of sharp fangs on the tip of my tail told me that the fight was almost over. I tensed for a desperate, futile sideways roll.

I sprang and rolled. But the expected heavy body didn't land on me; the expected fangs and claws didn't shred me. Coming to my paws, I saw that Shrubfur had given up at the same instant and escaped in the opposite direction.

Wobbling on our legs, we glared at each other. My quick side glance showed me Runt was clinging to Pamayers' hindleg. Pamayers wasn't watching the fight, but Ralphayers was, standing as immobile as a statue. The spectators had been noisily enjoying the best fight they had seen in a long time; now they were eager for the big finish.

Borrowing a move from the herdfolk, I charged Shrubfur. Based on our confrontation at Coldcrag I expected her to spring aside. Unfortunately her resolve was stiffer this time. She held her ground and we crashed into each other.

We fell tangled to the ground. Dizzy and disoriented, I was helpless for a pawful of heartbeats. But Shrubfur's fangs sinking into my shoulder cleared my head instantly. She was doing her best to chew through to my shoulder blade.

I tried to shake her off, but she clung to me like a bloodpuller worm. I scrambled to my paws, but she got up with me. Whimpers of pain escaped from my gritted teeth. My legs were turning to mud; a gray fog was obscuring my sight.

Sure of her victory at last, Shrubfur neglected her defense for a split-heartbeat. I slammed my forepaw down on the bloody back of her neck as hard as I could. A tremor shot through her and the jaws gnawing my shoulder went slack. Stunned, she sagged to the ground at my paws.

I reached down with my foreclaws to keep my promise.

And stopped.

I felt dizzy with sudden insight. I finally knew what the High Priest had meant, what it had taken all of my miserable exile to learn. Considering the source, I should have realized that the circle I had to complete wasn't physical or chronological. It was moral. The original evil had been mine: forcing others to my will. I had tried to flee from it, to blame others for it, then to atone for it. But the only right trail was to undo it.

If only I could. Shrubfur would die with honor, but I had clawed mine to shreds. I wouldn't survive the second challenge. The humans would die too; without me their ignorance would eventually cause them to give fatal offense. Their valuable knowledge, even the notion of cooperation which might be the most valuable of all, would be lost. My faith in cooperation had only been half-wrong, but I had been too proud to bend rather than break. Now I understood. Too late, though. My fate was set.

Or was it? I wasn't an animal or a wild adult. I was a Weigher, with a lifetime of accumulated experience. I thought hard and fast, searched my memories, fitted ideas together like puzzle pieces . . .

A lot went on in my mind during the pawful of heartbeats that I crouched over Shrubfur. Then I slowly straightened up. The spectators were staring at me in rapt silence, eager for the kill, wondering at my delay. Runt, Ralphayers, even Pamayers were watching closely.

I knew what I had to do, but just thinking about it hurt worse than everything Shrubfur had done to me. Shrubfur coughed; she was beginning to wake up. I walked over to where I had dropped my belongings. Getting out my *twilga* book, I carried it back to Shrubfur. My paw shook as I dropped it beside her.

There was a moment of shocked silence, then a hundred whispers set the ring of spectators abuzz. The reek of disgust made me gag. Better get used to it, I told myself.

Half-conscious, Shrubfur lurched to her wobbily legs to continue the fight. Then she saw my *twilga* book. Picking it up, she glared at it, then at me.

Irongut strode out to join us. He didn't look at me; his scent and expression were unreadable. The situation was an extremely unusual one, but he knew his Weigher lore. In a voice loud enough for everybody to hear he announced, "The challenge is settled."

Then he showed me his tail and walked away.

The ring was breaking up as the spectators hurried to leave the scene of my utter disgrace. Even my former friends wouldn't look at me. Everybody was discussing my action; they would be for a long time. What they were saying would have been challengeable if it hadn't been true. Shrubfur gave me a confused look, then staggered off to where her doctor and *tagnami* were waiting.

When everybody else was gone, Runt and the humans hurried over to me. "How badly are you hurt?" Pamayers demanded.

Kraal's own agony radiated from my shoulder through my entire body. My right hindleg wasn't working very well and I had lost several pawfuls of fur and meat from my hindquarters. Blood from my wounds was dripping on the ground. I was weak and dizzy and my head throbbed blindingly. "I'll live," I growled.

"What happened when you gave Shrubfur your _twilga_ book?" Ralphayers asked.

"I was surrendering to her." Each word hurt. "Everything I had left—my _twilga_, even my carrysack and beltpouch—belongs to her now."

"Does that include Runt?" Pamayers asked sharply.

"Of course not. _Tagnami_ are too much of an obligation to be considered an asset."

Speaking of _tagnami_, Runt was hugging Pamayers' hindleg and staring up at me fearfully. I must have been quite a sight.

"Why did you surrender?"

Several heartbeats passed before I could answer. "To survive. I realized that I have work to do—work which is more important than my property or even my honor."

"If you say so," Ralphayers replied, scratching his head. "But how are you going to get by without _twilga_ or a territory?"

My face hurt too much to grin. "I won't have to do without either. It's time for us to settle up for my services today on your behalf. Freeing you from the challenge, getting your territory and property back, and saving your lives should be worth the price of a modest territory plus some basic necessities."

"Of course," Pamayers agreed quickly. "As long as you include medical treatment at the top of your list. You've lost a lot of blood."

I was swaying and the gray fog was thickening. "A very good idea. I'll have to hurry to buy the patch job, territory and supplies before sunset. Then we should stay out of town for a few days, to let things calm down."

I hoped I could find some people willing to do

business with me. When I surrendered to Shrubfur, I had publicly branded myself as a coward. No self-respecting person would want to stain her pelt with my blood. I had lost all of my friends (except the humans). Brokering alien knowledge would be my only trade; Weighing was closed to me forever. In time I might win back some friends and respect, but for now I would be clinging precariously to the bottom of the dominance ranking.

I found myself staring at the humans. Their solicitude had a wary, impersonal scent very much at odds with their usual eager friendship. An invisible wall had gone up between us. They had the most reason to be pleased, but they weren't. I wondered why.

It finally came to me that the humans might have sensibilities which my behavior during the past pawful of days may have offended. In my weakness I had treated them improperly; I remembered my attack on Pamayers with shame. I would have to settle with them. And I would have to do it in accordance with their own bizarre moral code. I thought hard for a pawful of heartbeats and came up with a notion crazy enough to work.

"Pamayers, Ralphayers," I said formally, "I forgot for awhile that you're my friends. I apologize and . . . ask you to forgive me."

Pamayers' face twisted into a weird alien smile. "Apology accepted."

"Spoken like a true friend," Ralphayers added.

That left one victim of my impropriety to settle with. Looking down at Runt, my heart ached as I realized that what I had killed could probably never be resurrected. Love and innocence were as fragile as a newborn. I would try to reassure Runt that I still loved him and that I would be the best parent I could be. But if he wanted Pamayers to be his parent, I would sell him to her and hide my grief.

Runt was staring wet-eyed at my wounds. I

suddenly realized that his scent wasn't fear *of* me, but fear *for* me. Letting go of Pamayers, he came tentatively over to me. He started licking my injured hindleg, trying to make it feel better.

It felt a lot better.

# CHAPTER TWENTY-TWO

The sun was going to ground beyond the river, setting the horizon ablaze with its fire. The air was still and cool. Spring was just around the bend in the trail.

I took a break from my log-caulking to enjoy the sunset. Twelve days had passed since the fight with Shrubfur and I had spent most of that time making the dilapidated cabin of my new territory a fit home for Runt and myself.

The panoramic view of my new territory should have been a depressing sight, but it filled me with an eagerness almost like pre-fight excitement. The paw of the mountains south-east of Coalgathering was the home of those at the bottom of the dominance ranking. Even cloaked in snow the rocky slopes and patches of meager vegetation looked stark, forbidding. Game ranged from scarce to non-existent; feeding ourselves tested my hunting skills and was quickly developing Runt's.

But it wasn't going to stay that way. The humans had told me about techniques which could remake land into what you wanted it to be. A blasting magic called gunpowder could turn rock into rubble, sculpt meadows and vales, and divert streams to water them.

305

River muck, fertilizer and dirt from the Wild could bring barren ground to life. Flora and fauna could be planted and stocked to suit. The task would be long and hard, not to mention expensive, but someday Runt would own the finest territory in Coalgathering.

My shoulder and hindleg throbbed dully, I moved with a definite limp, and I tended to tire quickly. A third of my pelt was covered with bandages. But I felt considerably better than I had; working on the cabin was helping me get back in fighting shape. Stubbytail predicted a full recovery.

"All done, Mommy!"

I looked upslope. Runt was scampering out of the fireclaw bushes and stunted tangletrees surrounding the cabin clearing. The stream which ran through the cabin was clogged in many places from years of abandonment. I had sent Runt to clear the obstructions so it would flow freely come spring.

He skidded to a stop in front of me. "All done!" he repeated, panting from exertion and excitement. "I dig up rocks and branches and stuff, throw them out of stream like you say. I go all the way to boundary!"

"Good job." Smiling fondly, I patted his head. "Tomorrow you can collect the branches for firewood. Now go play until dinnertime."

"Okay!" Snow flying in his wake, he headed for the steep slope down which he loved to slide.

Watching him go, I wondered what the future held for him. He would continue my work with the humans after I was gone, bridging the gap between the ways of our two worlds. He already understood the humans better than I did and was learning more with my blessing. But he had to be an honorable and dominant person, too.

Which was why he would be returning to Bentback's school as soon as we were settled in. The interruption in his *tagnami* training had slowed his development. He would have to study hard to catch up; Bentback and I would see that he did. The old predator didn't think much of me these days, but he was dedicated to his students and my *twilga* was still good.

I was just getting back to packing clay into the gaps between lower-wall logs when the tuskhorn imitation of an entry request howl blared from the northern boundary. I had been expecting the humans to come calling today. Putting down my trowel and bucket, I went around to the front of the cabin to welcome them.

I smelled them before I saw them and wondered what they were doing with a pair of runlegs. When they entered the clearing, my jaw hit the ground.

They were *riding* the runlegs.

Small blankets were draped across the runlegs' backs and the humans sat straddling them in a way that would have done my tail serious damage. Miniature versions of boat reins ran from the runlegs' mouths to the humans' forepaws; presumably they were for steering, too. Hindpaws applied to the runlegs' flanks told them when to lumber forward. The notion of a person riding on top of an animal struck me as unnatural, but then so were the humans.

"Good afternoon, Slasher," Pamayers said when the runlegs stopped in front of me. Ralphayers echoed her.

"Afternoon, Pamayers, Ralphayers," I replied. "What in Kraal's name are you up to now?"

"You mean our four-pawed transportation?" Ralphayers patted his runleg's neck. "We needed a quicker, easier way to get around than walking. We didn't think you would want the job again, so we bought these in town a couple of days ago."

My back ached as it remembered the flight from Coldcrag. "You thought right. How do you get the runlegs to go where you want?"

"It isn't easy," Pamayers admitted. "They aren't

horses, but they are bred for docility and trained to pull wagons. We're getting better at it."

"They already beat walking—in most ways," Ralphayers added, rubbing where his tail should have been.

"Would you like to come inside out of the cold?" I offered.

"Thanks, but no thanks," Ralphayers replied. "We have to get home—these things don't ride worth a damn in the dark."

I could believe that. "How did your consultations go today?"

"Three more satisfied customers. The skyboat solved the problem with Rubbertail's dryeye vaccine, the carpenter from Oldtown got his improved formula for weatherproofing, and we swapped yarns with the traveling storyteller. Don't suppose we made a profit on that last one."

"You underestimate me—half the *twilga* he earned telling his tales in town yesterday belongs to us. Now, about tomorrow. Will you be available for a late morning and a mid-afternoon consultation?"

"No problem. But the day after is out—we've bought permission to study a couple of breeding operations."

I noted the information in my broker's book. It would mean chasing around town and territories tomorrow, rescheduling clients. They wouldn't appreciate the delay; on the other paw, scarcity increased value. "By the way, a traveler dropped off a letter for you from a savant in some town east of Mountainhole."

"Our fame is spreading."

I passed the letter up to Pamayers. Then we all got out our *twilga* books and settled up for the day.

"Business is picking up," I commented. The town's shock at my disgrace was fading and the news of our return was spreading. "A good thing, too. I need every *twil* I can wrap my paws around to fix up this miserable excuse for a territory."

"Enough about business," Pamayers exclaimed. "We have some important news!"

I peered closely at her. She was smiling. Indeed, though it might have been some trick of the golden sunset, her face seemed to be glowing with an inner light. "Well, quit grinning like a drunken nutcheek," I teased her. "Out with it."

"I'm going to have a baby!"

I remembered carrying and dropping my own cubs. "You have my sympathy. Remember, it's only a temporary inconvenience."

The humans looked stunned. What had I said wrong now? Thinking fast, I remembered that humans kept the cubs they dropped. That being the case, parental love might actually begin at conception. Which would explain their reaction.

"Excuse my misunderstanding," I said quickly. "Congratulations on your impending parenthood. I'm sure your *tagnami* will make you proud."

Pamayers' glow and Ralphayers' good humor returned. "Thank you," Pamayers replied. "We're very excited about it."

"I imagine this will mean major changes in your living customs." My curiosity-itch was back. After all her interference in my raising of Runt, I would look forward to seeing how well she did.

"Absolutely. I'm glad we had the opportunity to do some traveling—it'll be a long time before we do again."

It couldn't be too long for me.

"Observing Runt and our child growing up together will be a fascinating experiment in cross-culturalization," Pamayers went on. "Our child will continue our research and I hope Runt will help him."

"He will. But considering how long you told me humans take to reach adulthood, your cub will be growing up with Runt and *his tagnami*."

Pamayers laughed. "We still have a lot to learn about each other."

"Could we do it some other time?" Ralphayers asked, eyeing the setting sun.

"You could come over tomorrow after your last consultation," I suggested to Pamayers. "We could have a good female-to-female chat."

"Thank you. I'd love it."

Ralphayers' face twisted. "Only if I get to try Runt's slide."

"Agreed," I replied. Males.

We bid each other good night, then the humans rode their runlegs back toward Coldcrag. Watching them, I realized that their friendship almost made up for everything I had lost. I didn't know what the future held for me, but with them around it was bound to be interesting.

There wasn't enough light left to finish the caulking job. Time to fetch Runt and do our best to hunt up some dinner.

That was when I heard another entry permission howl. One I had never expected to hear again.

Trembling from surprise, I howled back my permission to enter. Then I rushed inside the cabin to run a quick comb through my pelt. Why was Irongut here? To warn me that the town wouldn't accept me back as Weigher even if I managed to defeat him on the challenge lawn? (I knew it and had no intention of trying.) Or for a more personal reason? Hopes and fears fought in my mind.

I met Irongut in front of the cabin; I wasn't sure that I wanted to invite him inside or that he would have accepted. I got my first good scent of him since my return. (I had been somewhat distracted at the challenge lawn.) He looked as lithe and handsome as I remembered, but older than my pawful of ten-days of traveling would account for. He carried himself with more maturity, a higher degree of self-control.

trees. The fresh wind in my face washed away the last
of my doubt, my pain.

Springing away from the cabin, we raced like twin
shadows across the newly fallen snow.

# THE END